KU-153-864

The Watsons

The Watsons

*Jane Austen
and Another*

BOOK CLUB ASSOCIATES

This edition published 1977 by
Book Club Associates
By arrangement with Peter Davies Limited

© 1977 by Peter Davies Limited
First published 1977

Printed and bound in Great Britain by
Cox & Wyman Ltd,
London, Fakenham and Reading

CHAPTER 1

THE FIRST WINTER ASSEMBLY in the town of Dorking in Surrey was to be held on Tuesday, October 13th and it was generally expected to be a very good one. A long list of county families was confidently run over as sure of attending, and sanguine hopes were entertained that the Osbornes themselves would be there. The Edwards' invitation to the Watsons followed of course. The Edwards were people of fortune who lived in the town and kept their coach. The Watsons inhabited a village about three miles distant, were poor and had no close-carriage; and ever since there had been balls in the place, the former were accustomed to invite the latter to dress, dine and sleep at their house on every monthly return throughout the winter. On the present occasion, as only two of Mr Watson's children were at home, and one was always necessary as companion to himself, for he was sickly and had lost his wife, one only could profit by the kindness of their friends. Miss Emma Watson, who was very recently returned to her family from the care of an aunt, who had brought her up, was to make her first public appearance in the neighbourhood; and her eldest sister, whose delight in a ball was not lessened by ten years' enjoyment, had some merit in cheerfully undertaking to drive her and all her finery in the old chair to Dorking on the important morning.

As they splashed along the dirty lane Miss Watson thus instructed and cautioned her inexperienced sister:

'I dare say it will be a very good ball, and among so many officers you will hardly want partners. You will find Mrs Edwards' maid very willing to help you, and I would advise you to ask Mary Edwards' opinion if you are at all at a loss, for she has a very good taste. If Mr Edwards does not lose all his money at cards, you will stay as late as you can wish for; if he does, he will hurry you home perhaps — but you are sure of some comfortable soup. I hope you will be in good looks. I should not be surprised if you were to be thought one of the prettiest girls in the room, there is a great deal in novelty. Perhaps Tom Musgrave may take notice of you; but I would advise you by all means not to give him any encouragement. He generally pays attention to every new girl, but he is a great flirt and never means anything serious.'

'I think I have heard you speak of him before,' said Emma. 'Who is he?'

'A young man of very good fortune, quite independent, and remarkably agreeable, a universal favourite wherever he goes. Most of the girls hereabouts are in love with him, or have been. I believe I am the only one amongst them that have escaped with a whole heart; and yet I was the first he paid attention to when he came into this country six years ago; and very great attention indeed did he pay me. Some people say that he has never seemed to like any girl so well since, though he is always behaving in a particular way to one or another.'

'And how came *your* heart to be the only cold one?' said Emma, smiling.

'There was a reason for that,' replied Miss Watson, changing colour. 'I have not been very well used, Emma, among them; I hope you will have better luck.'

'Dear sister, I beg your pardon, if I have unthinkingly given you pain.'

'When we first knew Tom Musgrave,' continued Miss Watson without seeming to hear her, 'I was very much attached to a young man of the name of Purvis, a particular friend of Robert's, who used to be with us a great deal. Everybody thought it would have been a match.'

A sigh accompanied these words, which Emma respected in silence; but her sister after a short pause went on:

'You will naturally ask why it did not take place, and why he is married to another woman, while I am still single. But you must ask him — not me — you must ask Penelope. Yes, Emma, Penelope was at the bottom of it all. She thinks everything fair for a husband. I trusted her; she set him against me, with a view

2

to gaining him herself, and it ended in his discontinuing his visits, and soon after marrying somebody else. Penelope makes light of her conduct, but *I* think such treachery very bad. It has been the ruin of my happiness. I shall never love any man as I loved Purvis. I do not think Tom Musgrave should be named with him in the same day.'

'You quite shock me by what you say of Penelope,' said Emma. 'Could a sister do such a thing? Rivalry, treachery between sisters! I shall be afraid of being acquainted with her. But I hope it was not so; appearances were against her.'

'You do not know Penelope. There is nothing she would not do to get married. She would as good as tell you so herself. Do not trust her with any secrets of your own, take warning by me, do not trust her; she has her good qualities, but she has no faith, no honour, no scruples, if she can promote her own advantage. I wish with all my heart she was well married. I declare I would rather have her well married than myself.'

'Than yourself! Yes, I can suppose so. A heart wounded like yours can have little inclination for matrimony.'

'Not much indeed — but you know we must marry. I could do very well single for my own part; a little company, and a pleasant ball now and then, would be enough for me, if one could be young for ever; but my father cannot provide for us, and it is very bad to grow old and be poor and laughed at. I have lost Purvis, it is true; but very few people marry their first loves. I should not refuse a man because he was not Purvis. Not that I can ever quite forgive Penelope.'

Emma shook her head in acquiescence.

'Penelope, however, has had her troubles,' continued Miss Watson. 'She was sadly disappointed in Tom Musgrave, who afterwards transferred his attentions from me to her, and whom she was very fond of; but he never means anything serious, and when he had trifled with her long enough, he began to slight her for Margaret, and poor Penelope was very wretched. And since then, she has been trying to make some match at Chichester — she won't tell us with whom; but I believe it is a rich old Dr Harding, uncle to the friend she goes to see; and she has taken a vast deal of trouble about him and given up a great deal of time to no purpose as yet. When she went away the other day she said

3

it should be the last time. I suppose you did not know what her particular business was at Chichester, nor guess at the object which could take her away from Stanton just as you were coming home after so many years' absence.'

'No indeed, I had not the smallest suspicion of it. I consider her engagement to Mrs Shaw just at that time as very unfortunate for me. I had hoped to find all my sisters at home, to be able to make an immediate friend of each.'

'I suspect the Doctor to have had an attack of the asthma, and that she was hurried away on that account. The Shaws are quite on her side — at least, I believe so; but she tells me nothing. She professes to keep her own counsel; she says, and truly enough, that "Too many cooks spoil the broth".'

'I am sorry for her anxieties,' said Emma; 'but I do not like her plans or her opinions. I shall be afraid of her. She must have too masculine and bold a temper. To be so bent on marriage — to pursue a man merely for the sake of situation — is a sort of thing that shocks me; I cannot understand it. Poverty is a great evil; but to a woman of education and feeling it ought not, it cannot be the greatest. I would rather be teacher at a school (and I can think of nothing worse) than marry a man I did not like.'

'I would rather do anything than be teacher at a school,' said her sister. '*I* have been at school, Emma, and know what a life they lead; *you* never have. I should not like marrying a disagreeable man any more than yourself; but I do not think there *are* many very disagreeable men; I think I could like any good-humoured man with a comfortable income. I suppose my aunt brought you up to be rather refined.'

'Indeed I do not know. My conduct must tell you how I have been brought up. I am no judge of it myself. I cannot compare my aunt's methods with any other person's, because I know no other.'

'But I can see in a great many things that you are very refined. I have observed it ever since you came home, and I am afraid it will not be for your happiness. Penelope will laugh at you very much.'

'*That* will not be for my happiness, I am sure. If my opinions are wrong, I must correct them; if they are above my situation, I

4

must endeavour to conceal them. But I doubt whether ridicule —
has Penelope much wit?'

'Yes; she has great spirits, and never cares what she says.'

'Margaret is more gentle, I imagine?'

'Yes; especially in company; she is all gentleness and mildness
when anybody is by. But she is a little fretful and perverse among
ourselves. Poor creature! She is possessed with the notion of
Tom Musgrave's being more seriously in love with her than he
ever was with anybody else, and is always expecting him to come
to the point. This is the second time within this twelvemonth that
she has gone to spend a month with Robert and Jane on purpose
to egg him on by her absence; but I am sure she is mistaken, and
that he will no more follow her to Croydon now than he did last
March. He will never marry unless he can marry somebody very
great; Miss Osborne, perhaps, or somebody in that style.'

'Your account of this Tom Musgrave, Elizabeth, gives me very
little inclination for his acquaintance."

'You are afraid of him; I do not wonder at you.'

'No indeed; I dislike and despise him.'

'Dislike and despise Tom Musgrave! No, *that* you never can.
I defy you not to be delighted with him if he takes notice of you.
I hope he will dance with you; and I dare say he will, unless the
Osbornes come with a large party, and then he will not speak to
anybody else.'

'He seems to have most engaging manners!' said Emma.
'Well, we shall see how irresistible Mr Tom Musgrave and I find
each other. I suppose I shall know him as soon as I enter the
ballroom; he *must* carry some of his charm in his face.'

'You will not find him in the ballroom, I can tell you; you will
go early, that Mrs Edwards may get a good place by the fire, and
he never comes till late; if the Osbornes are coming, he will wait
in the passage and come in with them. I should like to look in
upon you, Emma. If it was but a good day with my father, I
would wrap myself up, and James should drive me over, as soon
as I had made tea for him; and I should be with you by the time
the dancing began.'

'What! Would you come late at night in this chair?'

'To be sure I would. There, I said you were very refined; and
that's an instance of it.'

5

Emma for a moment made no answer. At last she said:

'I wish, Elizabeth, you had not made a point of my going to this ball; I wish you were going instead of me. Your pleasure would be greater than mine; my enjoyment, therefore, must be very doubtful. Yours, among all your acquaintance, would be certain. It is not too late to change. Very little apology would be requisite to the Edwards, who must be more glad of your company than of mine, and I should most readily return to my father; and should not be at all afraid to drive this quiet old creature home. Your clothes I would undertake to find means of sending to you.'

'My dearest Emma,' cried Elizabeth warmly, 'do you think I would do such a thing? Not for the universe! But I shall never forget your good nature in proposing it. You must have a sweet temper indeed! I never met with anything like it! And would you really give up the ball, that I might be able to go to it? Believe me, Emma, I am not so selfish as that comes to. No, though I am nine years older than you are, I would not be the means of keeping you from being seen. You are very pretty, and it would be very hard that you should not have as fair a chance as we have all had to make your fortune. No, Emma, whoever stays at home this winter, it shan't be you. I am sure I should never have forgiven the person who kept me from a ball at nineteen.'

Emma expressed her gratitude, and for a few minutes they jogged on in silence. Elizabeth first spoke:

'You will take notice who Mary Edwards dances with?'

'I will remember her partners if I can; but you know they will be all strangers to me.'

'Only observe whether she dances with Captain Hunter more than once — I have my fears in that quarter. Not that her father or mother like officers; but if she does, you know, it is all over with poor Sam. And I have promised to write him word who she dances with.'

'Is Sam attached to Miss Edwards?'

'Did you not know *that*?'

'How should I know it? How should I know in Shropshire what is passing of that nature in Surrey? It is not likely that circumstances of such delicacy should have made any part of the scanty communication which passed between you and me for the last fourteen years.'

'I wonder I never mentioned it when I wrote. Since you have been home, I have been so busy with my poor father and our great wash that I have had no leisure to tell you anything; but, indeed, I concluded you knew it all. He has been very much in love with her these two years, and it is a great disappointment to him that he cannot always get away to our balls; but Mr Curtis won't often spare him, and just now it is a sickly time at Guildford.'

'Do you suppose Miss Edwards inclined to like him?"'

'I am afraid not: you know she is an only child, and will have at least ten thousand pounds.'

'But still she may like our brother.'

'Oh, no! The Edwards look much higher. Her father and mother would never consent to it. Sam is only a surgeon, you know. Sometimes I think she does like him. But Mary Edwards is rather prim and reserved; I do not always know what she would be at.'

'Unless Sam feels on sure grounds with the lady herself, it seems a pity to me that he should be encouraged to think of her at all.'

'A young man must think of somebody,' said Elizabeth, 'and why should he not be as lucky as Robert, who has got a good wife and six thousand pounds?'

'We must not all expect to be individually lucky,' replied Emma. 'The luck of one member of a family is luck to all.'

'Mine is all to come, I am sure,' said Elizabeth, giving another sigh to the remembrance of Purvis. 'I have been unlucky enough; and I cannot say much for you, as my aunt married again so foolishly. Well, you will have a good ball, I daresay. The next turning will bring us to the turnpike: you may see the church-tower over the hedge, and the White Hart is close by it. I shall long to know what you think of Tom Musgrave.'

Such were the last audible sounds of Miss Watson's voice, before they passed through the turnpike-gate and entered on the pitching of the town, the jumbling and noise of which made further conversation most thoroughly undesirable. The old mare trotted heavily on, wanting no direction of the reins to take the right turning, and making only one blunder, in proposing to stop at the milliner's, before she drew up towards Mr Edwards' door. Mr Edwards lived in the best house in the street, and the best in the place, if Mr Tomlinson, the banker, might be indulged in calling his newly erected house at the end of the town, with a shrubbery and sweep, in the country.

Mr Edwards' house was higher than most of its neighbours with four windows on each side of the door; the windows guarded by posts and chain, and the door approached by a flight of stone steps.

'Here we are,' said Elizabeth, as the carriage ceased moving, 'safely arrived, and by the market clock we have been only five and thirty minutes coming; which I think is doing pretty well, though it would be nothing for Penelope. Is not it a nice town? The Edwards have a noble house, you see, and they live quite in style. The door will be opened by a man in livery with a powdered head, I can tell you.'

Emma had seen the Edwards only one morning at Stanton; they were therefore all but strangers to her; and though her spirits were by no means insensible to the expected joys of the evening, she felt a little uncomfortable in the thought of all that was to precede them. Her conversation with Elizabeth, too, giving her some very unpleasant feelings with respect of her own family, had made her more open to disagreeable impressions from any other cause, and increased her sense of the awkwardness of rushing into intimacy on so slight an acquaintance.

There was nothing in the manner of Mrs and Miss Edwards to give immediate change to these ideas. The mother, though a very friendly woman, had a reserved air, and a great deal of formal civility; and the daughter, a genteel-looking girl of twenty-two, with her hair in papers, seemed very naturally to have caught something of the style of her mother who had brought her up. Emma was soon left to know what they could be, by Elizabeth's being obliged to hurry away; and some very, very languid remarks on the probable brilliancy of the ball were all that broke at intervals a silence of half an hour before they were joined by the master of the house. Mr Edwards had a much easier and more communicative air than the ladies of the family; he was

8

fresh from the street, and he came ready to tell whatever might interest. After a cordial reception of Emma, he turned to his daughter with:

'Well, Mary, I bring you good news: the Osbornes will certainly be at the ball tonight. Horses for two carriages are ordered from the White Hart to be at Osborne Castle by nine.'

'I am glad of it,' observed Mrs Edwards, 'because their coming gives credit to our assembly. The Osbornes being known to have been at the first ball, will dispose a great many people to attend the second. It is more than they deserve; for, in fact, they add nothing to the pleasure of the evening, they come so late and go so early; but great people have always their charm.'

Mr Edwards proceeded to relate many other little articles of news which his morning's lounge had supplied him with, and they chatted with greater briskness, till Mrs Edwards' moment for dressing arrived, and the young ladies were carefully recommended to lose no time. Emma was shown to a very comfortable apartment, and as soon as Mrs Edwards' civilities could leave her to herself, the happy occupation, the first bliss of a ball, began. The girls, dressing in some measure together, grew unavoidably better acquainted. Emma found in Miss Edwards the show of good sense, a modest unpretending mind, and a great wish of obliging; and when they returned to the parlour where Mrs Edwards was sitting, respectably attired in one of the two satin gowns which went through the winter, and a new cap from the milliner's, they entered it with much easier feelings and more natural smiles than they had taken away. Their dress was now to be examined: Mrs Edwards acknowledged herself too old-fashioned to approve of every modern extravagance, however sanctioned; and though complacently viewing her daughter's good looks, would give but a qualified admiration; and Mr Edwards, not less satisfied with Mary, paid some compliments of good-humoured gallantry to Emma at her expense. The discussion led to more intimate remarks, and Miss Edwards gently asked Emma if she was not often reckoned very like her youngest brother. Emma thought she could perceive a faint blush accompany the question, and there seemed something still more suspicious in the manner in which Mr Edwards took up the subject.

9

'You are paying Miss Emma no great compliment, I think, Mary,' said he hastily. 'Mr Sam Watson is a very good sort of young man, and I dare say is a very clever surgeon; but his complexion has been rather too much exposed to all weathers to make a likeness to him very flattering.'

Mary apologized in some confusion. She had not thought a strong likeness at all incompatible with very different degrees of beauty. There might be resemblance in countenance, and the complexion and even the features be very unlike.

'I know nothing of my brother's beauty,' said Emma, 'for I have not seen him since he was seven years old; but my father reckons us alike.'

'Mr Watson!' cried Mr Edwards; 'well, you astonish me. There is not the least likeness in the world; your brother's eyes are grey, yours are brown; he has a long face, and a wide mouth. My dear, do *you* perceive the least resemblance?'

'Not the least: Miss Emma Watson puts me very much in mind of her eldest sister, and sometimes I see a look of Miss Penelope, and once or twice there has been a glance of Mr Robert, but I cannot perceive any likeness to Mr Samuel.'

'I see the likeness between her and Miss Watson,' replied Mr Edwards, 'very strongly, but I am not sensible of the others. I do not much think she is like any of the family *but* Miss Watson; but I am very sure there is no resemblance between her and Sam.'

This matter was settled, and they went to dinner.

'Your father, Miss Emma, is one of my oldest friends,' said Mr Edwards, as he helped her to wine, when they were drawn round the fire to enjoy their dessert. 'We must drink to his better health. It is a great concern to me, I assure you, that he should be such an invalid. I know nobody who likes a game of cards, in a social way, better than he does, and very few people that play a fairer rubber. It is a thousand pities that he should be so deprived of the pleasure. For now we have a quiet little Whist Club that meets three times a week at the White Hart; and if he could but have his health, how much he would enjoy it!'

'I dare say he would, sir; and I wish with all my heart he were equal to it.'

'Your club would be better fitted for an invalid,' said Mrs

Edwards, 'if you did not keep it up so late.' This was an old grievance.

'So late, my dear! What are you talking of?' cried the husband, with sturdy pleasantry. 'We are always at home before midnight. They would laugh at Osborne Castle to hear you call *that* late; they are but just rising from dinner at midnight.'

'That is nothing to the purpose,' retorted the lady, calmly. 'The Osbornes are to be no rule for us. You had better meet every night, and break up two hours sooner.'

So far the subject was very often carried; but Mr and Mrs Edwards were so wise as never to pass that point; and Mr Edwards now turned to something else. He had lived long enough in the idleness of a town to become a little of a gossip, and having some anxiety to know more of the circumstances of his young guest than had yet reached him, he began with:

'I think, Miss Emma, I remember your aunt very well, about thirty years ago; I am pretty sure I danced with her in the old rooms at Bath the year before I married. She was a very fine woman then, but like other people, I suppose, she is grown somewhat older since that time. I hope she is likely to be happy in her second choice.'

'I hope so; I believe so, sir,' said Emma, in some agitation.

'Mr Turner has not been dead a great while, I think?'

'About two years, sir.'

'I forget what her name is now.'

'O'Brien.'

'Irish! Ah! I remember; and she is gone to settle in Ireland. I do not wonder that you should not wish to go with her into *that* country, Miss Emma; but it must be a great deprivation to her, poor lady! After bringing you up like a child of her own.'

'I was not so ungrateful, sir,' said Emma, warmly, 'as to wish to be anywhere but with her. It did not suit Captain O'Brien that I should be of the party.'

'Captain!' repeated Mrs Edwards. 'The gentleman is in the army then?'

'Yes, ma'am.'

'Aye, there is nothing like your officers for captivating the ladies, young or old. There is no resisting a cockade, my dear.'

11

'I hope there is,' replied Mrs Edwards gravely, with a quick glance at her daughter; and Emma had just recovered from her own perturbation in time to see a blush on Miss Edwards' cheek, and in remembering what Elizabeth had said of Captain Hunter, to wonder and waver between his influence and her brother's.

'Elderly ladies should be careful how they make a second choice,' observed Mr Edwards.

'Carefulness and discretion should not be confined to elderly ladies, or to a second choice,' added his wife. 'They are quite as necessary to young ladies in their first.'

'Rather more so, my dear,' replied he; 'because young ladies are likely to feel the effects of it longer. When an old lady plays the fool, it is not in the course of nature that she should suffer from it many years.'

Emma drew her hand across her eyes, and Mrs Edwards, on perceiving it, changed the subject to one of less anxiety to all.

With nothing to do but to expect the hour of setting off, the afternoon was long to the two young ladies; and though Miss Edwards was rather discomposed at the very early hour which her mother always fixed for going, that early hour itself was watched for with some eagerness. The entrance of the tea-things at seven o'clock was some relief; and luckily Mr and Mrs Edwards always drank a dish extraordinary and ate an additional muffin when they were going to sit up late, which lengthened the ceremony almost to the wished-for moment.

At a little before eight o'clock the Tomlinsons' carriage was heard to go by, which was the constant signal for Mrs Edwards to order hers to the door; and in a very few minutes the party were transported from the quiet and warmth of a snug parlour to the bustle, noise, and draughts of air of a broad entrance passage of an inn. Mrs Edwards, carefully guarding her own dress, while she attended with yet greater solicitude to the proper security of her young charges' shoulders and throats, led the way up the wide staircase, while no sound of a ball but the first scrape of one violin blessed the ears of her followers; and Miss Edwards, on hazarding the anxious enquiry of whether there were many people come yet, was told by the waiter, as she knew she should, that 'Mr Tomlinson's family were in the room.'

12

In passing along a short gallery to the assembly room, brilliant in lights before them, they were accosted by a young man in a morning-dress and boots, who was standing in the doorway of a bed-chamber, apparently on purpose to see them go by.

'Ah! Mrs Edwards, how do you do? How do you do, Miss Edwards?' he cried, with an easy air. 'You are determined to be in good time, I see, as usual. The candles are but this moment lit.'

'I like to get a good seat by the fire, you know, Mr Musgrave,' replied Mrs Edwards.

'I am this moment going to dress,' said he. 'I am waiting for my stupid fellow. We shall have a famous ball. The Osbornes are certainly coming; you may depend on *that*, for I was with Lord Osborne this morning —'

The party passed on. Mrs Edwards' satin gown swept along the clean floor of the ballroom to the fireplace at the upper end, where one party only were formally seated, while three or four officers were lounging together, passing in and out from the adjoining card-room. A very stiff meeting between these near neighbours ensued, and as soon as they were all duly placed again, Emma, in a low whisper, which became the solemn scene, said to Miss Edwards:

'The gentleman we passed in the passage was Mr Musgrave, then? He is reckoned remarkably agreeable, I understand.'

Miss Edwards answered hesitatingly. 'Yes; he is very much liked by many people; but *we* are not very intimate.'

'He is rich, is not he?'

'He has about eight or nine hundred a year, I believe. He came into possession of it when he was very young, and my father and mother think it has given him rather an unsettled turn. He is no favourite with them.'

CHAPTER 2

THE COLD AND EMPTY APPEARANCE of the room, and the demure air of the small cluster of females at one end of it, began soon to give way. The inspiriting sound of other carriages was heard, and continual accessions of portly chaperones, and strings of smartly dressed girls, were received, with now and then a fresh gentleman straggler, who, if not enough in love to station himself near any fair creature, seemed glad to escape into the card-room.

Among the increasing number of military men, one now made his way to Miss Edwards with an air of *empressement* which decidedly said to her companion, 'I am Captain Hunter'; and Emma, who could not but watch her at such a moment, saw her looking rather distressed, but by no means displeased, and heard an engagement formed for the first two dances, which made her think her brother Sam's a hopeless case.

Emma in the meanwhile was not unobserved or unadmired herself. A new face, and a very pretty one, could not be slighted. Her name was whispered from one party to another, and no sooner had the signal been given by the orchestra's striking up a favourite air, which seemed to call the young to their duty, and people the centre of the room, than she found herself engaged to dance with a brother officer, introduced by Captain Hunter.

Emma Watson was not more than of the middle height, well made and plump, with an air of healthy vigour. Her skin was very brown, but clear, smooth and glowing, which, with a lively eye, a sweet smile, and an open countenance, gave beauty to attract, and expression to make the beauty improve on acquaintance. Having no reason to be dissatisfied with her partner, the evening began very pleasantly to her; and her feelings perfectly

14

coincided with the reiterated observation of others, that it was an excellent ball. The two first dances were not quite over when the returning sound of carriages after a longer interruption called general notice, and 'The Osbornes are coming the Osbornes are coming!' was repeated round the room. After some minutes of extraordinary bustle without and watchful curiosity within, the important party, preceded by the attentive master of the inn to open a door which was never shut, made their appearance. They consisted of Lady Osborne; her son, Lord Osborne; her daughter, Miss Osborne; Miss Carr, her daughter's friend; Mr Howard, formerly tutor to Lord Osborne, now clergyman of the parish in which the castle stood; Mrs Blake, a widow sister, who lived with him; her son, a fine boy of ten years old; and Mr Tom Musgrave, who, probably imprisoned within his own room, had been listening in bitter impatience to the sound of the music for the last half-hour. In their progress up the room they paused almost immediately behind Emma to receive the compliments of some acquaintance, and she heard Lady Osborne observe that they had made a point of coming early for the gratification of Mrs Blake's little boy, who was uncommonly fond of dancing. Emma looked at them all as they passed, but chiefly and with most interest on Tom Musgrave, who was certainly a genteel, good-looking young man. Of the females, Lady Osborne had by much the finest person; though nearly fifty, she was very handsome, and had all the dignity of rank.

Lord Osborne was a very fine young man; but there was an air of coldness, of carelessness, even of awkwardness about him, which seemed to speak him out of his element in a ballroom. He came, in fact, only because it was judged expedient for him to please the borough; he was not fond of women's company, and he never danced. Mr Howard was an agreeable-looking man, a little more than thirty.

At the conclusion of the two dances, Emma found herself, she knew not how, seated among the Osborne set; and she was immediately struck with the fine countenance and animated gestures of the little boy, as he was standing before his mother, wondering when they should begin.

'You will not be surprised at Charles's impatience,' said Mrs Blake, a lively, pleasant-looking little woman of five or six and thirty, to a lady who was standing near her, 'when you know what a partner he is to have. Miss Osborne has been so very kind as to promise to dance the two first dances with him.'

'Oh yes! We have been engaged this week,' cried the boy, 'and we are to dance down every couple.'

On the other side of Emma, Miss Osborne, Miss Carr, and a party of young men were standing engaged in very lively consultation; and soon afterwards she saw the smartest officer of the set walking off to the orchestra to order the dance, while Miss Osborne, passing before her to her little expecting partner, hastily said, 'Charles, I beg your pardon for not keeping my engagement, but I am going to dance these two dances with Colonel Beresford. I know you will excuse me, and I will certainly dance with you after tea.' And without staying for an answer, she turned again to Miss Carr, and in another minute was led by Colonel Beresford to begin the set. If the poor little boy's face had in its happiness been interesting to Emma, it was infinitely more so under this sudden reverse. He stood the picture of disappointment with crimsoned cheeks, quivering lips, and eyes bent on the floor. His mother, stifling her own mortification, tried to soothe his, with the prospect of Miss Osborne's second promise; but, though he contrived to utter with an effort of boyish bravery, 'Oh, I do not mind it!' it was very evident by the unceasing agitation of his features that he minded it as much as ever.

Emma did not think or reflect; she felt and acted.

'I shall be very happy to dance with you, sir, if you like it,' said she, holding out her hand with the most unaffected good humour. The boy, in one moment restored to all his first delight, looked joyfully at his mother, and stepping forward with an honest, simple 'Thank you, ma'am,' was instantly ready to attend his new acquaintance. The thankfulness of Mrs Blake was more diffuse; with a look most expressive of unexpected pleasure and lively gratitude, she turned to her neighbour with repeated and fervent acknowledgements of so great and condescending a kindness to her boy. Emma with perfect truth could assure her that she could not be giving greater pleasure than she felt herself, and Charles being provided with his gloves and charged to keep them on, they joined the set which was now rapidly forming, with nearly equal complacency. It was a partnership which could not be noticed without surprise. It gained her a broad stare from Miss Osborne and Miss Carr as they passed her in the dance. 'Upon my word, Charles, you are in luck,' said the former, as she turned to him; 'you have got a better partner than me,' to which the happy Charles answered, 'Yes!'

Tom Musgrave, who was dancing with Miss Carr, gave her many inquisitive glances; and after a time Lord Osborne himself came, and under pretence of talking to Charles, stood to look at his partner. Though rather distressed by such observation, Emma could not repent what she had done, so happy had it made both the boy and his mother; the latter of whom was continually making opportunities of addressing her with the warmest civility. Her little partner she found, though bent chiefly on dancing, was not unwilling to speak, when her questions or remarks gave him anything to say; and she learnt, by a sort of inevitable enquiry, that he had two brothers and a sister, that they and their mamma all lived with his uncle at Wickstead, that his uncle taught him Latin, that he was very fond of riding, and had a horse of his own given him by Lord Osborne; and that he had been out once already with Lord Osborne's hounds.

At the end of these dances Emma found they were to drink tea. Miss Edwards gave her a caution to be at hand, in a manner which convinced her of Mrs Edwards' holding it very important to have them both close to her when she moved into the tea-room; and Emma was accordingly on the alert to gain her proper station. It was always the pleasure of the company to have a little bustle and crowd when they adjourned for refreshment. The tea-room was a small room within the card-room; and in passing through the latter, where the passage was straitened by tables, Mrs Edwards and her party were for a few moments hemmed in. It happened close by Lady Osborne's casino table; Mr Howard, who belonged to it, spoke to his nephew; and Emma, on perceiving herself the object of attention both to Lady Osborne and him, had just turned away her eyes in time to avoid seeming to hear her young companion exclaim delightedly aloud, 'Oh, uncle! Do look at my partner. She is so pretty!' As they were immediately in motion again, however, Charles was hurried off without being able to receive his uncle's suffrage. On entering

17

the tea-room in which two long tables were prepared, Lord Osborne was to be seen quite alone at the end of one, as if retreating as far as he could from the ball, to enjoy his own thoughts and gape without restraint. Charles instantly pointed him out to Emma: 'There's Lord Osborne, let you and I go and sit by him.'

'No, no,' said Emma, laughing, 'you must sit with my friends.'

Charles was now free enough to hazard a few questions in his turn. What o'clock was it?

'Eleven.'

'Eleven! and I am not at all sleepy. Mamma said I should be asleep before ten. Do you think Miss Osborne will keep her word with me when tea is over?'

'Oh yes, I suppose so'; though she felt that she had no better reason to give than that Miss Osborne had *not* kept it before.

'When shall you come to Osborne Castle?'

'Never, probably. I am not acquainted with the family.'

'But you may come to Wickstead and see mamma, and she can take you to the castle. There is a monstrous curious stuffed fox there, and a badger, anybody would think they were alive. It is a pity you should not see them.'

On rising from tea, there was again a scramble for the pleasure of being first out of the room, which happened to be increased by one or two of the card-parties having just broken up and the players being disposed to move exactly the different way. Among these was Mr Howard, his sister leaning on his arm; and no sooner were they within reach of Emma, than Mrs Blake, calling her notice by a friendly touch, said, 'Your goodness to Charles, my dear Miss Watson, brings all his family upon you. Give me leave to introduce my brother, Mr Howard.'

Emma curtsied, the gentleman bowed, made a hasty request for the honour of her hand in the two next dances, to which as hasty an affirmative was given, and they were immediately impelled in opposite directions. Emma was very pleased with the circumstances; there was a quietly cheerful, gentlemanlike air about Mr Howard which suited her; and in a few minutes afterwards the value of her engagement increased, when, as she was sitting in the card-room, somewhat screened by a door, she heard

18

Lord Osborne, who was lounging on a vacant table near her, call Tom Musgrave towards him and say, 'Why do not you dance with that beautiful Emma Watson? I want you to dance with her, and I will come and stand by you.'

'I was determined on it this very moment, my lord; I'll be introduced and dance with her directly.'

'Aye, do; and if you find she does not want much talking to, you may introduce me by and by.'

'Very well, my lord. If she is like her sisters, she will only want to be listened to. I will go this moment. I shall find her in the tea-room. That stiff old Mrs Edwards has never done tea.'

Away he went, Lord Osborne after him; and Emma lost no time in hurrying from her corner, exactly the other way, forgetting in her haste that she left Mrs Edwards behind.

'We had quite lost you,' said Mrs Edwards, who followed her with Mary, in less than five minutes. 'If you prefer this room to the other there is no reason why you should not be here, but we had better all be together.'

Emma was saved the trouble of apologizing, by their being joined at the moment by Tom Musgrave, who requesting Mrs Edwards aloud to do him the honour of presenting him to Miss Emma Watson, left that good lady without any choice in the business, but that of testifying by the coldness of her manner that she did it unwillingly. The honour of dancing with her was solicited without loss of time, and Emma, however she might like to be thought a beautiful girl by lord or commoner, was so little disposed to favour Tom Musgrave himself that she had considerable satisfaction in avowing her previous engagement. He was evidently surprised and discomposed. The style of her last partner had probably led him to believe her not overpowered with applications.

'My little friend, Charles Blake,' he cried, 'must not expect to engross you the whole evening. We can never suffer this. It is against the rules of the assembly, and I am sure it will never be patronized by our good friend here, Mrs Edwards; she is much too nice a judge of decorum to give her licence to such a dangerous particularity.'

'I am not going to dance with Master Blake, sir.'

19

The gentleman, a little disconcerted, could only hope he might be more fortunate another time, and seeming unwilling to leave her, though his friend Lord Osborne was waiting in the doorway for the result, as Emma with some amusement perceived, he began to make civil enquiries after her family.

'How comes it that we have not the pleasure of seeing your sisters here this evening? Our assemblies have been used to be so well treated by them that we do not know how to take this neglect.'

'My eldest sister is the only one at home, and she could not leave my father.'

'Miss Watson, the only one at home! You astonish me! It seems but the day before yesterday that I saw them all three in this town. But I am afraid I have been a very sad neighbour of late. I hear dreadful complaints of my negligence wherever I go, and I confess it is a shameful length of time since I was at Stanton. But I shall *now* endeavour to make myself amends for the past.'

Emma's calm curtsy in reply must have struck him as very unlike the encouraging warmth he had been used to receive from her sisters, and gave him probably the novel sensation of doubting his own influence, and of wishing for more attention than she bestowed. The dancing now recommenced; Miss Carr being impatient to *call*, everybody was required to stand up; and Tom Musgrave's curiosity was appeased on seeing Mr Howard come forward and claim Emma's hand.

'That will do as well for me,' was Lord Osborne's remark, when his friend carried him the news, and he was continually at Howard's elbow during the two dances.

The frequency of his appearance there was the only unpleasant part of the engagement, the only objection she could make to Mr Howard. In himself, she thought him as agreeable as he looked; though chatting on the commonest topics, he had a sensible, unaffected way of expressing himself, which made them all worth hearing, and she only regretted that he had not been able to make his pupil's manners as unexceptionable as his own. The two dances seemed very short, and she had her partner's authority for considering them so. At their conclusion, the Osbornes and their train were all on the move.

20

'We are off at last,' said his lordship to Tom; 'how much longer do you stay in this heavenly place? — till sunrise?'

'No, faith! my lord, I have had quite enough of it. I assure you I shall not show myself here again when I have had the honour of attending Lady Osborne to her carriage. I shall retreat in as much secrecy as possible to the most remote corner of the house, where I shall order a barrel of oysters, and be famously snug.'

'Let me see you soon at the Castle; and bring me word how she looks by daylight.'

Emma and Mrs Blake parted as old acquaintances, and Charles shook her by the hand and wished her good-bye at least a dozen times. From Miss Osborne and Miss Carr she received something like a jerking curtsy as they passed her; even Lady Osborne gave her a look of complacency, and his lordship actually came back after the others were out of the room, to 'beg her pardon', and look in the window-seat behind her for the gloves which were visibly compressed in his hand. As Tom Musgrave was seen no more, we may suppose his plan to have succeeded, and imagine him mortifying with his barrel of oysters in dreary solitude, or gladly assisting the landlady in her bar to make fresh negus for the happy dancers above. Emma could not help missing the party by whom she had been, though in some respect unpleasantly, distinguished, and the two dances which followed and concluded the ball were rather flat in comparison with the others. Mr Edwards having played with good luck, they were some of the last in the room.

'Here we are back again, I declare,' said Emma sorrowfully, as she walked into the dining-room, where the table was prepared, and the neat supper maid was lighting the candles. 'My dear Miss Edwards, how soon it is at an end! I wish it could all come over again.'

A great deal of kind pleasure was expressed in her having enjoyed the evening so much; and Mr Edwards was as warm as herself in the praise of the fullness, brilliancy, and spirit of the meeting, though as he had been fixed the whole time at the same table in the same room, with only one change of chairs, it might have seemed a matter scarcely perceived. But he had won four rubbers out of five and everything went well. His daughter felt the advantage of this gratified state of mind, in the course of the remarks and retrospections which now ensued over the welcome soup.

'How came you not to dance with either of the Mr Tomlinsons, Mary?' said her mother.

'I was always engaged when they asked me.'

'I thought you were to have stood up with Mr James the last two dances; Mrs Tomlinson told me he was gone to ask you, and I heard you say two minutes before that you were *not* engaged.'

'Yes, but there was a mistake; I had misunderstood; I did not know I was engaged. I thought it had been for two dances after, if we stayed so long; but Captain Hunter assured me it was for those very two.'

'So you ended with Captain Hunter, Mary, did you?' said her father. 'And whom did you begin with?'

'Captain Hunter,' was repeated, in a very humble tone.

'Hum! That is being constant, however. But who else did you dance with?'

'Mr Norton and Mr Styles.'

'And who are they?'

'Mr Norton is a cousin of Captain Hunter's.'

'And who is Mr Styles?'

'One of his particular friends.'

'All in the same regiment,' added Mrs Edwards. 'Mary was surrounded by red-coats all the evening. I should have been better pleased to see her dancing with some of our old neighbours, I confess.'

'Yes, yes; we must not neglect our old neighbours. But if these soldiers are quicker than other people in a ballroom, what are young ladies to do?'

'I think there is no occasion for their engaging themselves so many dances beforehand, Mr Edwards.'

'No, perhaps not; but I remember, my dear, when you and I did the same.'

Mrs Edwards said no more, and Mary breathed again. A good deal of good-humoured pleasantry followed, and Emma went to bed in charming spirits, her head full of Osbornes, Blakes, and Howards.

22

CHAPTER 3

THE NEXT MORNING BROUGHT a great many visitors. It was
the way of the place always to call on Mrs Edwards the morning
after a ball, and this neighbourly inclination was increased in
the present instance by a general spirit of curiosity on Emma's
account, as everybody wanted to look at the girl who had been
admired the night before by Lord Osborne. Many were the eyes,
and various the degrees of approbation with which she was
examined. Some saw no fault, and some no beauty. With some
her brown skin was the annihilation of every grace, and others
could never be persuaded that she was half so handsome as Elizabeth Watson had been ten years ago. The morning passed quickly
away in discussing the merits of the ball with all this succession
of company, and Emma was at once astonished by finding it two
o'clock, and considering that she had heard nothing of her
father's chair. After this discovery she had walked to the window
to examine the street, and was on the point of asking leave to
ring the bell and make enquiries, when the light sound of a
carriage driving up to the door set her heart at ease. She stepped
up to the window again, but instead of the convenient though
very un-smart family equipage perceived a neat curricle. Mr
Musgrave was shortly afterwards announced; and Mrs Edwards
put on her very stiffest look at the sound. Not at all dismayed,
by her chilling air, he paid his compliments to each of the ladies
with no unbecoming ease, and continuing to address Emma presented her a note, which he had the honour of bringing from
her sister, but to which he must observe a verbal postscript from
himself would be requisite.'

The note, which Emma was beginning to read rather *before*
Mrs Edwards had entreated her to use no ceremony, contained a

few lines from Elizabeth importing that their father, in consequence of being unusually well, had taken the sudden resolution
of attending the visitation that day, and that as his road lay quite
wide from Dorking, it was impossible for her to come home till
the following morning, unless the Edwards would send her,
which was hardly to be expected, or she could meet with any
chance conveyance, or did not mind walking so far. She had
scarcely run her eye through the whole, before she found herself
obliged to listen to Tom Musgrave's further account.

'I received that note from the fair hands of Miss Watson only
ten minutes ago,' said he. 'I met her in the village of Stanton,
whither my good stars prompted me to turn my horses' heads.
She was at that moment in quest of a person to employ on the
errand, and I was fortunate enough to convince her that she
could not find a more willing or speedy messenger than myself.
Remember, I say nothing of my disinterestedness. My reward is
to be the indulgence of conveying you to Stanton in my curricle.
Though they are not written down, I bring your sister's orders for
the same.'

Emma felt distressed; she did not like the proposal — she did
not wish to be on terms of intimacy with the proposer — and yet,
fearful of encroaching on the Edwards, as well as wishing to go
home herself, she was at a loss how entirely to decline what he
offered. Mrs Edwards continued silent, either not understanding
the case, or waiting to see how the young lady's inclination lay.
Emma thanked him, but professed herself very unwilling to give
him so much trouble. 'The trouble was of course honour,
pleasure, delight — what had he or his horses to do?' Still she
hesitated. 'She believed she must beg leave to decline his assistance — she was rather afraid of the sort of carriage — the
distance was not beyond a walk.' Mrs Edwards was silent no
longer. 'We shall be extremely happy, Miss Emma, if you can
give us the pleasure of your company till tomorrow; but if you
cannot conveniently do so, our carriage is quite at your service,
and Mary will be pleased with the opportunity of seeing your
sister.'

This was precisely what Emma had longed for, and she
accepted the offer most thankfully, acknowledging that as Eliza-

beth was entirely alone, it was her wish to return home to dinner. The plan was warmly opposed by their visitor —

'I cannot suffer it, indeed. I must not be deprived of the happiness of escorting you. I assure you there is not a possibility of fear with my horses. You might guide them yourself. *Your sisters* all know how quiet they are; they have none of them the smallest scruple in trusting themselves with me, even on a race-course. Believe me,' added he, lowering his voice, '*you* are quite safe — the danger is only *mine*.'

Emma was not more disposed to oblige him for all this.

'And as to Mrs Edwards' carriage being used the day after a ball, it is a thing quite out of rule. I assure you — never heard of before; the old coachman will look as black as his horses — won't he, Miss Edwards?'

No notice was taken. The ladies were silently firm, and the gentleman found himself obliged to submit.

'What a famous ball we had last night!' he cried, after a short pause. 'How long did you keep it up after the Osbornes and I went away?'

'We had two dances more.'

'It is making it too much of a fatigue, I think, to stay so late. I suppose your set was not a very full one.'

'Yes; quite as full as ever, except the Osbornes. There seemed no vacancy anywhere, and everybody danced with uncommon spirit to the last.'

Emma said this, though against her conscience.

'Indeed! Perhaps I might have looked in upon you again, if I had been aware of as much, for I am rather fond of dancing than not. Miss Osborne is a charming girl, is not she?'

I do not think her handsome,' replied Emma, to whom all this was chiefly addressed.

'Perhaps she is not critically handsome, but her manners are delightful. And Fanny Carr is a most interesting little creature. You can imagine nothing more *naïve* or *piquante*; and what do you think of Lord Osborne, Miss Watson?'

'That he would be handsome even though he were *not* a lord, and, perhaps, better bred; more desirous of pleasing, and showing himself pleased in a right place.'

'Upon my word, you are severe upon my friend! I assure you Lord Osborne is a very good fellow.'

'I do not dispute his virtues, but I do not like his careless air.'

'If it were not a breach of confidence,' replied Tom, with an important look, 'perhaps I might be able to win a more favourable opinion of poor Osborne.'

Emma gave him no encouragement, and he was obliged to keep his friend's secret. He was also obliged to put an end to his visit, for Mrs Edwards having ordered her carriage, there was no time to be lost on Emma's side in preparing for it. Miss Edwards accompanied her home, but as it was dinner-time at Stanton, stayed with them only a few minutes.

'Now, my dear Emma,' said Miss Watson, as soon as they were alone, 'you must talk to me all the rest of the day without stopping, or I shall not be satisfied. But first of all Nanny shall bring in the dinner. Poor thing! You will not dine as you did yesterday, for we have nothing but some fried beef. How nice Mary Edwards looks in her new pelisse! And now tell me how you like them all, and what I am to say to Sam. I have begun my letter; Jack Stokes is to call for it tomorrow, for his uncle is going within a mile of Guildford next day.'

Nanny brought in the dinner.

'We will wait upon ourselves,' continued Elizabeth, 'and then we shall lose no time. And so you would not come home with Tom Musgrave?'

'No. You had said so much against him that I could not wish either for the obligation or the intimacy which the use of his carriage must have created. I should not even have liked the appearance of it.'

'You did very right; though I wonder at your forbearance, and I do not think I could have done it myself. He seemed so eager to fetch you that I could not say no, though it rather went against me to be throwing you together, so well as I knew his tricks; but I did long to see you, and it was a clever way of getting you home. Besides, it won't do to be too nice. Nobody could have thought of the Edwards letting you have their coach, after the horses being out so late. But what am I to say to Sam?'

'If you are guided by me, you will not encourage him to think of Miss Edwards. The father is decidedly against him, the mother shows him no favour, and I doubt his having any interest with Mary. She danced twice with Captain Hunter, and I think shows him in general as much encouragement as is consistent with her disposition and the circumstances she is placed in. She once mentioned Sam, and certainly with a little confusion — but that was perhaps merely owing to the consciousness of his liking her, which may very probably have come to her knowledge.'

'Oh! dear, yes — she has heard enough of *that* from us all. Poor Sam! He is out of luck, as well as other people. For the life of me, Emma, I cannot help feeling for those that are crossed in love. Well, now begin, and give me an account of everything as it happened.'

Emma obeyed her, and Elizabeth listened with very little interruption till she heard of Mr Howard as a partner.

'Dance with Mr Howard. Good heavens! You don't say so! Why, he is quite one of the great and grand ones. Did you not find him very high?'

'His manners are of a kind to give *me* much more ease and confidence than Tom Musgrave's.'

'Well, go on. I should have been frightened out of my wits to have had anything to do with the Osbornes' set.'

Emma concluded her narration.

'And so you really did not dance with Tom Musgrave at all? But you must have liked him — you must have been struck with him altogether.'

'I do *not* like him, Elizabeth. I allow his person and air to be good; and that his manner to a certain point — his address rather — is pleasing. But I see nothing else to admire in him. On the contrary, he seems very vain, very conceited, absurdly anxious for distinction, and absolutely contemptible in some of the measures he takes for being so. There is a ridiculousness about him that entertains me; but his company gives me no other agreeable emotion.'

'My dearest Emma! You are like nobody else in the world. It is well Margaret is not by. You do not offend *me*, though I hardly know how to believe you; but Margaret would never forgive such words.'

'I wish Margaret could have heard him profess his ignorance

of her being out of the country; he declared it seemed only two days since he had seen her.'

'Aye, that is just like him; and yet this is the man she *will* fancy so desperately in love with her. He is no favourite of mine, as you well know, Emma, but you must think him agreeable. Can you lay your hand on your heart, and say you do not?'

'Indeed I can, both hands; and spread to their widest extent.'

'I should like to know the man you *do* think agreeable.'

'His name is Howard.'

'Howard! Dear me; I cannot think of *him* but as playing cards with Lady Osborne, and looking proud. I must own, however, that it *is* a relief to me to find you can speak as you do of Tom Musgrave; my heart did misgive me that you would like him too well. You talked so stoutly beforehand, that I was sadly afraid your brag would be punished. I only hope it will last, and that he will not come on to pay you much attention; it is a hard thing for a woman to stand against the flattering ways of a man when he is bent upon pleasing her.'

As their quietly sociable little meal concluded, Miss Watson could not help observing how comfortably it had passed.

'It is so delightful to me,' said she, 'to have things going on in peace and good humour. Nobody can tell how much I hate quarrelling. Now, though we have had nothing but fried beef, how good it has all seemed. I wish everybody were as easily satisfied as you; but poor Margaret is very snappish, and Penelope owns she would rather have quarrelling going on than nothing at all.'

Mr Watson returned in the evening not the worse for the exertion of the day, and consequently pleased with what he had done and glad to talk of it over his own fireside. Emma had not foreseen any interest to herself in the occurrences of a visitation; but when she heard Mr Howard spoken of as the preacher, and as having given them an excellent sermon, she could not help listening with a quicker ear.

'I do not know when I have heard a discourse more to my mind,' continued Mr Watson, 'or one better delivered. He reads extremely well, with great propriety, and in a very impressive manner, and at the same time without any theatrical grimace or violence. I own I do not like much action in the pulpit; I do not like the studied air and artificial inflexions of voice which your very popular and most admired preachers generally have. A simple delivery is much better calculated to inspire devotion, and shows a much better taste. Mr Howard read like a scholar and a gentleman.'

'And what had you for dinner, sir?' said his eldest daughter.

He related the dishes, and told what he had eaten himself. 'Upon the whole,' he added, 'I have had a very comfortable day. My old friends were quite surprised to see me amongst them, and I must say that everybody paid me great attention, and seemed to feel for me as an invalid. They would make me sit near the fire; and as the partridges were pretty high, Dr Richards would have them sent away to the other end of the table "that they might not offend Mr Watson", which I thought very kind of him. But what pleased me as much as anything was Mr Howard's attention. There is a pretty steep flight of steps up to the room we dine in, which do not quite agree with my gouty foot, and Mr Howard walked by me from the bottom to the top, and would make me take his arm. It struck me I had no claim to expect it; for I never saw him before in my life. By the by, he enquired after one of my daughters, but I do not know which. I suppose you know among yourselves.'

CHAPTER 4

ON THE THIRD DAY after the ball, as Nanny, at five minutes before three, was beginning to bustle into the parlour with the tray and knife-case, she was suddenly called to the front door by the sound of as smart a rap as the end of a riding-whip could give; and though charged by Miss Watson to let nobody in, returned in half a minute with a look of awkward dismay to hold the parlour door open for Lord Osborne and Tom Musgrave. The surprise of the young ladies may be imagined. No visitors would have been welcome at such a moment; but such visitors as these — such a one as Lord Osborne at least, a nobleman and a stranger — was really distressing.

He looked a little embarrassed himself, as, on being introduced by his easy, voluble friend, he muttered something of doing himself the honour of waiting upon Mr Watson. Though Emma could not but take the compliment of the visit to herself, she was very far from enjoying it. She felt all the inconsistency of such an acquaintance with the very humble style in which they were obliged to live; and having in her aunt's family been used to many of the elegancies of life, was fully sensible of all that must be open to the ridicule of richer people in her present home. Of the pain of such feelings, Elizabeth knew very little. Her simple mind, or juster reason, saved her from such mortification; and though shrinking under a general sense of inferiority, she felt no particular shame. Mr Watson, as the gentleman had already heard from Nanny, was not well enough to be downstairs. With much concern they took their seats; Lord Osborne near Emma, and the convenient Mr Musgrave, in high spirits at his own importance, on the other side of the fireplace with Elizabeth. *He* was at no loss for words; but when Lord

Osborne had hoped that Emma had not caught cold at the ball, he had nothing more to say for some time, and could only gratify his eye by occasional glances at his fair companion. Emma was not inclined to give herself much trouble for his entertainment, and after hard labour of mind, he produced a remark of its being a very fine day, and followed it up with the question of 'Have you been walking this morning?'

'No, my lord. We thought it too dirty.'

'You should wear half-boots.' After another pause :

'Nothing sets off a neat ankle more than a half-boot; nankeen, galoshed with black, looks very well. Do you not like half-boots?'

'Yes; but unless they are so stout as to injure their beauty, they are not fit for country walking.'

'Ladies should ride in dirty weather. Do you ride?'

'No, my lord.'

'I wonder every lady does not. A woman never looks better than on horseback.'

'But every woman may not have the inclination, or the means.'

'If they knew how much it became them, they would all have the inclination; and I fancy, Miss Watson, when once they had the inclination, the means would soon follow.'

'Your lordship thinks we always have our own way. *That* is a point on which ladies and gentlemen have long disagreed; but without pretending to decide it, I may say that there are some circumstances which even *women* cannot control. Female economy will do a great deal, my lord, but it cannot turn a small income into a large one.'

Lord Osborne was silenced. Her manner had been neither sententious nor sarcastic, but there was a something in its mild seriousness, as well as in the words themselves, which made his lordship think; and when he addressed her again, it was with a degree of considerate propriety totally unlike the half-awkward, half-fearless style of his former remarks. It was a new thing with him to wish to please a woman; it was the first time that he had ever felt what was due to a woman in Emma's situation; but as he was wanting neither in sense nor a good disposition, he did not feel it without effect.

'You have not been long in this country, I understand,'

said he, in the tone of a gentleman. 'I hope you are pleased with it.'

He was rewarded by a gracious answer, and a more liberal full view of her face than she had yet bestowed. Unused to exert himself, and happy in contemplating her, he then sat in silence for some minutes longer, while Tom Musgrave was chattering to Elizabeth, till they were interrupted by Nanny's approach, who, half-opening the door and putting her head in, said :

'Please, ma'am, master wants to know why he be'nt to have his dinner?'

The gentlemen, who had hitherto disregarded every symptom, however positive, of the nearness of that meal, now jumped up with apologies, while Elizabeth called briskly after Nanny to 'tell Betty to take up the fowls.'

'I am sorry it happens so,' she added, turning good-humouredly towards Musgrave, 'but you know what early hours we keep.'

Tom had nothing to say for himself, for he knew it very well, and such honest simplicity, such shameless truth, rather bewildered him. Lord Osborne's parting compliments took some time, his inclination for speech seeming to increase with the shortness of the term for indulgence. He recommended exercise in defiance of dirt; spoke again in praise of half-boots; begged that his sister might be allowed to send Emma the name of her shoemaker; and concluded with saying, 'My hounds will be hunting this country next week. I believe they will throw off at Stanton Wood on Wednesday at nine o'clock. I mention this in hopes of your being drawn out to see what's going on. If the morning's tolerable, pray do us the honour of giving us your good wishes in person.'

The sisters looked at each other in astonishment when their visitors had withdrawn.

'Here's an unaccountable honour!' cried Elizabeth at last. 'Who would have thought of Lord Osborne's coming to Stanton? He is very handsome; but Tom Musgrave looks all to nothing the smartest and most fashionable of the two. I am glad he did not say anything to me; I would not have had to talk to such a great man for the world. Tom was very agreeable, was he not? But did you hear him ask where Miss Penelope and Miss Margaret were, when he first came in? It put me out of patience. I am glad Nanny had not laid the cloth, however; it would have looked so awkward; just the tray did not signify.'

To say that Emma was not flattered by Lord Osborne's visit would be to assert a very unlikely thing, and describe a very odd young lady; but the gratification was by no means unalloyed. His coming was a sort of notice which might please her vanity, but did not suit her pride, and she would rather have known that he wished the visit without presuming to make it, than have seen him at Stanton.

Among other unsatisfactory feelings it once occurred to her to wonder why Mr Howard had not taken the same privilege of coming, and accompanied his lordship, but she was willing to suppose that he had either known nothing about it, or had declined any share in a measure which carried quite as much impertinence in its form as good breeding. Mr Watson was very far from being delighted when he heard what had passed; a little peevish under immediate pain, and ill-disposed to be pleased, he only replied :

'Phoo! Phoo! What occasion could there be for Lord Osborne's coming? I have lived here fourteen years without being noticed by any of the family. It is some fooling of that idle fellow Tom Musgrave. I cannot return the visit. I would not if I could.'

And when Tom Musgrave was met again, he was commissioned with a message of excuse to Osborne Castle, on the too sufficient plea of Mr Watson's infirm state of health.

CHAPTER 5

A WEEK OR TEN DAYS ROLLED quietly away after this visit before any new bustle arose to interrupt even for half a day the tranquil and affectionate intercourse of the two sisters, whose mutual regard was increasing with the intimate knowledge of each other which such intercourse produced. The first circumstance to break in on their security was the receipt of a letter from Croydon to announce the speedy return of Margaret, and a visit of two or three days from Mr and Mrs Robert Watson, who undertook to bring her home and wished to see their sister Emma.

It was an expectation to fill the thoughts of the sisters at Stanton, and to busy the hours of one of them at least; for, as Jane had been a woman of fortune, the preparations for her entertainment were considerable; and as Elizabeth had at all times more goodwill than method in her guidance of the house, she could make no change without a bustle. An absence of fourteen years had made all her brothers and sisters strange to Emma, but in her expectation of Margaret there was more than the awkwardness of such an alienation; she had heard the things which made her dread her return; and the day which brought the party to Stanton seemed to her the probable conclusion of almost all that had been comfortable in the house.

Robert Watson was an attorney at Croydon in a good way of business; very well satisfied with himself for the same, and for having married the only daughter of the attorney to whom he had been clerk, with a fortune of six thousand pounds. Mrs Robert was not less pleased with herself for having had that six thousand pounds, and for being now in possession of a very smart house in Croydon, where she gave genteel parties, and wore fine clothes. In her person there was nothing remarkable; her manners were pert and conceited. Margaret was not without beauty; she had a slight, pretty figure, and rather wanted countenance than good features; but the sharp and anxious expression of her face made her beauty in general little felt. On meeting her long-absent sister, as on every occasion of show, her manner was all affection and her voice all gentleness; continual smiles and a very slow articulation being her constant resource when determined on pleasing.

She was now 'so delighted to see dear, dear Emma', that she could hardly speak a word in a minute.

'I am sure we shall be great friends,' she observed, with much sentiment, as they were sitting together. Emma scarcely knew how to answer such a proposition, and the manner in which it was spoken she could not attempt to equal. Mrs Robert Watson eyed her with much familiar curiosity and triumphant compassion; the loss of the aunt's fortune was uppermost in her mind at the moment of meeting; and she could not but feel how much better it was to be the daughter of a gentleman of property in Croydon than the niece of an old woman who threw herself away on an Irish captain. Robert was carelessly kind, as became a prosperous man and a brother; more intent on settling with the post-boy, inveighing against the exorbitant advance in posting, and pondering over a doubtful half-crown, than on welcoming a sister who was no longer likely to have any property for him to get the direction of.

'Your road through the village is infamous, Elizabeth,' said he, 'worse than ever it was. By heaven! I would indict it if I lived near you. Who is surveyor now?'

There was a little niece at Croydon to be fondly enquired after by the kind-hearted Elizabeth, who regretted very much her not being at the party.

'You are very good,' replied her mother, 'and I assure you it went very hard with Augusta to have us come away without her. I was forced to say we were only going to church, and promise to come for her directly. But you know it would not do to bring her without her maid, and I am as particular as ever in having her properly attended to.'

35

'Sweet little darling,' cried Margaret. 'It quite broke my heart to leave her.'

'Then why were you in such a hurry to run away from her?' cried Mrs Robert. 'You are a sad, shabby girl. I have been quarrelling with you all the way we came, have not I? Such a visit as this I never heard of! You know how glad we are to have any of you with us, if it be for months together; and I am sorry (with a witty smile) we have not been able to make Croydon agreeable this autumn.'

'My dearest Jane, do not overpower me with your raillery. You know what inducements I had to bring me home. Spare me, I entreat you. I am no match for your arch sallies.'

'Well, I only beg you will not set your neighbours against the place. Perhaps Emma may be tempted to go back with us and stay till Christmas, if you don't put in your word.'

Emma was greatly obliged. 'I assure you we have very good society at Croydon. I do not much attend the balls, they are rather too mixed; but our parties are very select and good. I had seven tables last week in my drawing-room. Are you fond of the country? How do you like Stanton?'

'Very much,' replied Emma, who thought a comprehensive answer most to the purpose. She saw that her sister-in-law despised her immediately. Mrs Robert Watson was indeed wondering what sort of a home Emma could possibly have been used to in Shropshire, and setting it down as certain that the aunt could not have had six thousand pounds.

'How charming Emma is,' whispered Margaret to Mrs Robert in her most languishing tone. Emma was quite distressed by such behaviour; and she did not like it better when she heard Margaret five minutes afterwards say to Elizabeth in a sharp, quick accent, totally unlike the first, 'Have you heard from Pen since she went to Chichester? I had a letter the other day. I don't find she is likely to make anything of it. I fancy she'll come back "Miss Penelope" as she went.'

Such she feared would be Margaret's common voice when the novelty of her own appearance were over; the tone of artificial sensibility was not recommended by the idea.

The ladies were invited upstairs to prepare for dinner. 'I hope you will find things tolerably comfortable, Jane,' said Elizabeth, as she opened the door of the spare bed-chamber.

'My good creature,' replied Jane, 'use no ceremony with me, I entreat you. I am one of those who always take things as they find them. I hope I can put up with a small apartment for two or three nights without making a piece of work. I always wish to be treated quite *en famille* when I come to see you. And now I do hope you have not been getting a great dinner for us. Remember we never eat suppers.'

'I suppose,' said Margaret rather quickly to Emma, 'you and I are to be together; Elizabeth always takes care to have a room to herself.'

'No — Elizabeth gives me half hers.'

'Oh!' (in a softened voice, and rather mortified to find that she was not ill-used) 'I am sorry I am not to have the pleasure of your company, especially as it makes me nervous to be much alone.'

Emma was the first of the females in the parlour again; on entering it she found her brother alone.

'So, Emma,' said he, 'you are quite the stranger at home. It must be odd for you to be here. A pretty piece of work your Aunt Turner has made of it! By heaven! A woman should never be trusted with money. I always said she ought to have settled something on you, as soon as her husband died.'

'But that would have been trusting *me* with money,' replied Emma, 'and *I* am a woman too.'

'It might have been secured to your future use, without your having any power to use it now. What a blow it must have been to you! To find yourself, instead of an heiress of eight thousand or nine thousand pounds, sent back a weight upon your family, without a sixpence. I hope the old lady will smart for it.'

'Do not speak disrespectfully of her — she was very good to me; and if she has made an imprudent choice, she will suffer more from it herself than *I* can possibly do.'

'I do not mean to distress you, but you know everybody must think her an old fool. I thought Turner had been reckoned an extraordinarily sensible, clever man. How the devil did he come to make such a will?'

'My uncle's sense is not at all impeached in my opinion by his attachment to my aunt. She had been an excellent wife to him. The most liberal and enlightened minds are always the most confiding. The event has been unfortunate, but my uncle's memory is, if possible, endeared to me by such a proof of tender respect for my aunt.'

'That's odd sort of talking. He might have provided decently for his widow, without leaving everything that he had to dispose of, or any part of it, at her mercy.'

'My aunt may have erred,' said Emma warmly. 'She *has* erred, but my uncle's conduct was faultless. I was her own niece, and he left to herself the power and the pleasure of providing for me.'

'But, unluckily, she has left the pleasure of providing for you to your father, and without the power. That's the long and short of the business. After keeping you at a distance from your family for such a length of time as must do away with all natural affection among us, and breeding you up (I suppose) in a superior style, you are returned upon their hands without a sixpence.'

'You know,' replied Emma, struggling with her tears, 'my uncle's melancholy state of health. He was a greater invalid than my father. He could not leave home.'

'I do not mean to make you cry,' said Robert, rather softened — and after a short silence, by way of changing the subject, he added: 'I am just come from my father's room; he seems very indifferent. It will be a sad break-up when he dies. Pity you can none of you get married! You must come to Croydon as well as the rest, and see what you can do there. I believe if Margaret had had a thousand or fifteen hundred pounds, there was a young man who would have thought of her.'

Emma was glad when they were joined by the others; it was better to look at her sister-in-law's finery than listen to Robert, who had equally irritated and grieved her. Mrs Robert, exactly as smart as she had been at her own party, came in with apologies for her dress.

'I would not make you wait,' said she, 'so I put on the first thing I met with. I am afraid I am a sad figure. My dear Mr W.

38

(to her husband) you have not put any fresh powder in your hair.'

'No, I do not intend it. I think there is powder enough in my hair for my wife and sisters.'

'Indeed you ought to make some alteration in your dress before dinner when you are out visiting, though you do not at home.'

'Nonsense.'

'It is very odd you should not like to do what other gentlemen do. Mr Marshall and Mr Hemmings change their dress every day of their lives before dinner. And what was the use of my putting up your last new coat, if you are never to wear it?'

'Do be satisfied with being fine yourself, and leave your husband alone.'

To put an end to this altercation and soften the evident vexation of her sister-in-law, Emma (though in no spirits to make such nonsense easy) began to admire her gown. It produced immediate complacency.

'Do you like it?' said she. 'I am very happy. It has been excessively admired, but sometimes I think the pattern too large. I shall wear one tomorrow that I think you will prefer to this. Have you seen the one I gave Margaret?'

Dinner came, and except when Mrs Robert looked at her husband's head, she continued gay and flippant, chiding Elizabeth for the profusion on the table, and absolutely protesting against the entrance of the roast turkey, which formed the only exception to 'You see your dinner.' 'I do beg and entreat that no turkey may be seen today. I am really frightened out of my wits with the number of dishes we have already. Let us have no turkey I beseech you.'

'My dear,' replied Elizabeth, 'the turkey is roasted, and it may just as well come in as stay in the kitchen. Besides, if it is cut, I am in hopes my father may be tempted to eat a bit, for it is rather a favourite dish.'

'You may have it in, my dear, but I assure you I shan't touch it.'

Mr Watson had not been well enough to join the party at dinner, but was prevailed on to come down and drink tea with them.

39

'I wish he may be able to have a game of cards tonight,' said Elizabeth to Mrs Robert, after seeing her father comfortably seated in his armchair.

'Not on my account, my dear, I beg. You know I am no card-player. I think a snug chat infinitely better. I always say cards are very well sometimes, to break a formal circle, but one never wants them among friends.'

'I was thinking of its being something to amuse my father,' said Elizabeth, 'if it was not disagreeable to you. He says his head won't bear whist, but perhaps if we made a round game he may be tempted to sit down with us.'

'By all means, my dear creature, I am quite at your service, only do not oblige me to choose the game, that's all. *Speculation* is the only round game at Croydon now, but I can play anything. When there is only one or two of you at home, you must be quite at a loss to amuse him. Why do you not get him to play cribbage? Margaret and I have played at cribbage most nights that we have not been engaged.'

A sound like a distant carriage was at this moment caught. Everybody listened; it became more decided; it certainly drew nearer. It was an unusual sound for Stanton at any time of the day, for the village was on no very public road, and contained no gentleman's family but the Rector's. The wheels rapidly approached; in two minutes the general expectation was answered; they stopped beyond a doubt at the garden-gate of the Parsonage. Who could it be? It was certainly a post-chaise. Penelope was the only creature to be thought of. She might perhaps have met with some unexpected opportunity of returning. A pause of suspense ensued. Steps were distinguished, first along the paved footway which led under the window of the house to the front door, and then within the passage. They were the steps of a man. It could not be Penelope. It must be Samuel. The door opened, and displayed Tom Musgrave in the wrap of a traveller. He had been in London and was now on his way home, and he had come half a mile out of his road merely to call for ten minutes at Stanton. He loved to take people by surprise with sudden visits at extraordinary seasons; and, in the present instance, had had the additional motive of being able to tell the Miss Watsons, whom he depended on finding sitting quietly employed after tea, that he was going home to an eight o'clock dinner.

As it happened, he did not give more surprise than he received when, instead of being shown into the usual little sitting-room, the door of the best parlour (a foot larger each way than the other) was thrown open, and he beheld a circle of smart people, whom he could not immediately recognize, arranged with all the honours of visiting round the fire, and Miss Watson seated at the best Pembroke table, with the best tea-things before her. He stood a few seconds in silent amazement. 'Musgrave!' ejaculated Margaret, in a tender voice. He recollected himself, and came forward, delighted to find such a circle of friends, and blessing his good fortune for the unlooked-for indulgence. He shook hands with Robert, bowed and smiled to the ladies, and did everything very prettily, but as to any particularity of address or emotion towards Margaret, Emma, who closely observed him, perceived nothing that did not justify Elizabeth's opinion, though Margaret's modest smiles imported that she meant to take the visit to herself. He was persuaded without much difficulty to throw off his great-coat and drink tea with them. For 'Whether he dined at eight or nine,' as he observed, 'was a matter of very little consequence'; and without seeming to seek he did not turn away from the chair close by Margaret which she was assiduous in providing him. She had thus secured him from her sisters, but it was not immediately in her power to preserve him from her brother's claims; for as he came avowedly from London, and had left it only four hours ago, the last current report as to public news, and the general opinion of the day, must be understood before Robert could let his attention be yielded to the less national and important demands of the women. At last, however, he was at liberty to hear Margaret's soft address, as she spoke her fear of his having had a most terrible cold, dark, dreadful journey —

'Indeed you should not have set out so late.'

'I could not be earlier,' he replied. 'I was detained chatting at the Bedford by a friend. All hours are alike to me. How long have you been in the country, Miss Margaret?'

'We only came this morning; my kind brother and sister brought me home this very morning. 'Tis singular — is not it?'

41

'You were gone a great while, were you not? A fortnight, I suppose?'

'*You* may call a fortnight a great while, Mr Musgrave,' said Mrs Robert smartly, 'but *we* think a month very little. I assure you we bring her home at the end of a month much against our will.'

'A month! Have you really been gone a month? 'Tis amazing how time flies.'

'You may imagine,' said Margaret, in a sort of whisper, 'what are my sensations in finding myself once more at Stanton. You know what a sad visitor I make. And I was so excessively impatient to see Emma; I dreaded the meeting, and at the same time longed for it. Do you not comprehend the sort of feeling?'

'Not at all,' cried he aloud; 'I could never dread a meeting with Miss Emma Watson, or any of her sisters.'

It was lucky that he added that finish.

'Were you speaking to me?' said Emma, who had caught her own name.

'Not absolutely,' he answered; 'but I was thinking of you, as many at a greater distance are probably doing at this moment. Fine open weather, Miss Emma! Charming season for hunting.'

'Emma is delightful, is not she?' whispered Margaret. 'I have found her more than answer my warmest hopes. Did you ever see anything more perfectly beautiful? I think even *you* must be a convert to a brown complexion.'

He hesitated. Margaret was fair herself, and he did not particularly want to compliment her; but Miss Osborne and Miss Carr were likewise fair, and his devotion to them carried the day.

'Your sister's complexion,' said he at last, 'is as fine as a dark complexion can be; but I still profess my preference of a white skin. You have seen Miss Osborne? She is my model for a truly feminine complexion, and she is very fair.'

'Is she fairer than me?'

Tom made no reply. 'Upon my honour, ladies,' said he, giving a glance over his own person, 'I am highly indebted to your condescension for admitting me in such *déshabille* into your drawing-room. I really did not consider how unfit I was to be here, or I hope I should have kept my distance. Lady Osborne would tell me that I was growing as careless as her son, if she saw me in this condition.'

The ladies were not wanting in civil returns, and Robert Watson, stealing a view of his own head in an opposite glass, said with equal civility:

'You cannot be more in *deshabille* than myself. We got here so late that I had not time even to put a little fresh powder into my hair.'

Emma could not help entering into what she supposed her sister-in-law's feelings at the moment.

When the tea-things were removed, Tom began to talk of his carriage; but the old card-table being set out, and the fish and counters, with a tolerably clean pack, brought forward from the buffet by Miss Watson, the general voice was so urgent with him to join their party that he agreed to allow himself another quarter of an hour. Even Emma was pleased that he would stay, for she was beginning to feel that a family party might be the worst of all parties; and the others were delighted.

'What's your game?' cried he, as they stood round the table.

'Speculation, I believe,' said Elizabeth. 'My sister recommends it, and I fancy we all like it. I know *you* do, Tom.'

'It is the only round game played at Croydon now,' said Mrs Robert; 'we never think of any other. I am glad it is a favourite with you.'

'Oh! me!' said Tom. 'Whatever you decide on will be a favourite with *me*. I have had some pleasant hours at speculation in my time; but I have not been in the way of it for a long while. Vingt-un is the game at Osborne Castle. I have played nothing but vingt-un of late. You would be astonished to hear the noise we make there — the fine old lofty drawing-room rings again. Lady Osborne sometimes declares she cannot hear herself speak. Lord Osborne enjoys it famously — he makes the best dealer without exception that I ever beheld — such quickness and spirit! He lets nobody dream over their cards. I wish you could see him overdraw himself on both his own cards — it is worth anything in the world!'

'Dear me!' cried Margaret, 'why should not we play vingt-un? I think it is a much better game than speculation. I cannot say I am very fond of speculation.'

Mrs Robert offered not another word in support of the game. She was quite vanquished, and the fashions of Osborne Castle carried it over the fashions of Croydon.

'Do you see much of the Parsonage family at the Castle, Mr Musgrave?' said Emma, as they were taking their seats.

'Oh! yes; they are almost always there. Mrs Blake is a nice, little, good-humoured woman; she and I are sworn friends; and Howard's a very gentlemanlike good sort of fellow! You are not forgotten, I can assure you, by any of the party. I fancy you must have a little cheek-glowing now and then, Miss Emma. Were you not rather warm last Saturday about nine or ten o'clock in the evening? I will tell you how it was — I see you are dying to know. Says Howard to Lord Osborne —'

At this interesting moment he was called on by the others to regulate the game, and determine some disputable point; and his attention was so totally engaged in the business, and afterwards by the course of the game, as never to revert to what he had been saying before; and Emma, though suffering a good deal from curiosity, dared not remind him.

He proved a very useful addition at their table. Without him it would have been a party of such very near relations as could have felt little interest and perhaps maintained little complaisance, but his presence gave variety and secured good manners. He was, in fact, excellently qualified to shine at a round game; and few situations made him appear to greater advantage. He played with spirit, and had a great deal to say; and though with no wit himself, could sometimes make use of the wit of an absent friend, and had a lively way of retailing a commonplace, or saying a mere nothing, that had great effect at a card-table. The ways and good jokes of Osborne Castle were now added to his ordinary means of entertainment; he repeated the smart sayings of one lady, detailed the oversights of another, and indulged them even with a copy of Lord Osborne's overdrawing himself on both cards.

The clock struck nine while he was thus agreeably occupied; and when Nanny came in with her master's basin of gruel, he had the pleasure of observing to Mr Watson that he should leave him at supper while he went home to dinner himself. The carriage was ordered to the door, and no entreaties for his staying longer could now avail; for he well knew that if he stayed he would have to sit down to supper in less than ten minutes, which to a man whose heart had been long fixed on calling his next meal a dinner, was quite insupportable. On finding him determined to go, Margaret began to wink and nod at Elizabeth to ask him to dinner for the following day; and Elizabeth, at last, not able to resist hints which her own hospitable social temper more than half seconded, gave the invitation — 'Would he give Robert the meeting, they should be very happy?'

'With the greatest pleasure,' was his first reply. In a moment afterwards, 'That is, if I can possibly get here in time; but I shoot with Lord Osborne, and therefore must not engage. You will not think of me unless you see me.' And so he departed, delighted in the uncertainty in which he had left it.

Margaret, in the joy of her heart under circumstances which she chose to consider as peculiarly propitious, would willingly have made a confidante of Emma when they were alone for a short time the next morning, and had proceeded so far as to say, 'The young man who was here last night, my dear Emma, and returns today, is more interesting to me than perhaps you may be aware —' but Emma, pretending to understand nothing extraordinary in the words, made some very inapplicable reply, and jumping up, ran away from a subject which was odious to her. As Margaret would not allow a doubt to be repeated of Musgrave's coming to dinner, preparations were made for his entertainment much exceeding what had been deemed necessary the day before; and taking the office of superintendence entirely from her sister, she was half the morning in the kitchen herself directing and scolding.

After a great deal of indifferent cooking and anxious suspense, however, they were obliged to sit down without their guest. Tom Musgrave never came; and Margaret was at no pains to conceal her vexation under the disappointment, or repress the peevishness of her temper. The peace of the party for the remainder of that day and the whole of the next, which comprised the length of Robert and Jane's visit, was continually invaded by her fretful displeasure and querulous attacks. Elizabeth was the usual object of both. Margaret had just respect enough for her brother's and sister's opinion to behave properly by *them*, but Elizabeth and the maids could never do right; and Emma, whom she seemed no longer to think about, found the continuance of the gentle voice beyond calculation short. Eager to be as little among them as possible, Emma was delighted with the alternative of sitting above with her father, and warmly entreated to be his constant companion each evening; and as Elizabeth loved company of any kind too well not to prefer being below at all risks, as she had rather talk of Croydon with Jane, with every interruption of Margaret's perverseness, than sit with only her father, who frequently could not endure talking at all, the affair was so settled, as soon as she could be persuaded to believe it no sacrifice on her sister's part. To Emma, the change was most acceptable and delightful. Her father, if ill, required little more than gentleness and silence, and, being a man of sense and education, was, if able to converse, a welcome companion. In *his* chamber Emma was at peace from the dreadful mortifications of unequal society and family discord; from the immediate endurance of hardhearted prosperity, low-minded conceit, and wrong-headed folly, engrafted on an untoward disposition. She still suffered from them in the contemplation of their existence, in memory and in prospect, but for the moment she ceased to be tortured by their effects. She was at leisure; she could read and think, though her situation was hardly such as to make reflection very soothing. The evils arising from the loss of her uncle were neither trifling nor likely to lessen; and when thought had been freely indulged in contrasting the past and the present, the employment of mind and dissipation of unpleasant ideas which only reading could produce, made her thankfully turn to a book.

The change in her home society and style of life, in consequence of the death of one friend and the imprudence of another, had indeed been striking. From being the first object of hope and solicitude to an uncle who had formed her mind with the care of a parent, and of tenderness to an aunt whose amiable temper had delighted to give her every indulgence, from being the life and spirit of a house where all had been comfort and elegance, and the expected heiress of an easy independence, she was become of importance to no one — a burden on those whose affections she could not expect, an addition in a house already overstocked, surrounded by inferior minds, with little chance of domestic comfort, and as little hope of future support. It was well for her that she was naturally cheerful, for the change had been such as might have plunged weak spirits in despondence.

She was very much pressed by Robert and Jane to return with them to Croydon, and had some difficulty in getting a refusal accepted, as they thought too highly of their own kindness and situation to suppose the offer could appear in a less advantageous light to anybody else. Elizabeth gave them her interest, though evidently against her own, in privately urging Emma to go.

'You do not know what you refuse, Emma,' said she, 'nor what you have to bear at home. I would advise you by all means to accept the invitation; there is always something lively going on at Croydon; you will be in company almost every day, and Robert and Jane will be very kind to you. As for me, I shall be no worse off without you than I have been used to be; but poor Margaret's disagreeable ways are new to *you*, and they would vex you more than you think for, if you stay at home.'

Emma was of course uninfluenced, except to greater esteem for Elizabeth, by such representations, and the visitors departed without her.

CHAPTER 6

'WHAT ARE YOU GOING TO DO this morning, Elizabeth?' enquired Margaret, in a voice between languor and peevishness.

'Oh, I have a hundred things to do,' cried Miss Watson, turning from the window where she had watched her brother and his wife drive off. 'I must go and see about helping Nanny put away the best china and glass, and I must pin up the curtains, and put by all the things in the best bedroom which were had out for Jane's use; and I want to try that recipe she gave me for a pudding for my father — and fifty other things beside.'

'Then you will not think of walking, I presume, shall you, Emma?'

'I am not sure, is it not very dirty?'

'Good gracious, Emma!' cried Margaret sharply. 'I hope you are not such a fine lady as to mind stepping out in a little mud, or what is to become of me — I cannot bear walking alone, and Elizabeth is sure to be busy when I want her company.'

'Perhaps,' said Emma gently, rather afraid of giving offence by suggesting so evident a duty, 'if we were to help Elizabeth, she would have done in time to join you and enjoy the fine weather.'

'I don't suppose she wants us a bit.'

'Thank you, Emma,' replied her eldest sister, without listening to Margaret, 'but do not put off your walk on my account, I am used to these things, and mind the trouble no more than you do threading your needle, or finding your place in a book.'

'There, I told you so,' said Margaret as her sister left the room. 'I knew Elizabeth disdains all assistance, and hates to be interfered with in her housekeeping: I believe she would rather go through any trouble herself, than allow us to share it for half an hour. Now just make haste, do, and put your pelisse on; I like the finest part of the day.'

Emma still hesitated —

'I am not sure that I can go with you — perhaps my father may want me.'

'My father want you!' repeated Margaret in a tone of astonishment. 'Why what in all the world should he want *you* for?'

'I read to him a great deal,' replied Emma, colouring slightly.

'What a bore that must be,' continued Margaret — 'and now you use that as an excuse for not walking with me. If you don't want to come you might just as well say so at once.'

'Indeed I shall be very happy to walk with you,' said Emma in a soothing tone, 'if my father can spare me; I will run up and see, and if so, we can go directly.'

Mr Watson happened to be occupied by letters of business, in which he did not need Emma's help, and accordingly the sisters set off together. They took the road towards the town, Margaret saying nothing as to their object, and Emma making no enquiries. Indeed it did not occur to her that her sister had any other motive for walking than the desire of air and exercise.

'I have hardly had time to talk to you, Emma, since I came home; but the fact is, Jane is so fond of me, that when we are together she seldom can spare me ten minutes. She is an amazingly clever woman, I assure you, and one of the best judges of character and manners I ever saw.'

This assertion, though Emma believed it might be perfectly true, did not convey to her mind precisely the idea which Margarget expected; it rather convinced her of the narrow circle in which her sister had always moved, than the depth of Mrs Robert's penetration, or the extent of Margaret's own virtues. She did not, however, dissent from the praise, and her sister went on complacently.

'I am sure, Emma, you must be struck with Tom Musgrave's manners — is he not delightful?'

'I cannot say that I admire him at all,' replied Emma firmly.

'Not admire him!' cried Margaret, for a moment aghast at such heresy — then recollecting herself, she added, 'Ah, I suppose you mean he did not admire *you* — he did not dance with you at all at the ball I know; I dare say, too, he was not in spirits

— if I had been there it would have been different; if you knew him as well as I do, and had received as much attention from him, you would see him with very different eyes.'

'I shall be quite satisfied to view him always with as much indifference as I do now,' said Emma, 'and I trust, even if his manners should improve, or my taste alter, I shall be able to look on him without causing you any anxiety by excessive admiration. Elizabeth tells me he has made inroads on the peace of most young ladies hereabouts; I hope he will spare me, as I suppose I must not flatter myself with being wiser or steadier than other girls.'

'Elizabeth only says so from jealousy,' cried Margaret indignantly, 'he never paid her any attentions, and so — but good gracious, Emma' — interrupting herself and looking behind — 'there he is coming, and some others with him. Who can they be? Only one wears a red coat — I did not expect them so soon.'

'Did you expect him at all?' said Emma with astonishment. 'Is it possible you walked here to meet him?'

'Well, and where's the harm if I did — I wish you would just look at those other two gentlemen, and tell me if you know who they are!'

'Indeed,' replied Emma, vexed and embarrassed, 'I do not like to look round in that way; it does not seem — at least I have been told it is not ladylike to turn round and stare at people. But Margaret, is it really the case, that you came here with this in view?'

'Pooh pooh, how can you be so tiresome. Didn't you know as well as me that the hounds were to meet at Ashley Lodge? I thought most likely that Tom Musgrave would come this way — it is his direct road; but I wish I could make out who it is with him; they are just putting their horses into a trot — I declare I believe it is Lord Osborne and Mr Howard — how tiresome now — for Tom will not stop when Lord Osborne is there — how very provoking!'

'If I had known this,' said Emma, 'nothing would have persuaded me to come this way. They will think we did it to meet them.'

The gentlemen were now come so near, that Emma's conclud-

50

ing words were lost in the noise produced by the sharp trot of several horses. She was thinking rather uncomfortably about what Mr Howard would think, and whether *he* would suppose she had walked out to throw herself in Lord Osborne's way, when the gentlemen suddenly drew up beside the high, narrow footpath on which the sisters were walking.

'Miss Emma Watson,' cried Lord Osborne, as he threw himself from his horse, which he hastily resigned to the groom. 'By jove! How lucky I am to have come this way — so you are come out to see the hounds throw off? I am so glad to have met you.'

Tom Musgrave dismounted in imitation of his noble friend; but, as the path only admitted two, he was obliged to draw back — and, while Lord Osborne walked by the side of Emma, Tom was exposed, without defence, to the appealing glances and soft whispers of Margaret. Emma saw, with a sort of concern, which she could not exactly analyse, that Mr Howard remained on horseback, and only acknowledged his former partner by a bow. While she was wondering at the change, her companion was trying to be as agreeable as nature would allow him, and she could almost have laughed outright at the air of deference and attention with which the dashing Tom Musgrave listened to his lordship's remarks, and confirmed any of his statements which required support. Thus they had walked for more than five minutes, when another branch of the lane opened to them, which Emma knew would lead them almost directly home.

'Margaret,' said she, turning to her sister, 'I think we had better return this way; we may, perhaps, be wanted at home before we can reach it.'

'I am sure I am quite ready to go,' said Margaret, apparently on the point of bursting into tears at finding it useless to attempt to fix Tom's attention on herself.

'I thought you were come here on purpose to see the hounds throw off,' said Lord Osborne to Emma, 'and what's the use of going home before you reach the covert?'

'Indeed you were mistaken, my lord,' replied Emma calmly, but decidedly; 'for I was not aware till we saw you that the hounds met in this neighbourhood.'

'Well, but do come on now, you are so near — my sister

51

and Miss Carr are to be there, and I want to introduce you to them.'

'Your lordship must be perfectly aware that what you propose is impossible,' replied Emma. 'I have no claim to intrude on Miss Osborne's notice, and she would, probably, be far more surprised than pleased by such an extraordinary step.'

'No, indeed, 'pon my honour, my sister wishes to make your acquaintance. Tom Musgrave knows what she said about it last night — I believe I was wrong in what I said, which, I suppose, is what you mean; I want to introduce my sister to you — is that right? (Emma could not quite control a smile.) So now will you just come on with us, without stopping here any longer?'

'I am much obliged to you, my lord; but indeed, I cannot comply with your request; and as Miss Osborne would not be expecting to meet us today, she will experience no disappointment.'

Very reluctantly the young nobleman was obliged to give up his proposition; and, as they rode away, he suddenly turned towards Tom Musgrave after some minutes' silence, and exclaimed:

'I say, Musgrave, how is it you manage with women to make them worship you so? — Miss Emma Watson is the only girl I ever *tried* to please, and she seems to delight in refusing everything I propose. I can make no way with her.'

Tom's self-complacency was very near betraying him into a serious blunder at this speech; for he was on the point of assenting to the proposition that he was more successful in making fools of young women than Lord Osborne. Fortunately, he recollected in time that however agreeable a strenuous support to his lordship's opinions might be under ordinary circumstances, there were occasions when a well-turned negative was far more flattering. Lord Osborne, like many other people, might depreciate himself — but he could not wish his friends to take the same view of the subject; Mr Musgrave therefore replied judiciously that Miss Emma Watson had treated him in a precisely similar fashion, from which he concluded that it was her usual way.

The sisters, in the meantime, were pursuing their path homewards, whilst Margaret was raining questions on Emma concerning the commencement and progress of her acquaintance with Lord Osborne — an event which seemed to her so very astonishing, as only to be surpassed by the cool and composed manner with which Emma had treated the affair.

Tom Musgrave's intimacy at Osborne Castle had always greatly elevated his importance in her eyes; yet here was her own sister, who not only had walked side by side with the peer himself, but had positively refused to accompany him further, in spite of his entreaties; and she now wound it all up by coolly declaring that she thought Lord Osborne very far from an agreeable young man, and had no wish to see more of him. She was silently pondering on these extraordinary circumstances when she was roused by the angry bark of a fierce dog — which rushing from the farmyard, took up a position in the centre of the way, and seemed determined to dispute the passage. Margaret, screaming aloud, turned to run away, and Emma's first impulse was to follow her example; but a moment's consideration checked her, and she attempted to soothe or overcome the animal by speaking gently, and looking fixedly at him. She was so far successful, that his bark sunk into a low irritable growl, and Emma profited by the comparative silence to address a man in the farmyard, and beg him to call back the dog.

'He woant hurt thee, Missus,' was the reply of the countryman, who seemed, in reality, rather amused at the fright of the young ladies.

'But my sister is afraid to pass him,' said Emma, imploringly, looking round at Margaret who was standing at the distance of a hundred yards, and evidently prepared again to take flight at the smallest aggressive movement of the enemy.

'Thy sister must jist make up her moinde to pass as other foalk do — unless you choose to go athert the field yonder, to get out of him's way.'

Athert the field, Emma concluded, they must go, as Margaret would not advance; and she was reluctantly about to turn back, when the sound of horse's hoofs was heard, and the next moment Mr Howard appeared advancing towards them. A glance showed him the dilemma in which the ladies were placed, and he was as quick in overcoming as in comprehending their difficulties. A well-aimed blow of his whip sent the aggressor yelping to his kennel, and a sharp reproof to his master followed, for not interfering in their favour, accompanied with a hint about the necessity of confining his dog, if he did not wish to have it indicted.

Mr Howard was too well known for his word to be disputed or his reproofs to be resented; and the farmer promised it should not happen again — peace was restored, and under Mr Howard's protection, even Margaret ventured to pass.

'I thought you were going to hunt,' said Emma, in reply to his offer to see them safely out of reach of their terrible foe. Mr Howard said he had only ridden out for pleasure, not for so important and imperative a business as fox-hunting: it was evident, however, that he considered walking with the Miss Watsons quite as pleasant as riding, and that he was in no hurry to remount.

'Would you allow my sister to do herself the honour of calling on you?' said he, presently. 'Your kindness to her little boy has quite captivated her, and Charles is as anxious as herself to carry on the acquaintance so happily begun. She has been quite ill since the assembly or the offer would have been made sooner.'

Emma readily professed that it would give her great pleasure to become better acquainted with both Charles and his mother.

'I was almost afraid to propose it,' said Mr Howard, 'when I heard the ill success of Lord Osborne's negotiation for a similar point; I assure you, the wish was really expressed by Miss Osborne; and though my pupil blundered in making it known, I am certain it was entirely from want of self-possession, not from want of respect.'

Emma did not answer; she was trying to ascertain whether the gratified feeling she experienced at the moment arose from the wish ascribed to Miss Osborne, or the anxiety shown by Mr Howard to set those wishes in a proper light.

A pause soon afterwards occurring in the conversation, Margarget seized the opportunity, and leaning past her sister, addressed Mr Howard in an earnest and anxious manner —

'Is it really true, Mr Howard, that Miss Carr is so very beautifully fair?'

'She is certainly very fair,' replied he, rather astonished at the

54

question, 'I do not know that I ever saw a whiter skin; but is it possible that her complexion can be a subject of discussion or interest in your village?'

'I do not know,' replied Margaret, not at all understanding him. 'Mr Musgrave is a great deal at the castle, is he not?'

'Yes, often, I believe,' said Mr Howard quietly.

'I do not wonder at it — he must be a great favourite with the ladies, no doubt,' continued she; 'I should think his manners must recommend him everywhere.'

'I fancy his intimacy at the castle is more owing to Lord Osborne's partiality than that of his mother or sister,' said he, still in a reserved tone of voice, as if not wishing to discuss the domestic circle of the Osbornes.

Mr Howard did not leave the girls until they had reached their own gate, and then with a quiet but decided assurance that he would soon bring his sister, he mounted his horse and rode homewards.

'Well, Emma,' said Margaret, as they entered the parlour together, 'I wish everybody had your luck; I cannot see why I should not have such great friends, yet I dare say, I have been to fifty assemblies, and never was a bit nearer knowing Lord Osborne or any of his set — how you managed it, I am sure I cannot guess.'

'It was only because Emma is both good-natured and pretty,' said Elizabeth, looking up from the sofa-cover that she was assiduously mending.

'Emma is not the first pretty girl who has been seen in these rooms, I believe,' said Margaret sharply; 'and I should like to know what being good-natured has to do with it!'

'It made her offer to dance with little Charles Blake — and by that means please his uncle and mother; it was her kindness and good-nature did that.'

'No it was not; it was because she was so lucky as to sit next the boy; if she had been at the other end of the room, all the good-nature in the world would have been of no use — it was all her good luck.'

'And if you had sat next to him the whole evening, should you have thought of offering to be his partner, Margaret?' enquired Elizabeth.

'Very likely not — I hate dancing with boys. But I don't understand how Emma got acquainted with Lord Osborne.'

'And I cannot at all comprehend what makes your head so full of the Osbornes this morning,' replied Elizabeth.

Margaret explained, but her account was so tinctured with jealousy that Elizabeth, curious and unsatisfied, ran up after Emma who had left the room at the commencement of this discussion, to ascertain the truth from her.

Even when Emma had related everything to her sister, it seemed almost incredible — that Lord Osborne should have proposed such an introduction, and Mr Howard promised a visit from his sister, appeared more like events in a fariy tale than the sober realities of their everyday life.

'But why did you refuse the introduction, Emma?'

'What, to Miss Osborne? Because I think such unequal acquaintances are very undesirable and not likely to compensate for the trouble which accompanies them, by any pleasure they can afford.'

'I believe in my heart, Emma, you are very proud,' said Elizabeth in a doubting, puzzled tone that almost made her sister laugh.

'Too proud to become a hanger-on of Miss Osborne's, certainly,' answered she; 'much too proud to be condescended to, and encouraged, or patronized, or anything of the sort.'

'Well, if I had been you, I would have just seen what his lordship would do; suppose they had invited you to the castle — would you not have liked that?'

'No,' said Emma; 'I should only indulge in luxuries which would make my home uncomfortable from the contrast, or perhaps become envious from comparing their state with my own. But I cannot imagine the option will be given me; unless Miss Osborne seeks me, we shall not meet, for I shall certainly not throw myself in her way.'

'Well, I am less proud and less philosophical than you, Emma, and I own I would accept such an offer if it were made to me. But after all, you mean to let Mrs Blake visit you — where's your pride in that case?'

'Surely Elizabeth, you must see the difference. Mr Howard and his sister are in our rank of life, though their intimacy at the

Castle gives them artificial consequence. There would be no condescension on their part, and no obligation incurred by me, which a return visit would not fairly pay.'

'Well, I wish I knew what day they would come,' said Miss Watson, 'for we could sit in the drawing-room, and not cover the sofa and the carpet.'

'Pray do not do anything of the sort,' said Emma, in alarm; 'I hope it will not be the only visit they will pay — we cannot always sit in state to receive them.'

Elizabeth shook her head.

'You are very odd, Emma — what notions you have. I don't at all understand you yet.'

CHAPTER 7

IT WAS VERY EVIDENT by the result, that Mr Howard had not overstated his sister's anxiety to place her acquaintance with Emma on a footing which would secure its permanence and authorize an increase of its intimacy; for the next Monday after making the request, the visitors arrived. Elizabeth and Margaret were sitting together when they were announced — but the former immediately left the room to seek for Emma — although she would have been very glad if Margaret would have saved her the trouble. Margaret, however, was determined to see as much of these strangers from an unknown world as she could, and consequently would not stir. She was very anxious to improve the opportunity by immediately entering into conversation with Mr Howard, but she could find nothing to say, and so could not help feeling, in some degree, obliged by the well-bred manner in which Mrs Blake commenced the conversation.

'My brother has been telling me of your adventures on Saturday with the dog. I hope you suffered no further inconvenience from it.'

'Oh,' said Margaret, 'I was dreadfully frightened; I believe, but for Mr Howard's interference, I should have fainted; I am very nervous, and I declare I would rather have remained there the whole night than have ventured past the horrid animal.'

'My arrival there must be esteemed most fortunate,' said he, 'but I own I am astonished at the rudeness of the man in the farmyard, who contented himself with looking on.'

'Oh, he was a brute,' cried Margaret, 'no better than the dog — but what else can you expect from boors like him. They have no sentiment or feeling.'

'I do not agree with you,' replied Mr Howard. 'I assure you,

I have often been struck with instances of disinterestedness and generosity among the lower classes, which show them to be endowed with excellent feelings.'

'They have no delicacy or sentiment,' said Margaret. 'I own my partiality for the gentle and elegant in manner, the aristocratic in birth and breeding.'

'Still, I think you do our peasantry injustice, if you suppose them destitute of feeling, because they have not a refined way of expressing their thoughts in words,' replied Mr Howard. 'Their manners are of course uncultivated, and their habits are what you would call unrefined — but then no one would wish they should be cursed with the desire for elegancies.'

'I dare say that is very true,' replied Margaret, 'but I must say I think them very coarse and clownish; now and then one sees a pretty-looking girl, but the men are all detestable.'

'But, I assure you, I have met with poetical though uncultivated minds amongst labouring men.'

'It must be very odd poetry expressed in such gothic language,' said Margaret, laughing; as she had not the smallest poetical feeling herself, she could not comprehend what he meant when he talked of it, and concluded that the peasantry spoke in rhyme or, at least, in blank verse.

At this moment the entrance of the other young ladies cut short the discussion, and introduced a new subject. Charles, who had been standing by his mother, earnestly contemplating the crown of his hat, and drawing figures with his finger on the beaver, now looked up, all animation, as Emma greeted him as her 'first partner at her first ball.' His mother's eyes sparkled, as much as the little boy's, at her good-natured notice. A moment after, Mr Watson entered the room; his gout was better, and allowed him to come downstairs.

It was Emma who rolled his easy chair into the proper position, Emma who arranged his footstool, who drew the curtain to exclude the glare of the wintry sun, placed the screen to ward off the draught from the door, and laid his spectacles, snuff-box, and writing-case on precisely the proper spots of the proper table next to him.

Mr Watson's comforts were soon arranged, and when he had carefully adjusted his spectacles, and taken a survey of the room, he turned to Mr Howard, and enquired, who was that nice young woman talking to Elizabeth.

On being answered that it was his sister, he civilly apologized for not having known her, which, as he had never seen her before, he remarked, was not wonderful; but Elizabeth ought to have introduced him before he sat down, as really the gout made it extremely difficult to move across the room.

Mrs Blake, however, made it all easy, and soothed Mr Watson's discomposure at such a breach of etiquette, by the good-natured and respectful manner in which she now addressed him.

Whilst they were sitting in pleasant chat, Tom Musgrave again appeared amongst them. Emma really began to hate the sight of him on Margaret's account, as her sister's manner whilst in his company cost her many blushes; and her increase of fretfulness after his departure occasioned discomfort to the whole party. It was some gratification to discover from Mr Watson's manner, that he was very far from looking on Tom Musgrave as the amiable and elegant gentleman that he aspired to be considered.

'Well, Master Tom,' said he, 'what foolish thing have you been doing lately — breaking any more horses' knees or dinner engagements? Your genius cannot have been idle since I saw you last — let's hear about it.'

'No indeed, sir,' replied Tom; 'I have been doing nothing worth chronicling, at least to such a *judge* as you. I have had my own little amusements, but they are not worth detailing. By the bye, Howard, I dare say Osborne did not tell you how completely I beat him at Fives the other day.'

'Lord Osborne seldom entertains me with accounts of his sports, whether defeated or victorious,' replied Mr Howard coolly.

'When you have the gout in your foot,' observed Mr Watson, 'it will be consolatory to you to remember that you could once beat Lord Osborne at Fives.'

'Aye, sir, I dare say I shall have my turn by-and-bye, I expect to have it early — Osborne tells me *his* father had it at five-and-twenty. It's an aristocratic complaint.'

'Unless you have reason to suppose that the late Lord Osborne

60

was *your* father likewise,' resumed Mr Watson drily, 'I don't see what either his gout or his aristocracy have to do with you.'

'Do you feel any symptoms already?' whispered Margaret; 'you really ought to take care of yourself — who would be so much missed if you were laid up with that dreadful disorder! And who would you get to nurse you in your hours of suffering.'

'Oh, I'll take care of myself, Miss Margaret, gout makes one a prisoner, which is bad — I hate all confinement, and bonds of every kind, especially fire-side bonds. — By the bye, Howard,' he continued, breaking in upon a very agreeable conversation which that gentleman was carrying on aside with Emma, 'I knew you were here when I came in, by that curious vehicle standing at the door. Positively it must have belonged to your great-grandfather — nobody more modern could have built such a conveyance.'

'One thing is certain,' said Mr Watson, 'Mr Howard *had* a great-grandfather to whom it might have belonged — it is more than everyone can say.'

'Perhaps it is not the most elegant conveyance in the world,' replied its owner good-humouredly, 'but it carries us very safely and the most fashionable curricle would do no more. Lord Osborne has promised to give me a new carriage when either he or I marry, and I mean to make mine serve till that event.'

'And are you come wooing now in person or as proxy?' whispered Tom, quite loud enough for Emma to hear.

'Mr Musgrave,' said Howard in his particularly quiet but decisive way, 'you are welcome to laugh at my carriage, but remember there are subjects on which jesting is indelicate, and places where it is insulting.' He turned away as he spoke and addressed Mr Watson, to give Emma's cheek time to recover from the glow which betrayed that she had heard more than was pleasant.

Tom looked a little foolish, and after a moment's hesitation, addressed Emma with an enquiry as to whether she had been walking that forenoon. He only gained a monosyllable in reply; and then Emma, drawing little Charles towards her, began a confidential conversation with him on the subject of his garden and companions at school, and the comparative merits of stool-ball and cricket. Tom was repulsed, so turning to Elizabeth, he cried:

'Well, I must be going, Miss Watson, for I have an engagement. I promised to meet Fred Russell and Beauclerc and another fellow presently — so I must be off. They want my opinion about some greyhounds Beauclerc has taken a fancy to, but wouldn't buy until I had had time to see them. They are monstrous good fellows, and must not be kept waiting — great friends of Osborne's, I assure you.'

Nobody opposed his design, and as the sound of his curricle wheels died away in the distance, Mr Watson observed :

'There goes a young man, who if he had had to work for his bread might have been a useful member of society. But unfortunately the father made a fortune, so the son can only make a fool of himself.'

CHAPTER 8

'I SUPPOSE SOME OF YOU GIRLS will be for going over to return Mrs Blake's visit,' said Mr Watson to his daughters, the next day. 'I have no objection to your visiting her, but you must go tomorrow, if you go at all this week, for I cannot spare the horse after that day.'

'Well, Emma,' said Margaret directly, 'I will drive you over tomorrow if you like — you don't drive, I dare say.'

'I think,' said Emma, 'that Elizabeth ought to go, because as it is a first visit, and she is the eldest — it will seem more complimentary.'

'Certainly,' cried Elizabeth, who was quite as anxious as Margaret to pay the visit, 'you and I, Emma, must go at all events.'

'But then *I* can't,' exclaimed Margaret, 'and why am I to be left out? If Elizabeth goes, because *she* is the eldest, I have the best right to go too, when Pen is away, for I am older than Emma at all events.'

'But as the visit was paid especially to Emma,' rejoined Elizabeth, 'it is quite impossible that she should give it up to you. She *must* go.'

'Oh, yes, everybody must go but me; that is always the way — it's very hard.'

'Would not the chaise hold three?' suggested Emma, anxious for a compromise. 'Margaret is so slight, and I am not large, I am sure we could sit so.'

'I dare say you could,' replied her father, 'but I can tell you, you would have to sit in the stable-yard if you did, for the old horse could not draw you, and should not make the attempt. No, no, if Margaret wants to go she may wait till next time — if you pay visits at all, you shall pay them properly.'

The consequence of this decision was such an increase of fretfulness in Margaret for the rest of the day, as to make Emma inclined to think the society of her new acquaintance would be dearly bought at such a penalty. Elizabeth bore it with the indifference produced by long habit.

'It is no use minding her,' said she to Emma as they made ready for bed that night. 'She is always the same; if you give up one thing, she will quarrel with another; you can do no good to her by sacrificing every thing to her wishes, and you had much better take your own way when you can, and mind her crossness as little as possible.'

Margaret's ill-humour was as apparent next morning, but it was some consolation to her that the day was exceedingly cold with a heavy canopy of clouds overhead, and occasional slight sprinklings of snow, which promised anything but a pleasant drive to her sisters.

Wrapping themselves up as well as they could, they set off; but before they came in sight of Osborne Castle, for the Parsonage was within the park, a very heavy fall of snow overtook them.

They found Mrs Blake sitting alone, and were received by her with warmth and ease.

'It is very good, indeed, of you to come through such weather to see us. I am sure you must be half-frozen — what can I give you to make you comfortable?'

Elizabeth looked round the room with surprise and admiration. It was not larger nor better than their own — and the furniture was, apparently, neither more expensive, nor more plentiful — but there was an air of comfort and tidiness which their sitting-room never had.

They had not sat there many minutes, when Mr Howard entered from his little study which faced the entrance. He had seen their arrival, but would not gratify his wishes of immediately presenting himself till he had ascertained that their horse was properly attended to, and the carriage placed under cover to shelter it from the now thickly descending snow.

Half an hour passed rapidly, but when the sisters, after glancing at each other as a signal for departure, began to look rather anxiously at the weather, they found that it had changed decidedly for the worse since their entrance, although their attentions had been too much engrossed to perceive it before.

'What can we do?' said Emma, as she contemplated the scene in some alarm. 'Do you think you could drive in such a storm, Elizabeth?'

'Oh, I should not mind venturing,' said Miss Watson, 'but I am afraid for you; you know you had a cold this morning and to encounter such a storm would make you worse.'

An encounter with the storm was denounced immediately as impossible, not to be mentioned or thought of, much less put in practice — they must wait a little while, if they wished *very much* to return home; in case it did not mend, they might send a message if they feared Mr Watson would be uneasy — but indeed Mr Howard thought they had better give up all idea of returning at once, and allow him immediately to dispatch someone to answer for their safety to their father's house.

With the most friendly warmth, every possible accommodation was placed at their disposal; every objection done away as soon as stated; every difficulty proved to be a vain fancy of its originator. The idea of the addition to their circle at dinner did not seem at all to discompose Mrs Blake; and the minor arrangements, the things to be lent for their use and comfort, appeared rather to bring her positive enjoyment. In a short time, the young ladies felt themselves quite domesticated in the house; their cloaks and bonnets removed, their hair smoothed, and their thick boots exchanged for comfortable slippers of their new friend, they found themselves again seated comfortably in the pretty parlour and busily employed in helping Mrs Blake in the agreeable occupation of sewing certain little coloured silk bags which Mr Howard and Charles afterwards filled with deliciously scented pot-pourri, from the large china jar in the corner of the room. Now, their only subject of uneasiness, besides the dread of giving too much trouble, was the fear that their father's comfort would suffer in their absence, as they knew only too well how little Margaret contributed towards his amusement, or sought to spare him trouble.

Dinner-time came, and Elizabeth was surprised to find that, although they lived in the vicinity of Osborne Castle, their hour of dining was no later than that to which she was accustomed, and still more surprised that the simple meal — the single joint, and the plain, but certainly well-made, pudding which followed it — was considered quite sufficient in itself, and needed no apologies. Not that she expected anything more elegant or uncommon, much less wished for it, but she felt that had *she* been the host, she would certainly have regretted the absence of further luxuries. The hour of dusk which followed the dinner was particularly agreeable, as they drew their chairs round the comfortable fire, and chatted with the easy good nature which such a situation and such a combination of characters is sure to promote.

Charles very freely expressed his extreme satisfaction at the turn events had taken — appealing to his uncle to confirm his assertion that nothing could be more delightful than the fact of the two Miss Watsons being forced to remain in the house, and to join in his hope that the snow would keep them prisoners for a week to come. Mr Howard readily assented to his view and only demurred from the doubt whether the young ladies would not find such a detention a severe penalty — in which case, he was sure, even Charles could not wish, for his own gratification, to inflict it on them.

'Oh, certainly not, if they did not like it,' cried Charles, 'only I am sure, Miss Emma, you are too good-natured to object to what would give us all so much pleasure.'

'If my opinion or wishes could make any difference to the snow, or serve to open the road, Charles, it would be reasonable to form a deliberate decision,' said Emma, 'but now I want you, in the meantime, to guess this riddle,' and she diverted his attention by proposing some charades and enigmas.

The diversion soon occupied the whole party, but presently a note was brought to Mr Howard, which after studying near a light for some time, he threw down on the table, and said :

'There, ladies, there is a riddle which I would almost defy you to read — look at it !'

His sister took it up.

'Oh ! I see — pray, Miss Watson, can you read that name?' And she held it out to Elizabeth who, with Emma, looked at it with great curiosity.

'Is that writing!' cried Emma, 'and can anyone expect it to be read; I do not understand a word, except the three first.'

'Yes,' said Elizabeth, 'one can read "my dear Mr Howard", but the rest appears as if the writer had dipped a stick in an ink bottle, and scribbled over the paper at random. You do not mean to say, you have read it, Mr Howard?'

'I made out its meaning,' said he, looking up from a writing table, at a little distance, 'and I am answering it at this moment. It is only to invite me to the Castle tonight, to make up their card-table, which I have refused.'

'Ah, how glad I am,' cried his sister, 'such a night, to ask you out, though only across the park! The Miss Watsons' company affords a sufficient apology even to Lady Osborne, I should think.'

'It is a sufficient one to myself,' said Mr Howard. 'Lady Osborne may be unable to calculate accurately what I gain by the refusal — but I know that I secure a pleasant party, and escape a dreadful walk, to say nothing of the tedium of the card-table itself; you see how deeply I am indebted to your presence, Miss Watson.'

'We always hear virtue is its own reward,' said Emma, 'and your hospitality to us now is repaid in kind; as you would not allow us to encounter the snow, it would have been unjust that you should be exposed to it yourself.'

The weather the next morning did not offer any prospect of a release to the young ladies, and to say the truth they evidently bore the involuntary absence from home without suffering very acutely, if either their air of complacency or their lively conversation might be considered indicative of their feelings. Breakfast passed pleasantly away, and the ladies were quietly sitting together afterwards, when the door opened and Lord Osborne's head appeared.

'May I come in?' said he, standing with his hand on the door. 'You look very comfortable.'

'You will not disturb us, my lord,' said Mrs Blake gently but good-naturedly, 'provided you have no dog with you.'

He advanced and paid his compliments to the ladies, then turned to the fire.

'That's nice,' said he, 'you cannot think how pleasant it is after the cold air'; then seating himself and holding out his feet to dry before the fire, he said to Emma, 'I heard you were snowed up here last night.'

'Did you, my lord?' said she very coolly.

'Yes; my mother *would* know who it was with Howard and so I learnt, and I am to give you my sister's compliments, or something of the sort, and as soon as the road is swept she will come and see you.'

'It's not such bad walking as you would think,' went on Lord Osborne, 'and the walk down here is screened from the wind; but you would be surprised to see how the snow has drifted in places: it will be impossible for you to get through the lanes today, Miss Watson.'

'We do not intend that they should attempt it,' said their hostess. 'Until we have ascertained that the roads are perfectly practicable, it would be inhuman to turn them out.'

A short silence ensued. Lord Osborne sat by the fire looking at Emma, who proceeded steadily with her work; presently Mrs Blake commenced, or rather resumed, a conversation with Elizabeth on the best methods of rearing domestic poultry.

Gradually as Miss Watson became hardened to the consciousness of being listened to by Lord Osborne, her faculties returned; and though at his first entrance she could not have told how young chickens should be fed, before the expiration of half an hour she was equal to imparting to her companion the deepest mysteries of the poultry yard.

Whilst they were thus sitting, Charles Blake suddenly rushed into the room and took up his station close to Emma's worktable.

'Why, Charles,' said Lord Osborne, 'don't you see me — aren't you going to speak to me this morning?' and he laid a firm grasp, as he spoke, on Charles's coat collar.

'I beg your pardon, my lord, I really did not see you,' replied Charles, twisting his person in the vain hope of eluding his lordship's grasp, and keeping his place.

'I say, Charles, how comes it lessons are over so early this morning — a holiday — hey — or uncle lazy — I thought you never finished till noon?'

'Oh, no, we have both been very industrious,' Charles

answered. 'We both worked as hard as we could to get lessons over because we wanted to come early into the drawing-room as the Miss Watsons were here.'

When Mr Howard entered the room, the eager step and open, happy look with which he was advancing, seemed to meet an unexpected shock at the sight of the visitor. His air was embarrassed as he paid him his compliments, and after standing for a moment, as if in hesitation, he drew a chair near Miss Watson and her sister, on the opposite side of the table to the others.

'It is not like your lordship's usual aversion to cold,' said he, at length, 'to venture out on foot in such a morning. I thought nothing could have tempted you to such an exertion.'

'One changes sometimes,' replied Lord Osborne, 'and one can do anything with sufficient motive — I mean to turn over a new leaf, as my nursery maids used to say — and you will hardly know me again.'

Another silence, during which his lordship crossed and uncrossed his legs repeatedly, then took up the poker and stirred the fire. Emma heartily wished him back at the Castle: his looks fixed on her were very unpleasant; and she hoped that his departure would release Mr Howard from the spell which appeared to overpower him.

It was evident, however, that the drawing-room at the Parsonage presented more charms to the young peer than the Castle halls, and he continued to sit in silent admiration of Emma long after Mr Howard had risen in despair and left the room.

The sound of the door-bell about noon brought some prospect of a change, eliciting from Mrs Blake an exclamation of wonder, and from Lord Osborne an interjection —

'I'll bet anything that's my sister.'

He was right. Wrapped in a furred mantle which might almost have defied the cold of a Siberian winter, Miss Osborne made her entry on purpose to call on Miss Emma Watson, as she declared immediately. Emma observed her with some curiosity. She was a small, young woman, with lively manners, a quick, dark eye, and good-humoured expression. Quite pretty enough, considering her birth, to be called beautiful, though had she been without the advantages of rank, fashion and dress — had she, in fact, been a Miss Watson, and not a Miss Osborne — she would, probably, not have been noticed a second time. She was extremely courteous and agreeable in her manners, chatting with volubility and animation, as if it was a relief to her to escape her mother's house to the unrestrained warmth and good-nature of the Parsonage.

'Where's your brother today, Mrs Blake?' said she presently. 'Has he run away from me — does he fancy we are charged with lectures for his desertion of our drawing-room last night? He need not be afraid. *I* think he was very excusable.'

'He was here just now. I do not think his conscience seems very uneasy — he is probably engaged in some business at present — I will let him know you are here.'

'Oh no, pray don't disturb him; I have too much regard for his credit, and the good of his parishioners. Let him write his sermon in peace.'

Mrs Blake assented. Probably Miss Osborne did not expect she would, for she presently added :

'*I* don't know, however, but that on the whole you had better summon him, because then he can give us his opinion on the proposal that I am charged to make, being nothing less than that you should *all* come and dine at the Castle this evening.'

Miss Osborne's proposal was followed by a short, hesitating silence amongst those to whom it was addressed.

'Perhaps,' said she perceiving this, 'you will like a moment's consideration. I do not wish to hurry for an answer. Pray deliberate on the case, Mrs Blake, but if you can, persuade your friends to conclude their deliberations in our favour.'

'I am afraid,' said Elizabeth, urged by the desperate nature of her feelings to some deliberate exertion, 'I am afraid we cannot have the pleasure — do ourselves the honour, I believe I ought to say — but indeed we were not prepared — we have no dress at all suitable for the occasion —' she stopped, afraid that she might have done wrong in exposing the real state of the case.

Miss Osborne looked surprised, as if the idea of not possessing a sufficient stock of gowns had never before entered her head.

'I am sorry there should be any difficulty,' she cried, 'gowns that are good enough for Mrs Blake and Mr Howard must surely be good enough for us. We shall not make the smallest objection to your coming as you are. You will be conferring on us a most important favour. You cannot imagine how miserably dull we find ourselves in this weather. Mama dozes over a fire-screen, and Miss Carr and I sit and look at each other, and long for a change of scene. Snow is always detestable, but at Osborne Castle it surpasses everything for deadening the faculties and damping the spirits. Come now, do think favourably of my request, how shall I dare to face Lady Osborne with a second refusal?'

'I hope her ladyship was not vexed at my brother's refusal last night?' said Mrs Blake with a little anxiety.

'I will not say she was not disappointed,' replied Miss Osborne gaily, 'we are so dreadfully dull and melancholy; but he has my full and entire forgiveness for his defalcation, on condition that he comes tonight to repair his errors, and brings you all with him.'

Lord Osborne had edged his chair closer to Emma and was in low tones pressing on her the request his sister had just made.

'Do come, you look too good-natured to say no — I am sure you must be monstrously obliging.' — Emma shook her head and tried not to smile — 'And as to what your sister says about dress, that's nonsense; that is, I don't mean she talks nonsense, but it's foolish to care about dress — you look very nice — you always do — and we don't the least mind about your gown. My mother and sister have such quantities of fine clothes themselves, that depend upon it they will not care the least for seeing any more.'

Emma thought this extremely probable, but yet it did not seem quite applicable to their case. How, indeed, could any young lady be expected to derive consolation from the idea that her appearance could be a matter of total indifference to her companions. It was evident to Miss Osborne that the ladies wished to discuss this question amongst themselves; she therefore dismissed the subject, with an assurance that if they decided in favour of the Castle, a carriage should be sent to fetch them.

Hardly was the house door closed on them, when Elizabeth, drawing a long breath, exclaimed:

'Dear Mrs Blake, do tell me what we had better do, I am sure I would much rather refuse if we can, but then perhaps it would not be thought right — and I must own if I were not so frightened I should rather like to see the inside of the Castle.'

71

'I do not think you need to be much alarmed,' replied Mrs Blake smiling. 'You will survive it I dare say, if you make up your mind to go. Lady Osborne *is* rather stiff certainly, but though she does nothing to make herself agreeable, she is not unpleasant. And I really think you would be more amused there than in our little drawing-room.'

'But we have no dress fit for company,' again urged Elizabeth.

'They are aware of the circumstances under which you came, and therefore must know you to be unprepared. I do not therefore think *that* need be an insurmountable objection. Your own inclination must decide it.'

At this moment Mr Howard re-entered the room. His sister immediately began to relate to him the fact of the visit and the invitation; but he cut her short by saying that he knew it; he had met Miss Osborne and her brother as they were leaving the house, and accompanied her part of the way home. His eyes were turned on Emma as he spoke and an idea which suddenly occurred to her caused her a sensation that brought the blood to her cheeks. Why she should colour and feel warm at the notion that he had any particular regard for Miss Osborne, she could not exactly decide. She was very much afraid that he would guess her thought.

This was an alarm entirely without foundation, as far from rightly guessing what was passing in her mind, Mr Howard's fancy went off in a totally different direction. He attributed her blushes to sentiments connected with the brother, not the sister, and supposed her to be pleased with the consciousness of these attentions being meant for her. For his own part he felt considerable surprise that Miss Osborne should so directly and decidedly countenance her brother's admiration. He was well acquainted both with Osborne pride and with the complacent indolence of his former pupil, but unaware that Lord Osborne's troubling himself to make Emma's acquaintance had already been the subject of discussion between Miss Osborne and Miss Carr. The two friends had concluded that this was a very passive sort of admiration unlikely to produce any positive results. Lady Osborne had made no objection to her daughter's proposal. Her card-table would thus be filled and Mr Howard would have no excuse for absenting himself. That was a matter to which she attached a growing importance as her daughter was now becoming somewhat anxious to observe.

Elizabeth suddenly turned to her sister and exclaimed:

'Emma, you have given no opinion on the subject — yet you are as much interested as the rest of us. What do you think of going — should you like it?'

'Yes, I think I should,' replied Emma honestly and boldly. 'I like what I have seen of Miss Osborne better than I expected, and really have rather a curiosity to see the inside of the Castle.'

'Ah, Emma, I am glad you have come down from your proud indifference, and condescended to be curious like the rest of us.'

'Did you think I affected indifference, Elizabeth?'

'I suspected it. For my part, I have no scruple in owning my wishes, and should like extremely to surprise Tom Musgrave by my acquaintance with the manners, amusements and ideas prevalent in Osborne Castle, of which he talks so much.'

'Then I may conclude it a settled affair,' observed Mrs Blake; 'and Charles shall run up to the castle with the note immediately. That shall be his share of the amusement.'

CHAPTER 9

AT SIX O'CLOCK THE PARTY started from the Parsonage,
Elizabeth in a flutter between curiosity and fear, which made her
pleasure in the undertaking rather doubtful to herself. Emma
would have thought more about it had she not been engrossed
with meditations on the change in Mr Howard's manners, which
somewhat perplexed her. There was a coldness in his tone when
he addressed *her*, quite at variance with his former warmth and
frankness. She was constantly fancying that she had done or said
something to lessen herself in his esteem, but she could not
imagine what it was. Occupied with these thoughts she scarcely
noticed the grandeur of the hall, the magnificent staircase, the
elegance of the ante-rooms as they approached, and was only
roused from her reverie by the overpowering blaze of light in
the drawing-room. Lady Osborne was alone in the room, seated
on a sofa from which she did not rise to receive them, but
graciously extended her thin and richly jewelled hand to Mrs
Blake, and bowed courteously to her companions.

Overawed by her near approach to such magnificence, Elizabeth drew back rather hastily, and after nearly upsetting Emma
by inadvertently treading on her toe, she dropped into the chair
which seemed most out of sight and endeavoured to recover her
composure.

Lady Osborne desired the other ladies to find seats, and then
observing that Mr Howard likewise drew back, and seemed to
meditate a retreat to one of the windows, she addressed a few
civil words to Mrs Blake, and then said:

'You have no footstool, Mrs Blake, take mine — I daresay Mr
Howard will bring me another.'

Thus appealed to, the gentleman was forced to approach and

74

immediately with eager civility was offered a seat on the sofa by herself.

Emma meantime was contemplating their hostess with some interest, and more wonder. Lady Osborne had been a celebrated beauty, and her dress showed that she had by no means given up all pretensions to her former claims. Jewels and flowers were mingled in her hair which was still remarkably abundant; her neck and shoulders were a good deal uncovered, her arms and hands were heavily hung with ornaments, and she smoothed down her rich dress with a hand which though thin was still white and delicate-looking. There was something in her manner to Mr Howard which particularly struck Emma — a wish to attract and engage him, that seemed very much at variance with her age and station. Not that she was an old woman, but as the mother of a grown-up son and daughter, and the widow of a peer, a grave and gentle deportment would have seemed more becoming in Emma's eyes.

Miss Osborne presented a remarkable contrast to her mother, from the studied plainness of her dress. She was entirely without ornament, except some beautiful flowers, and had evidently sought to assimilate her appearance as nearly as was suitable to what she knew her guests must present. She took a seat between the two strangers, and entered readily into conversation with Emma; but before many sentences had been exchanged, their party was completed by the appearance of Miss Carr at one door, and the young master of the house at another.

He paid his compliments to them all by a short bow, and a muttered, 'Glad to see you,' then walked towards his mother's sofa, and stationed himself by the end of it nearest Emma; here, leaning against the elbow, he could resume his apparently favourite amusement of staring at her face. Miss Carr, meanwhile, had approached the fender, and stood fluttering over the fire for some minutes, then advancing nearer to Lady Osborne, addressed to her some trifling question which diverted her attention from Mr Howard, to his evident relief. He immediately rose, and resigned his seat in her favour. Lady Osborne looked displeased, but to that Miss Carr was indifferent; she had secured a position at Lord Osborne's elbow, which was her own

75

object, and broken short a conversation, which she knew would please her friend.

Her position, however advantageous, was not long tenable. Before she had time to make more than one remark to Lord Osborne, the summons to dinner was given, cutting off his answer, though it was as short as he usually made his replies.

Lady Osborne rose in great state, and giving her hand to Mr Howard, proceeded to the dining-room through a long range of ante-rooms, where the large glasses on the walls seemed to be arranged for the purpose of exhibiting the lustre of her diamonds.

'How dingy we look compared to her ladyship and Miss Carr,' whispered Elizabeth to her sister. 'I really feel quite ashamed of myself.'

'I trust I shall be a little sheltered from her son's eyes,' rejoined Emma in a similar tone, 'his stare is quite overpowering; why does he not, sometimes, look at *you*.'

'Thank you, I do not wish it — gracious — six footmen — what can they all find to do in waiting.'

There was not a great deal said at dinner, and of that little a comparatively small portion fell to Emma's lot.

It was over at last, and when they had reached the drawing-room to which they were ushered, in almost as much style as they left it, Emma hoped she might find some little relief from insipidity; nor was she disappointed; whilst Lady Osborne was prosing to Mrs Blake, her daughter drew her younger guests into a smaller room, which she assured them was her own particular domain. Here establishing themselves comfortably round the ample fire, they fell into a lively and pleasant chat, as any four girls might be expected to do.

'I should think the gentlemen would not sit very long,' observed Miss Osborne, 'and when they come we must all adjourn to the drawing-room, for mama will wish to sit down to cards. I hope you can play cards.'

Her visitors assented, Elizabeth asserting that she was very fond of them.

'And you, Miss Emma Watson,' cried Miss Carr, 'do you not delight in cards — you answer with a degree of coldness that speaks rather of indifference on the subject.'

'I can play if necessary,' replied Emma, 'but there are many occupations I prefer.'

'But you shall not be obliged to make martyrs of yourselves,' said Miss Osborne good-humouredly. 'If you prefer it you shall sit here, either or both of you, but we do not play high.'

Nothing remarkable occurred during the rest of the evening; they played cards, but a dull, leaden state seemed to pervade everything, and both the Miss Watsons felt an inclination to yawn, which they had to restrain in Lady Osborne's august presence. They were very glad when the time for taking leave arrived, and the enlivening bustle of putting on cloaks and fur boots quite aroused them. Lord Osborne looked on whilst Mr Howard was wrapping up Emma, with a degree of attention which held out fair hopes of his soon learning such a lesson by heart.

'I shall come down and see you tomorrow,' said he.

'It seems warmer tonight,' observed Emma, 'don't you think we are going to have a thaw? Perhaps we may get home tomorrow.'

'I hope you are not weary of us,' said Mr Howard, in a cordial voice; 'if the weather does not change till *we* wish it, we shall keep you prisoner some days yet.'

'Thank you,' said Emma — she wanted to say something more but did not know exactly what, and they reached the carriage before she had made up her mind.

The bright fire which was burning in the comfortable little drawing-room at the Parsonage, irresistibly invited them to enter and draw round it, before separating for the night. Their drive had dispelled their sleepiness, and they were all four in good spirits.

'Well, Miss Watson,' said Mrs Blake, 'is your curiosity gratified? How do you like the Castle? Are you envious of their state?'

'No, I think not,' answered Elizabeth reflectingly, 'there are some things I should like, but much that would be troublesome. I dare say Lady Osborne has no worry about housekeeping, but then *I* should feel the responsibility of having so many dependent on me.'

'And what part would you choose of her ladyship's manner of

77

living?' asked Mr Howard. 'Her jewels perhaps — or her six footmen?'

'Neither,' replied Elizabeth, laughing a little. 'I am used to wait on myself, and should feel it a great restraint to be obliged to wait whilst others waited on me. I could not help thinking of what my father used to say, when Lady Osborne's maid was so long bringing her ladyship a shawl. "If you want to be served, send — if you want to be *well* served, go." That was his motto — and though he never acted on it himself, I think I do — and would rather run up three pairs of stairs than wait whilst another does it.'

'I admire the activity and independence of your spirit, Miss Watson,' replied Mr Howard. 'But you have not yet told me what it is you do envy.'

'No, and I do not mean to do it,' replied she; 'be satisfied with your own conjectures.'

'I must if you will say no more. And *you*, Miss Emma, how were you pleased with your evening?'

'Very much — I have come back much wiser than I went; I have made up my mind that the more elevated the situation the less pleasant it would be unless one had been brought up to it.'

'Then you would not change places with Lady Osborne?' said he, fixing a pair of very penetrating eyes on her.

'I think the supposition hardly a reasonable one; could you suppose I should wish to exchange with a woman old enough to be my mother — give up five and twenty years of life to be a wealthy middle-aged dowager in claret-coloured satin and diamonds?'

Mr Howard smiled.

'Remember,' continued Emma as if retracting, 'I mean no disparagement to your friend, who I have no doubt must be a very excellent and amiable woman, but I was speaking as she appeared to me today.'

'There have been young Lady Osbornes,' said he, almost in a whisper, and as if rather doubtful whether or not to speak the words.

'I suppose so,' replied Emma coolly, without the smallest embarrassment, but with a slight shade of reserve in her manner. He recognized it immediately and changed the subject.

'Then what do you think you require to make you happy?' he asked.

'A very comprehensive question — I should like to know whether you expect a serious answer.'

'A true one, if you please.'

'To be with those I love, and have money in my purse — I think that is sufficient: no — I think I should like a house too —'

'Very reasonable and moderate.'

'But preserve me from the slavery of living *en grande dame*; I was not brought up to it — and nothing but habit could make such bonds sit light and gracefully.'

'I believe you are right, and you must certainly be wise.'

He looked at her with unmistakable admiration; she could not meet his eyes, but coloured and fixed hers on the fender. In spite of her embarrassment, however, she felt a real pleasure in the friendly tone he had assumed, and hoped sincerely that the morning would not see him cold and formal again.

'Emma,' said Elizabeth after they had retired for the night, 'I am certain that Lord Osborne admires you very much.'

Emma only smiled in reply.

'What do you think about it?' continued Miss Watson.

'That I wish he would find some pleasanter way of testifying his admiration,' said Emma. 'I do not know whether he is the only man who ever admired me, but he is certainly the only one who ever looked at me so much.'

'Oh, we must not expect everything arranged just to our taste,' replied Elizabeth; 'and whilst you enjoy so much of his attention, you must not complain if he is not the most sprightly of admirers — the honour itself should suffice you. His rank is higher, if his wit is not brighter, than Mr Howard's.'

'To mention them in the same breath!' cried Emma; 'they are the antipodes of each other — as different in sense as in rank — what a pity their position cannot be reversed!'

'Oh, then your objection to being Lady Osborne is not after all to the rank but the man,' laughed Elizabeth, 'and you are less philosophic than you pretended to be. But if Mr Howard had been a peer, perhaps you would never have known him.'

'Very likely not,' said Emma calmly, 'but I do not see what that has to do with it.'

'Now don't pretend to be so very innocent and simple-minded, Emma; you know, as well as I do, that the two men are both in love with you.'

'How can you talk such nonsense, Elizazeth,' said Emma, colouring.

'No, it is you who are unreasonable, I am talking in the most matter-of-fact way imaginable.'

Emma was silent, and after waiting a minute, her sister began again:

'I wonder what Tom Musgrave will say when he hears we have dined at the Castle?'

'Some nonsense, I dare say; I believe his boastings were at the bottom of your curiosity to go there; you wished to surprise him.'

'Yes, I think I did — but was it as you expected? It was all so grand and formal that I felt quite uncomfortable. I am glad to have been, and still more glad to have come away.'

'I was not surprised at anything I saw; except that Lady Osborne would take the trouble of wearing so many jewels, and dress in so very juvenile a style.'

'I like Miss Osborne,' said Elizabeth, after a moment's pause.

'So do I,' replied her sister.

'Better than Miss Carr,' continued Miss Watson, 'I have a little fear of Miss Carr; but, Emma, I wonder how my father and Margaret get on, I am afraid he will find it very dull; she does not like backgammon or reading out loud — and this snow will prevent his getting the newspaper, or seeing anyone to amuse him.'

'Yes, I am afraid so,' sighed Emma, 'it is very pleasant here, but I wish we were home again.'

'I wish home were like this,' continued Miss Watson, 'as airy and cheerful and elegant-looking — what a nice room this is — we have no such room in our house — and I am sure our furniture never looks so well, take what care I can of it. You had better take this for your room when you are Mrs Howard.'

'I really wish you would not talk in that way, Elizabeth,'

remonstrated Emma, 'it can do no good, and it will make me feel very uncomfortable.'

'I beg your pardon, I will try not,' said her sister laughing.

Long after her sister was asleep, Emma herself was thinking over the events of the morning, and recalling to memory every tone and word and look of Mr Howard.

CHAPTER 10

MORE SNOW HAD FALLEN during the night, and the cutting wind which had accompanied it assured them that the lanes would be still less practicable than before. Noon brought a little note from Miss Osborne, reminding Emma of a wish expressed the night before to see the picture-gallery at the Castle, and offering, if Mr Howard would escort her up in time for luncheon, to go round with her afterwards.

'Do you think your brother could spare the time to accompany me?' said Emma to Mrs Blake, after communicating to her the contents of the note. 'I should be so much obliged if he would — because —' she added rather hesitatingly, 'I do not like to go alone, lest I should encounter the young lord.'

'And you do not like him, my dear?' said Mrs Blake with a bright look.

'I do not mind him much,' replied Emma; 'but I think I would rather not throw myself in his way: going alone would be almost like inviting his escort. Will you ask your brother?'

'I will go to him immediately — but I have no doubt of his acquiescence, and I can assure you in promising you Edward's company through the picture-gallery, Miss Osborne is securing you a *very* great pleasure.'

'It would, I am afraid, be encroaching too much on Mr Howard's time,' replied Emma, 'to exact his attentions as a cicerone. Miss Osborne has promised to go round with me herself.'

'Miss Osborne sometimes breaks her word,' said Mrs Blake coolly; 'and as she has usually a good many engagements perhaps you had better trust to my brother since you seem to shun hers.'

'I should not expect much intellectual gratification from Lord

Osborne's company, or his remarks on painting,' replied Emma, almost laughing at the idea.

Mrs Blake left the room to speak to her brother. She found him of course in his study, from whence Charles had just been dismissed.

'Edward, are you busy?'

'No, Anne, what do you want? I was just coming to the parlour.'

'It is not I, but Emma Watson who wants you.'

Mr Howard turned round to look at his sister with an expression half pleased, half incredulous.

'Yes indeed, so you need not stare so; Miss Osborne has sent to ask you to carry her to luncheon at the Castle, and go through the picture-gallery afterwards — that is to say, she has promised to go through the gallery, but you must be sure to accompany them.'

Mr Howard bent over his papers again for a moment in silence.

'Why do you not answer, Edward? There is nothing to prevent your going, is there? — and I am sure you cannot dislike it.'

'Oh no — but Emma — what did she say to it?'

'She begged me to come and engage you as her escort, that she might avoid falling into the company of Lord Osborne, who she seemed to apprehend might be lying in wait for her. Elizabeth Watson does not care for paintings, and means to remain with me.'

'It will give me the greatest pleasure,' said Mr Howard, starting up, and beginning to put away his books and papers. 'Now, or at any time she will name, I am quite at her service. When does she wish to go?'

'Immediately, I should think — that is, as soon as she can get herself ready. I will go back and give her your message at once.'

They were soon on their way. The air was bright and exhilarating — and it would have been very pleasant walking but for the ground being exceedingly slippery. It may be doubtful whether Mr Howard thought this an evil, since it compelled his companion to lean upon him for support, up the steep ascent which conducted them to the Castle. Even with the assistance of his arm, she was obliged to pause and take breath, at a point to which he led her which commanded a delightful prospect. The Parsonage and the church lay snugly at their feet, and the snow-clad country stretched out beyond, chequered with rich hanging woods of beech on the sides of the hills, and thick coppices of underwood down in the valley. Emma expressed her delighted admiration. Mr Howard assured her that if she would move a short distance along a path to the left, she would enjoy a still more splendid panorama. The snow had been swept off the gravel, and Emma could not resist the temptation, though it was diverging from their object. There was plenty of time — since they need not be at the Castle till one o'clock — and it was now little more than half an hour past noon. They turned into the path accordingly, and soon reached the spot he had mentioned. The Castle was now in view though still some way above them; and as they were standing there, Mr Howard observed:

'There is Lord Osborne just coming out at the side door, near his own rooms — do you see him?'

Emma perceived and watched him.

'I think he is taking the path to your house — is not he?'

'Yes, we shall meet him presently, if we turn and pursue our walk upwards.'

'Oh; then, pray, let us stay here till he is gone past,' said Emma hastily. 'I do not wish to meet him in the least.'

Mr Howard did not press the proposition to meet Lord Osborne. On the contrary, he acquiesced with very good grace in her wish to remain concealed till all danger of encountering him was past. As soon as the winding of the path hid him entirely from sight, they proceeded upwards and reached the Castle without incident, having only consumed half an hour in a walk which might have easily been accomplished in a third of that time. Yet Emma did not find the walk tedious, and Mr Howard never discovered the period it had occupied.

They were shown to Miss Osborne's own sitting-room, where they found her practising upon the harp. Miss Carr was reclining amongst the soft pillows of a comfortable chair — from which she hardly raised herself to address the visitors. Her friend was extremely good-natured and civil. She pressed Emma's hand affectionately — enquired tenderly after her health, and expressed herself excessively obliged by her coming.

'Luncheon is waiting,' she added. 'You will not meet mama — she is never to be seen of a morning — but did you not meet my brother?'

Emma did not answer immediately and Mr Howard replied:

'We saw him at a distance — but he did not join us.'

'I am surprised,' said Miss Carr, 'for I know he set off on purpose to escort Miss Emma Watson up here. Which way did you come, to pass him?'

'It is easily accounted for,' replied Emma, calmly. 'Mr Howard had taken me out of the direct road to show me a good view of the Castle — and Lord Osborne passed whilst we were looking at it.'

'It is a pity you did not stop him,' pursued Miss Carr, 'he would not then have had his walk for nothing.'

Emma made no answer. She did not think it necessary to inform Miss Carr that the honour of Lord Osborne's company was not a thing that she coveted.

When their luncheon was over, Miss Osborne renewed her offer of guiding Emma through the picture gallery — observing that they had better not lose time, as there was no light to spare in a winter's afternoon.

'But you must come too,' continued she, addressing Mr Howard. 'I am sure you know more about the pictures than I do — and are much better worth listening to on *that* subject, at least.'

'Your humility, Miss Osborne, is most commendable,' said he, with a playful bow.

'Oh, yes, I am the humblest creature in the world — there are some subjects in which I believe you and a few others are wiser than myself — Greek and mathematics for instance.'

The collection was really a very good one, and Emma was delighted. Miss Osborne looked at two or three pictures, then sauntered about the room — looked out of the window — and, at length, returning to her companions, said:

'I have just recollected an engagement, for which I must leave you — I will be back as soon as I can; do not hurry, and pray do not wait for me. You may be quite comfortable here, nobody will disturb you.'

Emma and her guide walked on together through the gallery.

She responded to all his comments on the pictures and showed an eager interest in all he had to tell about them. Almost an hour had passed before Emma felt in the least tired, and she then found herself seated beside Mr Howard on a sofa placed in one of the alcoves.

'You surely must have been used to look at good pictures,' he remarked.

'I do not pretend, I assure you, to be a connoisseur,' said Emma, 'but my uncle took me to every good collection and exhibition within our reach. He was at great pains to form and correct my taste, so that I ought rather to blush at knowing so little than receive compliments on the subject!'

'Of what uncle are you speaking?' asked Howard. 'You forget that I know almost nothing of your family.'

'The uncle who brought me up, Dr Turner.'

'Then you were not educated at Stanton.'

'I — oh no — my home was formerly in my uncle's house; I have not been more than two months resident in my father's family.'

'I dare say you think me a very stupid fellow for not being aware of this, but though I saw you were different from your sisters, and indeed most of the young ladies of the neighbourhood, the reason never occurred to me.'

'You supposed me a sort of Cinderella,' said Emma laughing, 'let out by some benevolent fairy on the occasion of one ball.'

'No, but I had not been in your father's house, and therefore had no reason to assign you to the kitchen in preference to the parlour. But I own I was surprised by your sudden apparition, since I had neither in street, town or country seen or heard of more than three Miss Watsons.'

'I can easily believe it — my absence had been so protracted.'

'May I ask if you are to return to your uncle's house?'

'Alas! no — my dear, kind uncle died nearly two years ago — my aunt has left England to settle in Ireland, and my home is now at my father's.'

'Is it not with rather a strange sensation that you meet your nearest relations; they must be almost unknown to you.'

'I have made acquaintance with one brother and two sisters,'

86

replied Emma with something like a sigh. 'But I have yet to meet another brother and sister.'

'It seems almost a pity,' said Mr Howard thoughtfully, 'to bring up one child apart and differently from the other members of a family, if they are ultimately to be rejoined. At least I feel in my own case how much I should have lost, had Anne been separated from me in childhood. I suppose it rarely happens that a brother and sister are so much together as we were — but we were orphans and everything to each other till her marriage.'

'It does not do, Mr Howard, to indulge in retrospective considerations if they tend to make one dissatisfied,' said Emma, with an attempt to check a tear or hide it by a smile; 'my family wished to do everything for the best, and if the result has been different from their intentions, they are not to blame. But I do not know that I should choose to repeat the experiment for one under my care.'

A pause ensued until Emma suddenly started from her reverie.

'It is almost dusk — we must really return home.'

'True, we can come again another day; I am sure you may come whenever you feel disposed — I shall be most happy to escort you.'

At this moment the door was thrown back and Lord Osborne appeared. After paying his compliments he paused a moment, and then observed :

'You must have a precious strong taste for pictures, Miss Watson, to like to remain in the gallery even when it is too dark to see.'

'We have stayed longer than we intended, my lord,' said Emma.

'It's a mighty fine thing to have such a lot of fine pictures, with all the fine names tacked on them. One or two I really like myself — there's one of some horses, by somebody, excellent — and a Dutch painting of dead game, which is so like you would really think them all alive. Howard knows all about them: he has the names and dates and all on the tip of his tongue. Don't you find it a deuced bore to listen to it?'

'On the contrary, I am much obliged to Mr Howard for the information.'

87

'Well, I should be glad, for my part, of a piece of information: how the — I beg pardon — I mean how did I contrive to miss you as I was going down the straight path to the Parsonage?'

'Because we did not come up the straight path, my lord.'

'Well, on my honour, I was astonished when I got there to hear you were gone — stole away, in fact. "Holloa! how can that be!" said I, "I did not meet them — no indeed." "Did you not?" cried Mrs Blake. "Well deuce take it, that is extraordinary."'

'Did she say so indeed,' said Emma with exemplary gravity.

'I don't mean to say she used those very words — she thought them, though, I'm sure, by her look.'

'But now, my lord, we must wish you good evening, or Mrs Blake will be waiting for dinner; and though I am not afraid of her swearing at us, I do not wish to annoy her.'

'Ah yes, Mrs Blake is mistress — I know — the parson there, like myself, is under petticoat government; nothing like a mother or sister to keep one in order. I'll be bound a wife is nothing to it. One cannot get away from a sister, and one cannot make her quiet and obedient —you see she has never undertaken any promise of that kind, as I understand wives do when one marries them.'

'But I have heard, my lord, that they sometimes break their word and rebel,' said Emma with a glance in the direction of Mr Howard.

'Ah, but that must be the husband's fault, he gives them too much rein — keep a strict hand on them, that's my maxim.'

'I recommend you, however, to keep it a secret, if you wish to find a wife; I assure you no woman would marry you if she knew your opinion.'

'Seriously — well, but I am sorry I said so then.'

'Oh never mind — there is no harm done, and now we must say good-bye to Miss Osborne.'

Emma was vexed to find the young peer insisted on escorting them homewards. Though his conversation had been much shorter than Mr Howard's she was far more weary of it. To hurry her walk was her only remedy, and the coldness of the air was a plausible excuse for this. The space which had occupied nearly half an hour in ascending, was now traversed in five minutes, and breathless but glowing, the party reached the door of the Parsonage. Here Lord Osborne was really obliged to leave them, and Emma hastened to her room to prepare for dinner.

'Well, Emma,' said Elizabeth, 'I should like to know what you have been doing all this time — what an age you have been gone!'

'Looking at pictures, Elizabeth — you know what I went for.'

'I know what you went for indeed, but do I know what you stayed for?'

Emma laughed.

'Of what do you suspect me, Elizabeth?'

'Which have you been flirting with?' demanded Elizabeth, taking her sister's hand, and closely examining her countenance. 'The peer or the parson, which of your two admirers do you prefer?'

'How can you ask?' returned Emma, laughing and struggling to disengage herself. 'Would you not hesitate yourself — is not Lord Osborne the most captivating, elegant, lively, fascinating young nobleman who ever made rank gracious and desirable? Would *you* not certainly accept him?'

'Why yes, I think I should — it would be something to be Lady Osborne — mistress of all those rooms and servants, carriages and horses. I think I should like it, but then I shall never have the choice!'

'If he makes you an offer, do not refuse it on my account.'

'Very well — and when I am Lady Osborne, I will be very kind to Mrs Howard — I will send and ask her to dine with me most Sundays, and some week days too.'

'I hope she will like it.'

'I will give her a new gown at Easter, and a pelisse or bonnet at Christmas.'

'Your liberality is most exemplary, but in the midst of your kind intentions to Mrs Howard, I fear you are forgetting Mrs Blake and her dinner. If you do not finish your dressing quickly you will keep them waiting.'

The evening was spent in quiet comfort, far removed from the stately grandeur of the yester-night's scene — they closed round the fire, chatting and laughing, cracking nuts and eating home-baked cakes with a zest which Osborne Castle and its lordly halls could not rival. They talked of the snow melting, and Charles and his uncle too persisted in the greatest incredulity on that subject. A hundred other things were discussed, made charming by the ease and good-humour with which they were canvassed, and then a book was produced. Shakespeare was placed in Mr Howard's hands, and he read with a degree of feeling and taste which made it very delightful to his listeners. Thus the evening passed peacefully and quickly, and when they separated for the night, it was with increased good will and affection between the parties.

CHAPTER 11

THE NEXT MORNING, though ushered in by no change of the weather, brought a very material alteration to the Miss Watsons. About eleven o'clock, as the ladies were working together, their attention was attracted by the sound of carriage wheels on the drive to the house. Presently a note was handed to Miss Watson, accompanied by an assurance that the carriage was waiting. With much surprise, Elizabeth opened the dispatch. It was from her father, and contained information to the effect, that wearied by their long absence, and finding that the lanes were still blocked, he had sent their man to the post town for a chaise, in which they could return home, by taking the high road which, although greatly adding to the distance, was the safest and most expeditious route they could adopt. He begged them to return immediately in the post-chaise, and Robert could follow with their own little vehicle later.

There were now many remonstrances on the subject of the dangerous nature of the expedition they were proposing to undertake. Charles repeatedly assured them that they would certainly be upset, until Emma declared her belief that his foreknowledge arose from having bribed the postillion to cause such a catastrophe. Mrs Blake's object seemed to be to overwhelm them with cloaks, furs, shawls and everything she could think of to fence the cold away, and Mr Howard obviated all difficulty of returning these articles by volunteering to drive over as soon as the weather permitted, and fetch them all back. Hopes of a continued friendship closed the visit, and they parted on the best possible terms.

Their return home was perfectly uneventful. Most cordial was the welcome they received from Mr Watson.

'I shall not let you young ladies go visiting again in a hurry,' he said. 'I began to think one of you must have eloped with Lord Osborne, and the other with Mr Howard. I assure you, we have been very dull without you.'

Margaret's salutation followed:

'Well, I hope you have been having pleasure enough — and that you will have brought home some news to enliven us. I am sure I am almost dead of stupidity and dullness. Not a creature have we seen — no one has come near us. Some people contrive to keep all the amusement to themselves.'

Her astonishment, when she heard the detail of what had occurred, was excessive; she was ready to cry with vexation and envy, to think of her sisters having so much to amuse them. She insisted upon knowing every particular, for the sake, apparently, of tormenting herself to the uttermost, and being as miserable and ill-used as possible.

Every dish at dinner — every jewel in Lady Osborne's necklace — every word spoken by the ladies at the Castle, and every amusement suggested by the inhabitants of the Parsonage, was an additional sting to her mind; and she was more than ever convinced that she had been victim of an act of the most barbarous injustice.

As soon as the roads became at all passable, Emma began to catch herself wondering when Mr Howard would redeem his promise of coming to fetch the articles with which his sister had supplied them. She likewise detected herself in what she considered another failing; this was looking round the untidy rooms of her father's home, with their dingy carpets, faded curtains, wallpapers soiled and tables marked and scratched, and contrasting them with the clean and cheerful aspect of the apartments where Mrs Blake was mistress. The grandeur of Osborne Castle had none of the charms in her eyes which Mrs Blake's little parlour presented, and she came to the conclusion that the happiest thing in the world must be to preside over such an establishment. Those feelings, however, she did not openly express. It was Elizabeth who repeatedly declared that she wished she could make their house resemble Mr Howard's.

One morning, shortly after their return home, Tom Musgrave was ushered into the parlour.

Margaret, who happened to be alone, was instantly all agitation and bustle, trying to persuade him to take her chair by the fire, as she was sure he must be cold, or to accept the loan of her father's slippers whilst his boots were sent to the kitchen to dry.

He persisted, however, in declining her tender attentions, declaring she wanted to make an old man of him before his time, and, placing himself on the hearth-rug with his back to the fire, and his hands behind him, half whistled an air.

Margaret sighed.

'It is long since we have seen you,' said she; 'and the time has passed very wearily.'

'Hum,' said Tom, stopping in his tune. 'Where are your sisters, Miss Margaret?'

'Oh, they are at home again,' replied Margaret. 'I believe Emma is with my father, and Elizabeth in the kitchen. Did you hear of their being away so long?'

'For how long?' asked Tom quickly.

'From Wednesday to Saturday: there was I left without a creature to speak to, except my father and the servants, snowed up in the house, and if they had only taken me with them, I should have enjoyed it as much as they did.'

'I dare say; but how came they to go?' said Tom, who knew nothing but was determined to learn all he could without betraying his ignorance.

'Oh, they wanted to return Mrs Blake's visit, and they went over in the pony-chaise, and then the snow came on and stopped them there all that time. I dare say they liked to stay, for I have no doubt but they might have come home had they tried. At last my father was obliged to send for a post-chaise to fetch them home in, and they came on Saturday.'

'And they liked it very much, did they?'

'Oh yes, of course — was it not hard I could not go too? I am always thwarted and ill-used.'

'I wish your sister Emma would come down; she is always shut up in your father's room; I called here on purpose to see her.'

'I dare say she will come presently — do sit down here; I am sure you ought to rest yourself; you seem to have had a very dirty ride.'

'Do you suppose you could call her?'

93

'Oh no, she will come when she has done reading to my father. Do take something — a biscuit and a glass of wine, or something of that kind?'

'Quite unnecessary, I have but just breakfasted. I do not keep such gothic hours as some of my friends do. I am able to please myself — a free and independent man.'

'Oh, Mr Musgrave, you are most fortunate. You cannot tell the misery, the low spirits, the —' But before Margaret could continue her pathetic address, Elizabeth entered the room and Tom interrupted it.

'So I understand, Miss Watson, you have been playing the truant, and been obliged to be brought back almost by force.'

'And are you come to congratulate or condole with me on our return?'

'I am come to wish you joy about being overwhelmed in the snow. I little thought when I was last at Osborne Castle we were such near neighbours.'

'When were you there?' cried Elizabeth.

'Let me see — I think it was Thursday. I am there very often, but I think Thursday was the last day. How droll it would have been had we met.'

'Emma,' cried Miss Watson, as her youngest sister just then entered the room, 'Mr Musgrave says he was at the Castle on Thursday.'

'Oh,' said Emma.

'I wonder we did not hear of it,' pursued Elizabeth. 'Miss Osborne never mentioned it.'

'How do you like Miss Osborne?' enquired Tom, who wanted to appear perfectly well informed of what had passed, and was, therefore, ashamed of asking questions which might betray his real ignorance.

'She seems a very pleasant, amiable young lady,' replied Elizabeth, 'don't you think so, Emma?'

'Yes,' replied she, quietly.

'Did she know you were friends of mine, Miss Watson? Miss Emma, did she not talk about me?'

'No indeed,' replied Emma, with some satisfaction; 'we never heard your name mentioned the whole time we were in company with her.'

94

'How did you hear we had been there?' enquired Elizabeth.

'I think Osborne mentioned it on Saturday, when I saw him for a minute.' Then seating himself by Emma, who was a little apart from the others, he whispered: 'He told me the beautiful, but obdurate Miss Watson had been at Howard's Parsonage. Why do you treat him with such scorn, Miss Emma? You will drive my poor friend to despair.'

'I should be very sorry to think that I merited your accusation, Mr Musgrave; scorn cannot be a becoming quality in a young lady.'

'Nay, there can be nothing unbecoming which you can do; youth and beauty have unlimited privileges,' whispered he again. 'Miss Osborne vows you eclipse Miss Carr in beauty, and she would rather have you for a friend. She is dying to be introduced to you.'

'It is quite unnecessary to inflict such a death upon her even in imagination, Mr Musgrave — for our acquaintance has progressed too far for that phrase to be at all applicable to it.'

'Yes now, I dare say; Osborne told me, but I forgot, you went over the Castle I think.'

'No, we did not.'

'You did not! That was unlucky; I wish I had known you were going, I would have been there, and I could have proposed it to Miss Osborne. I dare say she would have shown you all the rooms.'

'She offered to do so, but we put it off till another time; we thought we should be too hurried.'

'It's a pity you did not dine there; it's something quite grand to see all the plate — I quite enjoy it — they give such good dinners.'

'You do not seem aware that we *did* dine there,' replied Emma, 'and I saw nothing so very astonishing at their table.'

'You did dine there — yes — but that was in a family way; the thing to see is a regular great dinner — twenty people sitting down. I should like to have *you* for a neighbour at such a dinner.'

Emma was still obdurately silent, and Mr Musgrave, to recompense himself, turned to Elizabeth, and began to talk to her.

As soon as her attention was released Emma left the room, and throwing on a bonnet and cloak, determined to take refuge in the garden as the day was fine, and she longed for fresh air. Hardly had she quitted the entrance, however, when her attention was attracted by the sound of wheels in the lane, and she perceived with pleasure Mr Howard, come to redeem his promise. There was another object in his visit — he was the bearer of an invitation to herself and her sisters to attend a ball preceded by a concert, at the Castle. Miss Osborne hoped they would excuse her mother's not having called on them; she scarcely ever paid visits, never in the winter, or she would have accompanied her daughter to the Vicarage when they were there.

Emma read the note, which was addressed to herself, and felt very much pleased. It contained, besides the invitation to the concert and ball for herself and all her sisters, a most pressing request that she would pay a lengthened visit at the Castle; over this she pondered long, and then ended with coming to no conclusion, suddenly remembering that she was detaining Mr Howard out of doors, when she ought to have allowed him to enter the house.

'You will find Mr Tom Musgrave sitting with my sisters,' continued she; 'but if you will be so kind as *not* to mention the contents of the note before him, you will greatly oblige me.'

'Could I not see Mr Watson?' replied Howard; 'I wish to call on him, and perhaps when my visit to him is over your sisters will be disengaged.'

'Certainly; I am sure my father would have great pleasure in seeing you,' said Emma much gratified; 'allow me to show you the way.'

She ushered him accordingly to her father's dressing-room, and, having witnessed the very cordial reception which Mr Watson offered him, she was about to withdraw, but her father stopped her.

'I am sure you can have nothing particular to do, Emma, so you may just as well stay and talk to Mr Howard — I like very much to hear you, but you know I am not strong enough to converse myself.'

'I am sure, my dear father, nobody talks half so well when you are equal to it, but indeed you must not fancy yourself unwell, or you will frighten Mr Howard away.'

'When Mr Howard has reached my age, my dear, and felt half the pain that I do, from gout and dyspepsia, he will be very glad to set his daughter to talk for him; so I beg you will stay.'

'I wish I enjoyed the prospects of realizing your picture, my dear sir; a daughter exactly like Miss Emma Watson would indeed be a treasure.'

'But remember it is to be purchased at the expense of gout, and you must not look for it these thirty years, Mr Howard,' said Emma laughing. 'When the sacrifice is complete you will talk in a very different strain.'

Mr Howard *looked* very incredulous, but said nothing more on that subject.

Emma then mentioned the note she had received; her father began to murmur.

'The Osbornes will turn all your heads with their balls and their visits, child. I wish you had never known them.'

Emma looked down.

'I am sure I do not wish to go, if you dislike it,' she said, in a voice which faintly trembled.

It was evident to Mr Howard that she *did* wish it very much.

Mr Watson began again.

'What am I to do if you are going away for two or three days? You are but just come home as it is — I cannot do without you.'

'Then I, at all events, can stay with you,' replied Emma cheerfully, 'and my sisters can do as they please.'

Annoyed at the gentleman's selfishness, Mr Howard felt inclined to interpose, but doubted whether he would not do more harm than good.

Emma knew better, or acted more wisely in not contradicting him, for like many irritable people, the moment he found himself unopposed, Mr Watson began to relent, and said in a more placid voice, 'What's the invitation? Read it again, Emma, I am not quite clear about it.'

Emma complied.

'Well, I do not know; she does not want you all to stay over the ball — and as Elizabeth will be at home, perhaps I could spare you for a day or two.'

'Elizabeth would like to go to the ball too, papa.'

'Yes, yes, but then she and Margaret would come home at night, and I should not be all day alone. I think you might go — you must have a post-chaise and a pair of horses to take you, I suppose, and bring your sisters back again. Would you like it, my dear?'

'Very much, sir, if it does not disturb you.'

Like it indeed — the words served but coldly to express the pleasure with which her heart beat at the idea. It was so very kind of Miss Osborne to think of her in that way, and it was so very pleasant to see how much consequence Mr Howard attached to her acceptance of the offer. She had not dared to look straight at him; but the first glance she had ventured on, showed in his face an expression of deep interest, not to be mistaken, and now looking up, she met his eyes fixed on her with a look which immediately sunk hers again to the ground.

'I am sure,' said he, speaking hurriedly to relieve her embarrassment, 'Miss Osborne would have been exceedingly disappointed had you settled otherwise. I can venture to assert, sir, that Miss Osborne is very fond of your daughter, and extremely anxious to cultivate her acquaintance.'

'I dare say, I dare say, why should she not? But I hope dear Emma does not flatter her to win her good will.'

'I hope not, sir. I should despise myself if I did.'

'It is impossible that it should be necessary,' said Mr Howard. 'Miss Osborne is not to be propitiated by flattery, and it would require, on Miss Emma's part, nothing beyond her natural manners to produce a wish to carry on the acquaintance.'

'I suppose Miss Osborne desired you to make civil speeches for her,' said Mr Watson, laughing.

'No, I do it of my own free will, my dear sir.'

Mr Howard's visit was long and lively; Mr Watson was evidently cheered by it, and pressed him to renew it.

'I am afraid I ask what is not agreeable,' continued he; 'I dare say I am dull; but if you knew how much it benefits one to see cheerful faces, you would not wonder at my selfish wish. You, Mr Howard, and Emma do me good.'

There was something very pleasant to Emma's ears in hearing her name thus connected with Mr Howard's; and it was not unwelcome to the young man either, who warmly pressed her father's hand, and promised readily to come as often as he could.

'And mind, Emma, when he does come, you bring him to me,' said her father; 'it is not every young man that I care to see.'

After renewing his promise to be a regular and frequent visitor, Mr Howard was conducted by Emma to the parlour, from whence they found Tom Musgrave had departed. Her two sisters looked up as if surprised to see Emma and her companion; but their pleasure much exceeded their surprise, when they learnt the nature of the embassy with which he was charged. Margaret especially, who had formed most exalted ideas of the nature and felicity of a visit to the Castle, was at first in a perfect rapture. She was certain that the whole affair would be in the most superlative style of excellence; that Miss Osborne must be a lady of superior taste and talent; that the company would be select in an extraordinary degree, and in short that she should never have known what grandeur, beauty, elegance, and taste meant, but for Lady Osborne's invitation to the ball. It was not until after Mr Howard's departure, which took place after a visit of about ten minutes, that a cloud came over her bright vision. She then learnt the disagreeable fact that Emma was invited to remain at the Castle, but she herself was to return home.

This discovery made her very angry; she could comprehend no reason for such a marked preference; why should Miss Osborne invite Emma who was the youngest, and exclude herself; it really surpassed her comprehension; it was most extraordinary; she had a great mind not to go at all; she would let Miss Osborne see that she was not to be treated with neglect; she was not a person to come and go at any one's bidding; if Miss Osborne could ask Emma, why not herself too; she surely had as much claim to attention. She said everything which an irritated and jealous temper could suggest, and tormented Emma into tears at her crossness and ill-will.

'I wonder you mind her, Emma,' remonstrated Elizabeth, when she discovered that her sister's eyes were red, and wrung from her an acknowledgement of the cause. Elizabeth had not been present when the discussion which pained Emma so much had taken place. 'It's not the least use fretting about Margaret's ill-temper and teasing ways — she always was a plague and a torment from a child, and there's no chance of her being any better. She is so abominably selfish. But I cannot endure that she makes you cry.'

'I dare say you think me very foolish,' replied Emma, wiping her eyes, 'but I have never been used to be crossly spoken to, and it quite upsets me.'

'No, I don't think you foolish, Emma; you are only much too good and tender for this situation. I shall be glad when you are married and safe with Mr Howard, and nobody to scold you or make you spoil your beauty by crying.'

'Nonsense, Elizabeth.'

'It's not nonsense, Emma, I believe he is very good-natured, and I dare say you will be very happy with him. How long were you *tête-à-tête* with him, before you brought him into the parlour?'

'We came directly from my father's room.'

'Oh, you need not apologize; I think you were quite right to have a comfortable chat with him, before bringing him into Margaret's company. It is but little conversation you can have when she is by. I saw you with him in the garden.'

Emma blushed.

'I assure you we did not stay there five minutes; he came to call on my father, and we went to him immediately.'

Elizabeth only answered by a look; but it was a look which showed that she was not in the least convinced by Emma's assertions.

CHAPTER 12

THREE DAYS BEFORE THE PARTY at the Castle fell due, a very unexpected event threw the whole family into a ferment. Just as the two elder sisters were setting off to the town to see if their new bonnets were making the progress which was desirable, the sudden appearance of a post-chaise startled them. Emma, who was in her father's room as usual, was perfectly astonished the next minute by the uproar which resounded through the hall. Loud laughter, and a mingled clatter of tongues, convinced her that whatever was the origin, it was not of a tragic nature, but her awakened curiosity made her long to know the cause, though she feared to move, as her father had fallen into a gentle doze. A shriller exclamation suddenly roused him from his slumber, and starting up he demanded to know the reason for such unusual clamour.

Emma escaped from the room to obey his behest, and on reaching the turn of the stairs paused a moment to see who was there; just then she caught her own name.

'Emma is at home,' Margaret was saying. 'Pen, you can go and sit with her.'

'Very well, it's all the same to me,' replied a stranger, whom she inferred was her unknown sister, 'I am sure I don't want to keep you at home.' And as she spoke she turned again to the door, 'I say, driver, you just get that trunk lifted in, there's a good fellow, and see you don't turn it bottom upwards, my man, or I vow I won't give you a sixpence — do you hear?'

When satisfied with the care which he took of her property, she paid and dismissed him, and then turned to her sisters.

'There, now you may bundle off too, as fast as you please, my

101

bonnet and gown are in that trunk, and you shall not see them till I put them on, lest you should try and copy them.'

'How very ill-natured,' cried Margaret.

'No, it isn't, what becomes me would never suit you, so I only prevent you making a fright of yourself. Where's Emma? I want to see her.'

'Here I am,' said Emma, descending the final stairs.

'Here I am,' mimicked Penelope, advancing towards her, 'and how does your little ladyship do, pray? Why are you so long coming to welcome your new sister? I am sure you ought to have learnt more affection from Margaret.'

Emma did not know what to answer to this attack, but looked at Elizabeth rather distressed.

'Never mind Penelope,' replied Miss Watson, 'she always says what she pleases; well, Margaret is waiting in the chaise, so I must go; Emma, will you take Pen to my father?'

Penelope turned to her remaining sister, and surveyed her from head to foot —

'Well,' said she, 'I suppose I had better go and report myself first, and then I can settle about my things; upon my word, Emma, you are very pretty, I am so glad you have dark hair and eyes; Margaret makes me quite sick of fair skins, by her nonsense about her own.

'Here I am, sir,' she announced, advancing into her father's room, 'come to waken you all up; I am sure the old house looks as if it had gone to sleep since I went away, and there is the same fly on the window, I protest, as when I was last in the room. How do you do, my dear sir?'

'None the better for all the confounded clatter you have been making in the hall, I can tell you; I thought you had brought home a dozen children at your heels, judging from the uproar you occasioned. What mad freak has possessed you now, Penelope?'

'Oh, I came for two things — one was to go to the Osborne Castle ball — the other I'll tell you by and by.'

'You are always racing over the country, and bent on having your own way, I know.'

'So is everyone; but they don't all know how to get it, so well

102

as I do; but I see I'm disturbing you, so I shall go and unpack my rattle-traps — Emma come with me.'

Penelope went to the parlour, and stirring up the fire drew in a chair close to the chimney — placed her feet upon the fender, and then turning abruptly round to her sister, said :

'So it is all your doing, is it, our going to the Castle Ball? It is really something new — Margaret wrote me word you and Miss Osborne were bosom friends.'

Emma did not know what to say in reply.

'How sheepish you look, Emma,' cried her sister, 'one would think you were ashamed of it all; I am sure I think it vastly clever of you to get up a friendship with Miss Osborne, or a flirtation with her brother. I've a great respect for girls who know how to push their way and make the most of circumstances. What sort of young fellow is Lord Osborne?'

'Plain and quiet,' replied Emma.

'As if I did not know *that*,' cried Penelope, 'why I've seen him these dozens of times, child. I mean, is he pleasant? — can he talk nonsense? — does he know how to make himself agreeable?'

'That must depend upon taste,' replied Emma, 'he never was particularly pleasant to me; and, as to his talking, it's neither good sense, nor good nonsense.'

'Do you know what good nonsense is, Emma? Why, then I dare say you may not be quite detestable.'

'I should hope not,' said Emma, trying to smile.

'I thought your uncle might, perhaps, have made a Methodist of you, and that would not have suited me. Those musty old doctors of divinity have queer notions.'

'I must beg, Penelope, when you mention my late uncle, you will do so with respect,' said Emma with spirit.

Penelope looked surprised — and, for a moment, was silent; when she spoke it was to question Emma minutely, about the quality, price and texture of her dress, for the important day and night in prospect.

'I expect Margaret will be ready to expire with envy, when she sees the real Indian muslin I mean to wear; I am not going to tell you how I came by it — for that's a great secret for some days to come. Is not Margaret horribly jealous?'

103

Emma looked shocked.

'Oh, I see!' laughed Penelope, 'you are too good to abuse a sister — quite the Miss Charity of a good little girl's prize book. But, if you like to sit like a goose weighing every word you are about to utter, I can tell you that does not suit me at all. I always say what comes into my head, without caring for anybody.'

As Emma did not express how very unpleasant a course she considered it, the sisters did not quarrel then.

'How has Margaret got on with Tom Musgrave?' continued Penelope. 'By-the-bye, have you see Tom Musgrave, yourself?'

'A little,' said Emma.

'And how do you like him? — what do you think of him? — do you think he is in love with Margaret?' pursued Penelope.

'No,' replied Emma, answering only to the last question.

'Nor do I; I don't see that he is at all more in love with her than he has been with twenty other girls — myself included. But it's very amusing talking to him when he is in spirits. Emma, can you keep a secret?'

'Yes, I hope so, when necessary; but I would rather have none to keep.'

'How absurd — why, it's the best fun possible to have a good secret; I would tell no one, if you would promise not to betray it.'

'I shall be very happy to hear anything you like to tell me, and I am sure you would not ask me to do anything wrong.'

'Wrong! Are you such a little Methodist as to consider whether everything is wrong — it's my own affair, and how can there be anything wrong in my telling you if I like? If one always stops to meditate whether anyone would think a thing wrong, one might give over talking altogether.'

Emma was silent from not very well knowing what to say in reply; and, after a momentary pause, Penelope went on:

'Now, the only reason I want you not to tell is because I wish to surprise all the others by the news some day. You will promise not to mention it!'

'You had much better not tell me at all, Penelope; because then your secret will certainly be safe; if you, who are interested in it, cannot resist telling it — how can you expect me to be proof against such a temptation?'

'You are very much mistaken,' said Penelope, angrily tossing her head, 'if you suppose I cannot resist telling anything I wish to keep secret; I assure you, I am quite as discreet, when occasion requires, as your little ladyship can be, though I do not set up to be so superior to all my family, and give myself airs of superfine prudence.'

Emma saw that she had made her sister angry — though she did not know exactly how or why, and she attempted, but vainly, to apologize for the involuntary offence. Penelope was not to be propitiated.

'It's no use at all, your trying to be so grand and indifferent; it was not a trifling mark of my regard, what I was going to tell you, but, if you do not wish to hear it, you may let it alone. I dare say Margaret will show more interest in my concerns.'

And with these words, Penelope rose and hastily quitted the room, slamming the door after her.

During the three succeeding days every means was taken to raise a curiosity which would have flattered Penelope's self-importance. Elizabeth and Emma concluded that a secret which required so much exertion to give it importance could not be much worth knowing or that it would certainly soon become public.

CHAPTER 13

AT LAST THE DAY CAME for the four sisters to be transported to the scene of such great anticipation, and when they had sufficiently arranged their dresses and shaken out the creases, after being so very much squeezed in the carriage, they were marshalled up the grand staircase.

After passing through several state apartments, where they followed in the wake of many others, they arrived at the entrance of the music salon, to be received by Miss Osborne and her mother. The former broke off a conversation to offer her hand to Elizabeth and her youngest sister, to whom she expressed much pleasure at the meeting; she then said a few civil words to the two others, when Miss Watson named them. Both Elizabeth and Emma would have been glad to find quiet seats from which they might survey the company, and thus secure all the share in the amusement that they felt they had a right to expect. But the others were not so easily satisfied. They wanted to keep close to Miss Osborne, hoping for the distinction of further notice, and they both declared that they had no idea of being wedged into a corner where nobody could see them. To avoid attracting attention by their angry whispers, their sisters were obliged to comply, though they both felt uncomfortable at parading the rooms without any chaperone or gentleman to escort them, and yet did not like to attach themselves to Miss Osborne, lest she should think so large a body of followers troublesome.

Passing once more down one of the drawing-rooms, they for the first time perceived an acquaintance. This was Tom Musgrave, who was in the act of escorting a party of fashionable-looking ladies, and either did not, or would not see them. To pass him unobserved, however, suited neither Penelope nor Margaret, and the latter having failed to catch his eye, the former pulled his elbow to make him look at them.

His attention thus arrested, he could not avoid speaking — but his bow was as short and hurried as was possible, and he would again have turned to his party had Penelope or Margaret allowed it. But this they would not do.

'Bless me, Tom,' cried the elder sister; 'how many ages it is since we met, and yet you seem not to have a word to bestow on an old friend.'

His party passed on as she spoke, and as soon as they were sufficiently far off for him to be sure he should not be heard, he replied in a very short abrupt tone.

'I am much obliged for your notice, Miss Penelope, and vastly happy to see you, only for the present, as I am particularly engaged in escorting the daughters of Sir Anthony Barnard, I must beg you will excuse my further delay; your humble servant, Miss Margaret,' and he rushed away as he finished his sentence.

'How provoking,' muttered Penelope, 'I declare, Tom Musgrave seems to have become a perfect bear since I went away.'

'I wish our father was a baronet or a lord,' sighed Margaret, 'then he would care for us, too.'

'Then I am sure I should not care for him,' said Elizabeth, with much spirit. 'Who would value attentions dependent on such a circumstance?'

They now stood still, and seemed quite at a loss what to do, until of a sudden Mr Howard stood beside them and proposed that they should join his sister, who was in the music saloon.

The awkwardness of feeling, from which Emma had been suffering, was at once done away; they would belong to someone — they would have someone to address them — someone to make them feel comfortable and not out of place.

Mrs Blake was good-humoured and agreeable as ever — receiving the two strangers cordially, for the sake of their sisters, and immediately proposing that she should act as their chaperone at the ball.

To this, not even Margaret could make an objection, and Emma, with Mr Howard by her side, was now really happy. The happiness, however, was not of very long duration; scarcely

107

had she been seated five minutes, when she perceived Lady Osborne's eyeglass turned in their direction — and a moment after, a young man, to whom Miss Osborne had been paying much attention on their arrival, approached and said :

'Howard, you are wanted — her ladyship finds your assistance and presence indispensable — but, before you go, I pray you to bequeath to me your seat.'

With evident reluctance, he rose, and turning to Emma said :

'Since I must leave you — will you allow me to present to you my friend, Sir William Gordon — but, remember, Gordon,' he added, laughing, 'I shall expect my proxy to resign in my favour, the moment I return to claim the situation.'

'Do not build too much upon that,' said Sir William, whose demeanour would certainly have prepossessed Emma in his favour, had he not turned out Mr Howard, and who showed at once that there was no inclination wanting on his part to amuse her with conversation.

'Have you been often at the Castle?' he enquired. 'I do not remember to have seen you here; yet I think I should have noticed your face, had we met before.'

Emma informed him that she was a comparative stranger in the neighbourhood, and had rarely been at Osborne Castle.

'Then are you sure that you are acquainted with the Castle's politics? Are you conversant with the position of parties in the establishment?'

'On the contrary, I am quite ignorant — possessing no knowledge and little curiosity.'

'Oh, impossible! All women are curious, more or less. You must wish to have a peep behind the scenes, and it is necessary that you should, or you will transgress again.'

'Again!' said Emma, a little alarmed. 'Have I done so already then?'

'Certainly,' replied Sir William gravely. 'Were you not guilty of detaining Mr Howard by your side, when her ladyship needed him?'

'Indeed, no! He went directly she sent for him.'

'To send should have been on her part superfluous; to go on his, impossible; he should, instinctively, have sought her side, and placed himself in her service.'

108

'Surely not — Mr Howard is not the individual of highest rank; he is a free agent, and has, surely, the power of choice.'

'His choice cannot be questioned, but this is more a matter of her ladyship's choice.'

Emma looked a little puzzled.

'Howard is *my* intimate friend,' added Sir William, 'and I really wish him well; after all, there is no such disparity in their years — only fifteen or thereabouts — the jointure might be some time in his possession.'

'I should really be obliged if you would find some other subject of conversation, Sir William,' replied Emma decidedly.

'Suppose we talk of her daughter, then? Don't you think her rather over-dressed?'

'No,' said Emma, 'and I think you had better let the whole family alone.'

'I think I will follow your advice and choose another subject — what shall it be? — shall we talk of yourself? Confide to me all your peculiar tastes — your wonderful aversions — your never dying friendships. How many bosom friends have you, Miss Watson?'

'None, except my sister,' said Emma, amused.

'Your sister! Oh, fie! No one thinks of making a friend of a sister — that is quite a burlesque — a friend's brother is, of course, a favourite — but one's own brothers or sisters are quite out of the question.'

'Well, then, I am badly off indeed, for I have no friend.'

'Indeed! I wish you would take me as one.'

Emma shook her head.

'I assure you, I am very modest,' he insisted. 'I should make an excellent friend; only try me.'

She answered only by an incredulous look.

'Here comes Lord Osborne into the room,' continued he, 'looking as if he were going to be hanged. Just turn your eyes this way, Miss Watson.'

'Thank you,' replied Emma, without complying; 'but I will not add to Lord Osborne's modest confusion by looking at him.'

'His modest confusion —what a good idea. Why, he is the most impudent man in Great Britain. What bribe do you suppose his mother had to offer him, to induce him to come into the music saloon today?'

'It is difficult for me to guess. Agreeable company and excellent music, no doubt.'

'I cannot fancy either would gratify him. Look, he is making his way to his mama — what would you wager that he does not tread on six ladies' toes before he crosses the room?'

Emma could not help smiling, but would not turn round.

'Oh, it is not Lady Osborne, it is Howard he is addressing. I wonder what he is saying. Howard's countenance is a tell-tale, and it's something he does not like. Now they are both looking this way; upon my word his lordship is coming here. Do you think he is trying to find *me*, Miss Watson? Shall I vacate my place in favour of his lordship?'

'That must be as you please. Don't do it on my account, however.'

'What a perplexing answer; I don't know how to understand it; for though well aware that a lady's private opinion is usually the reverse of her public one, I am still left in ignorance of which of us you really prefer.'

All this conversation passed in whispers during the bustle of arrangement, and previous to the commencement of the overture; but now the full burst of the orchestra made a reply from Emma unnecessary.

The silence which followed between them proved a relief to her, and thinking that her companion's attention was engrossed by some other object, she stole a glance towards Lady Osborne's party. Her ladyship sat in state, and close by her stood Mr Howard; he was stooping to listen to some observation of his patroness, and the painful idea crossed her mind that perhaps after all those who suggested the possibility of an alliance between them were right. She could not imagine that he loved the dowager, but it was very possible that ambition, the desire of independence, or some other motive might influence him; and as for her ladyship, she must have given some ground for a conjecture so generally whispered.

A year ago, had Emma then known the parties, such an idea would have been rejected as absurd; but her aunt's marriage had given a shock to her feelings, which seemed to destroy her confidence in men and women, especially in middle-aged widows with large jointures. It was true that if Mr Howard's character were such as she supposed, he would be uninfluenced by such a consideration, but in this she might be mistaken, and where such a possibility of mistake existed, it became her not to risk her own happiness by encouraging her feeling of partiality for him. Now she determined to keep as much as possible out of his company, and so to restore her mind to a state of equanimity. Studiously she fixed her eyes on the orchestra, and was thus surprised by the sudden address of Lord Osborne, who had at length succeeded in approaching her.

'I have been trying to get to you this half hour, Miss Watson, but those fellows with their music make such a confounded hullabaloo, there is no knowing what one is doing here.'

There was nothing in Emma's calm and collected reception of him to encourage the notion of partiality on her part which Sir William Gordon had entertained. It was polite, but as far removed from the flutter of a gratified vanity as from the consciousness of a growing attachment.

'I wish you would make room for me to sit down,' he said presently. 'Gordon, I think you have been here quite long enough — go and make love to Miss Carr and you will be doing a double charity.'

'In what way, my lord?' said Sir William without moving an inch.

'By giving her something to do, and leaving a seat for me here.'

'Thank you, but in good truth I am not equal to the undertaking which your lordship has so successfully performed. I could not make my way across such a room, and must pray your leave to remain in the modest seclusion of this corner, as best suited to my humble capacities.'

'You abominably selfish fellow, you have the best seat in the room, and you know it — that's all.'

Sir William bowed.

'Then your lordship can hardly expect me to give it up; possession you know is everything.'

'I can make room for your lordship,' cried Margaret who had long been straining forward to try and catch his attention. She

111

was seated behind Emma and Elizabeth, by the side of Mrs Blake.

Lord Osborne did but turn his head and give her a momentary glance, then stooping towards Emma, enquired who was that thin girl behind her.

She informed him it was her sister.

'Indeed,' cried he; 'I should not have guessed that — she is not the least like you!'

At this moment a favourable movement was effected by Penelope, who had been seated at the extreme end of the form. Seeing the advantage of attaching Lord Osborne to their party, and too wise to expect to do so by superceding Emma, she quietly removed herself and left a vacant seat.

He immediately requested Elizabeth to make room for him, and in another moment he was established by Emma's side, in the long-desired position.

'What a remarkably good-natured girl,' observed he in a whisper; 'who is she?'

'Another sister, my lord.'

'Another sister! Why in the name of heaven, how many sisters have you in the room?'

'Only three.'

'Only three! And how many others have you?'

Emma assured him that that was all.

'Well, but three is too many,' replied he gravely. 'It must be very awkward having so many — don't you find it so?'

'I never looked upon it in that light, which is fortunate, perhaps, as I see no remedy.'

'That's true — you have them and cannot help it; but that does not make it less of an evil — one would not choose three sisters.'

Emma did not think it necessary to reply to this speech.

'Then your father has four daughters?' continued he, as if the result of profound calculation on his part.

'Your arithmetic is quite correct, my lord,' replied she, smiling a little.

'And how many sons are there?'

'Two only.'

112

That makes six children in all. It's a great draw-back certainly.'

'It does not make me unhappy at all.'

'That must be because you are so very good-tempered. I am not sure that I could bear it myself.'

'It is fortunate that you will not probably be called on to support such an infliction!'

'Unless I were to marry a woman who had a good many brothers and sisters.'

'It will be your own fault if you do that, and with so strong a prejudice against them, I should certainly advise you against it.'

A long pause ensued, during which everyone seemed occupied with the singing, and when, at the close, there was an opportunity again afforded for conversation, Emma's attention was claimed by Miss Osborne, who led her into another saloon, as she said, to enjoy a little chat with her.

'How do you find Sir William Gordon?' she began, turning away her face as she spoke, to examine some flowers near her.

'I have hardly seen enough to form a serious idea of him.'

'Are you engaged to Mr Howard for the first dance?'

'No, I have hardly seen him,' replied Emma, in her turn trying to conceal her countenance.

'That's unlucky; I wish he had asked you,' said Miss Osborne, subjecting Emma to a thoughtful scrutiny.

Her attention was diverted by the approach of her sisters, and now that they were standing under the immediate patronage of Miss Osborne, Tom Musgrave thought proper to approach and join them. Emma, of course, was his object, not only on her own account, but because her arm was linked in that of the Honourable Miss Osborne.

'How rejoiced I am to see you looking so well, Miss Emma Watson,' cried he. 'Stanton must certainly agree remarkably well with you; but it is a most unexpected pleasure to meet you under this noble roof; it is the first time I have had that satisfaction.'

Emma calmly admitted the fact.

'On what a magnificent scale our noble hostess entertains,' continued he. 'There is not such hospitality exercised in any other mansion where I visit. Does it not remind you of the old feudal times, when fair ladies held their court, and knights and squires vied with one another for their bright smiles.'

'I wish you would go and see for my brother, Mr Musgrave,' said Miss Osborne, looking quickly round.

Tom bowed low and obsequiously.

'Can you tell me where I shall find his lordship?' enquired he.

'No indeed; you must just have the goodness to search till you find him. But don't put yourself out of breath in the chase,' said Sir William. 'I am sure Miss Osborne will not require that of you.'

As soon as he was out of hearing, Miss Osborne said:

'I have been told that some women admire that young man prodigiously, but he is idle and has not an opinion of his own.'

'Upon my word, Miss Osborne,' said Sir William, 'if you express such very strong opinions, you will frighten me out of your company. If you treat Tom Musgrave with such severity, I wonder what character you would give me?'

'You! Sir William, I make no scruple in telling you how vain, disagreeable and idle you are. What else can you expect me to say? Do not you waste your days in fox hunting and coursing: your nights in drinking or flirting? Are you not well known as the worst master, the worst landlord, the worst magistrate, the worst member in the county? Your misdeeds are notorious; do you not pull down schools and destroy churches? Did I not hear of a fire on your estate where much damage was done — were you not supposed to be deeply concerned in that?'

'I pray your mercy, Miss Osborne; do not enumerate any more of my misdeeds, or you will indeed drive me away. Such public censure is more than I can stand.'

A summons soon came from Lady Osborne to her daughter, announcing that they were waiting for her to open the ball.

Emma now found herself with Lord Osborne at her side but he stood in silence without any apparent intention of proposing himself as her partner. She began to feel very uncomfortable, and to wish herself quietly in a corner out of sight, anywhere in fact but in a conspicuous station with none near her whom she knew, except their host.

At length she took courage to say that as they would probably be in the way where they now stood, she should be glad to find

Mrs Blake and sit with her. Before Lord Osborne had time to reply, the lady they were speaking of appeared accompanied by her brother.

Emma's surprise was very great when his lordship exclaimed: 'Oh, Howard, I'm monstrously glad you're come. You shall dance with Miss Emma Watson, I've been trying to get her a partner for this great while.'

Mr Howard, who had but recently escaped from the attentions required of him by Lady Osborne, and who had been searching for Emma with this very intention, felt all his expectation of pleasure die away at the sight of the young couple standing together. He knew enough of his pupil to be aware of the extraordinary interest he must take in his companion even to think of procuring her a partner, and he could hardly suppose that she would be quite undazzled by the devotion which was thus testified by a young nobleman. It was therefore with a grave though civil air that he took up the request that Lord Osborne had dictated and solicited the honour of her hand.

To refuse was out of the question, and yet she could not bear to accept what seemed so unwillingly proffered. She thought he disliked the proposition; he concluded she was disappointed in not having the young baron for her partner; this feeling produced on each side a natural coldness of manner. She could not explain how uncomfortable she had felt, whilst standing apart with Lord Osborne; and he seemed to be suddenly quite without all ideas productive of conversation. Their dance was as different as possible from that of the happy evening when they had first stood up together, and in spite of her philosophic resolutions to cultivate indifference towards him, she could not get over her regret at his manner. It was ended at last, and again she found Lord Osborne at her side, this time accompanied by his sister.

'Henrietta,' he said, 'I do not think Miss Watson was enjoying that dance. Next time you send her a partner, I hope he will be more to her mind. Suppose you were to dance with me, Miss Watson, and see whether I could not be agreeable; only, Henrietta, you must call a very easy dance, for I shall not be able to get through an intricate one.'

Miss Osborne looked rather surprised at this extraordinary exertion on her brother's part; Mr Howard turned away. Just at

115

this moment Mr Musgrave approached again, and Lord Osborne instantly addressing him, desired he would go and ask that good-natured Miss Watson to dance, as he felt particularly obliged to. her. It would have amused a spectator to watch his countenance on receiving this command; he could not make up his mind to disobey; indeed as he found the whole family so much in favour at the Castle, he intended to take them under his patronage likewise, but he wished to *dance* only with Emma and had come to seek her for that purpose. After a moment's hesitation he turned to her, and affecting to believe she was the one intended, requested the honour of her hand, in compliance equally with his own wishes, and his noble friend's commands. His friend, however, was by no means inclined to cede his prior claim in favour of Mr Musgrave, but plainly told him that the Miss Watson who he was to ask was an elder one, who had been very good-natured when he wanted a seat. Since he could not dance with Miss Osborne, who was likewise engaged, Musgrave thought the next thing must be to take the sister of Lord Osborne's partner, and he accordingly went to find the young lady whose good nature had made so deep an impression. But Penelope was engaged, and so on this occasion his duty lay in asking Margaret to dance.

Margaret received him with a flutter of gratified vanity and delight, which displayed itself in her looks and actions. She now felt certain that his affections were once more returning to her, and that, before long, he would become her avowed admirer.

Emma's dance was little more lively than her last; Lord Osborne was so very much occupied in keeping his feet in time, and in giving his *vis-à-vis* the proper hand at the proper moment, that he had no faculties to spare for engaging in conversation. She saw Mr Howard did not dance and more than once she met his eyes fixed on her with a look which she could not understand. It was not dislike or disapproval that his countenance expressed — she would rather have described it as depicting concern and a friendly interest. She tried to avoid looking at him, and was provoked with herself for thinking so much about his looks and manners, in spite of her resolutions to the contrary.

At the conclusion of this dance, there was a general movement to the supper-room, and Emma found herself escorted there by her late partner, rather to her own astonishment, as she could not help feeling that her place should have been occupied by one of the more distinguished guests. Indeed, she fancied, for a moment, that both his mother and his sister looked a little annoyed at his selection. She was quite separated from her own family, except Margaret, who, with Tom Musgrave, was placed nearly opposite to them. In fact, Emma saw, with some little surprise, that they were carrying on a very lively flirtation — which, as the excellent champagne took effect on Mr Musgrave, became every moment more tender.

CHAPTER 14

ON RISING FROM SUPPER, Miss Osborne again passed her arm under Emma's, and led her out of the room: complaining that she was tired and heated, she proposed adjourning to the conservatory. There, the chequered glimpses of a bright wintry moon played on the blossoms and shrubs. At the end of the conservatory was an alcove fitted up with sofas, and almost concealed from observation by a row of orange trees, whose blossoms perfumed the air. Into this recess Miss Osborne conducted her friend. They had been sitting only a few minutes when they heard voices approaching.

Miss Osborne whispered, 'It is only your sister and Mr Musgrave — sit still or we shall be plagued with his company.'

Trusting that they would not loiter long, the two young ladies remained concealed; and, in another moment, the couple approached so close as to enable them distinctly to hear what was said.

Margaret was speaking.

'But you need not envy us, I assure you, Mr Musgrave, we, poor weak women, who are afforded no pity for the wounds inflicted on us. We have to bear in silence; we dare not reveal the secrets of our hearts.'

'But women have so much more — I mean to say they are so much less — that is, you know, so tender, so angelic . . .' Tom's speech, by now thoroughly fuddled, tailed off into complete confusion.

'Very true, very true, we smile though there is a dagger in our heart,' went on Margaret, now launched on a flood-tide of romantic sentiment.

Tom, finding it impossible to sustain his part in this any longer, tried to change the subject.

'What are these heavenly blooms?' he asked, fingering the leaves of the shrub nearest to him.

'Do you not know they are orange blossoms — bridal flowers?'

'Are they indeed? — and when do *you* mean to wear them?'

'How can you ask — is such an event in the disposal of woman?'

'Do you wish to wear them?'

'Heartless creature — how can you ask?'

'Do not scold me for the deep interest I take in you.'

'You take an interest, indeed!' cried Margaret laughing affectedly. 'Ah, I know you better.'

'If you doubt my word, you don't know me at all — tell me, is there one of all those men in that bright assembly, for whom you would put on those mystic blossoms?'

'None, upon my word; but why should you ask; you do not care — you take no interest in me — you profess much indeed — but you are a man of professions.'

'You are unkind. I assure you I have the most feeling heart in the world and a deep and earnest devotion to you, fair Margaret.'

'Now you are jesting, Mr Musgrave.'

'In professing my admiration — my attachment — impossible! By this fair hand, I swear I love you beyond expression. Will you wear the orange blossoms for me?'

'Will I? Ah! dearest Tom — you little know my heart, if you doubt the willingness — but may I trust you?'

'I vow to you by the bright moon above us — by all the honour of my ancestors; by every thing that is dear to me, that you are the fairest, best, most amiable, lovely, perfect woman of my acquaintance.'

'Ah! dearest Tom. I sadly fear you flatter me with your sweet words.'

'Flatter you! — some I have flattered — but not *you* — that is impossible — tell me, Margaret, do you love me?'

'Doubt you my love? Can you question my feelings — would you probe my heart. Tom, I am yours in life and death.'

'You are mine and I am yours — but hush, there are voices — let us return to the dancing.'

With slow, and apparently reluctant step, Margaret was drawn away. The moment they were out of hearing, Miss Osborne turned to her companion and aroused her from the state of astonishment in which she was plunged by commencing a rapid, but whispered, apology for having become unintentionally the confidante of her sister's happy prospects. She assured her that it was entirely from feelings of friendship that she had sat silent — for had they started out and put the lovers out of countenance by their appearance, the declaration would have been interrupted, the whole affair disarranged. At the same time she promised to say nothing of the matter until it was generally published. She did not think it necessary to add how singularly absurd she had thought them.

That Tom Musgrave should propose marrying any woman without money or connexions, and especially Margaret, appeared to Emma almost miraculous. She was vexed that Miss Osborne should have overheard all the nonsense passing between them, for she could not help fearing that she would ridicule such affection and folly. Then too she felt very doubtful of her sister's happiness with a man whose present levity and idleness promised but ill for the future. Certainly Margaret loved him, but hers was a love which doubtless might have been transferred to some other object, and was but little likely to make her seriously unhappy.

All these thoughts passed through her mind whilst slowly accompanying her companion to the ballroom, where they neither sought nor saw the two whose conversation they had overheard.

The evening had given Emma decidedly more perplexity than pleasure. She had been disappointed in the conduct and manner towards her of Mr Howard which seemed rather to have enlarged a strange division between them than to have promoted their friendship. In Sir William Gordon she had become acquainted with a lively wit. It would have been a sorry affair, he asserted, if she had merely shone across his path like a meteor only to leave him plunged in darkness. Her orbit, Emma told him, was bound to be lonely and distant from his. It depended

120

solely on Miss Osborne that she was at the Castle and it was unlikely that their paths would cross again.

'Now tell me, do you think her pretty?' he asked.

'Exceedingly so,' replied Emma warmly; 'it is a countenance that improves on one so very much — surely you must admire her.'

Sir William did not return a direct answer, and Emma suspected that he would have been more ready with a reply had his admiration been merely superficial. Yet it had struck her that Miss Osborne's manner to him was cool and capricious, while Sir William was perhaps trying to hide his feelings and make a demonstration of amusing himself with others. Perhaps they were all amusing themselves at her expense by giving her the encouragement which had induced her to enter a society decidedly above her proper situation.

And so ended Emma's enjoyments of the ball at Osborne Castle, which were certainly less than her imagination had promised. She was convinced, on reflection, that this dissatisfaction must spring from some fault of her own mind; had her feelings been under proper regulation, she would have entered with contentment or satisfaction into the amusements before her, instead of wearying her spirit in wishes for what was withheld. Her tender interest in Mr Howard was the origin of all this; and if this incipient partiality already produced so much discontent it became her to check it at once, lest she should find herself permanently deprived of her peace of mind.

The conjoined effects of excitement of mind, and unusual dissipation, tended naturally to produce a restless and sleepless night, and finding early the next morning that her head would be better for fresh air, she resolved to try and find her way out of doors before the breakfast which would probably be at a very late hour.

The wintry sunbeams were sparkling on the hoar frost, the air was brisk and enlivening, and promising herself a pleasant ramble, she walked into the park. The path she chose lay along the side of a beautiful hanging wood of beech, and she pursued it in profound solitude for some time, hearing no other sound than the echo of her own foosteps on the hard, ringing gravel; but after walking a considerable distance, it struck her that there was a sound of other feet in her vicinity which seemed to be keeping parallel with herself, but farther in the wood. Supposing it might be some labourer or gamekeeper, she paused to listen, and allow them to pass on; but the steps likewise ceased when she did, and that so immediately as to make her doubt if it were not fancy altogether.

Again resuming her walk, she immediately heard the accompanying sound, and this time being convinced it was no delusion, she tried to see through the wood, and ascertain who was thus her silent companion, but the shrubs and underwood were too thick to allow her to see anything.

Not quite liking to be thus accompanied, she resolved to return, and an opening which appeared to her to lead in the direction of the Castle at that moment presenting itself, she unhesitatingly struck off in that direction. She no longer heard the footsteps but saw with a different kind of alarm that the rapidly gathering clouds predicted rain or snow. The turns and windings of that path began to perplex her, and she soon came to the conclusion that she had quite lost her way. The state of the weather became every moment more threatening.

Hoping to discover the turrets of the Castle amid the trees, she climbed up a small eminence, in order to obtain a more extensive prospect, and from this spot, though no view of Osborne Castle met her eyes, she saw in a little glen beneath a cottage, apparently belonging to a keeper or gardener, and there she determined to apply for directions.

During the momentary pause, whilst taking this survey of the landscape, her quick ear again caught the sound of the footsteps which had before seemed to follow her. Well aware that there could in reality be no cause for alarm, she overcame, as well as she could, an increase of nervous excitement, and listened attentively.

The tread was light and steady, evidently that of a gentleman, too light, she thought, for Lord Osborne, who was not remarkable for his grace in walking; and her heart suggested the idea that it might be Mr Howard.

She would not speak to him, if it were, that she was resolved upon; she would not allow him to be friendly only in private, whilst he was cold and distant before witnesses; but she thought she should like to ascertain if it were he, and to see how he would be disposed to behave.

The steps were now so close, another moment must reveal the figure; she would not seem to be waiting for him, and turned once more to look at the lodge below, to which a few large, heavy drops of rain made it advisable she should speedily retreat. Whilst her head was thus averted a few rapid bounds brought to her side Sir William Gordon.

The young man would in all probability have felt but little gratified had he known that the flush on her cheek at sight of him was entirely one of mortification and disappointment, for whatever she might try to persuade herself, she was really quite disappointed that the intruder was not Mr Howard as she had fancied.

She gave him as friendly a return to his salutation as she could force from her lips; whilst he professed most unbounded satisfaction at his good luck in thus overtaking her. She owned she had lost her way, and was proposing to take shelter in the cottage before them from the rapidly increasing rain.

'Do you require shelter?' he said; 'then let us hasten there at once; seeing you could do without rest, I naturally concluded you would be indifferent to the variations of the elements — proof against the storm —impervious to the rain.'

He begged to be allowed to show her the way, and as they descended the steep side of the glen together, she felt that she ought to be thankful for his arrival, as the path was so abrupt — in some places almost precipitous — that his support was, if not absolutely necessary, at least very convenient.

They were indeed glad when the door of the cottage opened in answer to their knock and they saw a bright fire burning on the hearth. The keeper's wife very hospitably pressed them to enter, exerted herself to dry Emma's cloak, and then after asking if they had breakfasted, set about preparing them a meal with all expedition.

Whilst she was preparing bread, butter, eggs and raspberry jam, an infant of a few months old awoke in its cradle near the chimney corner. Perceiving that the mother was too busy to attend to him, Emma volunteered to do so and took much pleasure in the occupation. Sir William looked at her with

123

admiration — he had been struck with her when dressed for the ball, and surrounded by a crowd of other elegant women, but here the effect was different. Emma's simple dress unencumbered by ornament, her dark hair now wetted by the rain carelessly pushed back from her glowing cheeks, her graceful movements as she played with the infant in her arms, struck him as forming the prettiest picture he had ever seen. He could not resist the temptation of trying a sketch of her figure on a leaf of his pocket-book.

'Can you see any prospect of the rain ceasing?' asked Emma without looking up.

'I assure you we shall not be missed these two hours,' said he, 'there is not the remotest chance of any one being risen in the Castle before noon, after such a ball as that of last night.'

'I should not like to spend many such nights. One soon tires of pleasure.'

'What sort of life would you have, Miss Watson, could you decide your lot with a wish — have you made up your mind?'

'Hardly, it is a point that requires reflection, and I cannot say that I have bestowed much on it.'

'Indeed — you don't say so — I thought all young ladies settled that beforehand — the situation, residence, fortune, even the name which the future was to bring them, do you not arrange that entirely?'

'If that is the case I am sadly behindhand.'

'It is never too late to mend, that must be your comfort; begin now — do you prefer the country, or are you ambitious of a house in town?'

'Oh, the latter of course; a house in town and ten thousand a year; you cannot imagine I should stop short if I once began wishing; what would be the good of that?'

'Bravo, I like to hear a lady speak her opinions boldly — so you are ambitious after all; I should not have thought that from your face; I am a great student of countenance.'

'But indeed you must blame yourself for my ambitious wishes,' retorted Emma. 'I am sure it was you who put them into my head; I told you I had never thought of anything of the kind.'

'Very well, I see you are a promising pupil, but to tell you the truth, I should have assigned you a quiet cot in the country, domestic cares and joys, a round of parochial duties, cheered by peace and content — a clever and well-educated companion, not a dashing or ambitious one. I read your feelings as I thought in your face, and should have expected you to choose such a lot; you see how the best physionomist may be mistaken.'

Emma blushed and then recovered herself with an effort.

'Are you aware, Sir William, how nearly you have drawn my lot — did you know I was the daughter of a country parson, and am situated nearly as you describe?'

'No indeed. I am after all then a better guesser than I took credit for; it is curious that I should have so closely described you. You live in the midst of content and peace, do you?'

'I have always thought content was an internal, not an external, blessing,' replied Emma, again evading his question, 'one which it became our duty to cultivate for ourselves, and I was blaming myself for feeling discontented at the detention in this cottage.'

'Well, I am certainly more amiable than you, Miss Watson, for I am as happy as possible, or nearly so at least. But now you mention it, it occurs to me that perhaps the rain may continue all day, in which case we should be really confined in our present refuge. Suppose we were to consult our hostess about a means of escape.'

'But what means can she suggest,' enquired Emma, 'except walking home? And in that case we shall certainly get wet through.'

'We might send to the Castle for a carriage; this seems to me the most simple remedy; do you object?'

Emma was rather startled at the idea of taking such a liberty, but Sir William knew the ways of the Castle best, and she did not raise any objection. Mrs Browning, the keeper's wife, when called into counsel, regretted extremely that she had no one about whom she could send on such an errand, her husband being out with the boy that helped; but she did have a little tilted cart in which they drove to church on Sunday.

'Well, and is not that at home — can we not have that? It would do admirably,' said Sir William.

'Certainly, sir, I could harness it for you, the horse is at home today luckily — I will go and see about it.'

'No, no, my good woman, let me go and see — I dare say I can manage the affair without troubling you,' said Sir William.

But she assured him her presence was necessary, at least to show him the way; if the young lady would be so kind again to hold the infant, they would soon have everything right. To this, of course, Emma readily agreed, and she soon, from the thinness of the partition, heard Sir William's voice joking with their hostess about the horse and harness.

In about ten minutes he returned.

'Miss Watson,' he said, 'your carriage is waiting — are you ready to undertake the expedition under my escort?'

Emma, after thanking the mother and kissing the child, was assisted into the neat little chay-cart.

At the porch of the Castle they were greeted by Lord Osborne.

'Hallo, what have you got there? Why, Gordon, when did you set up that handsome equipage?'

'I will tell you presently, Osborne — but I must first assist Miss Watson out,' replied Sir William gravely.

'Miss Watson! What sort of frolic is this? If you wanted to take a drive with Miss Watson, why did you not take her in your curricle?'

'Because, my good fellow, the curricle being uncovered, would have exposed us to the rain. You had better trust to me, Miss Watson, and let me lift you out — the step is very awkward for a lady — gently, now, there, you are safe,' as he set her down within the porch, 'I hope you are none the worse for your expedition. Do you not see, Osborne, this, our coach, is weather-proof — and, therefore, convenient on such a rainy day.'

'But where have you been?'

'Only driving in the park — surely you cannot object to so innocent a recreation.'

'Why did you not ask for one of the carriages,' said Lord Osborne reproachfully turning to Emma, who was trying not to laugh at his wondering look.

'We are exceedingly obliged to you,' replied Emma, but —'

'But,' interrupted Sir William, 'we were quite content with each other's society — and, as to our equipage, I defy you to produce one from your coach-house at all to be compared to this elegant vehicle. Miss Watson, were you ever in one you liked better?'

'Never in one for the loan of which I felt more obliged.'

'There, I knew it; only add you never had a better charioteer and then I shall be satisfied. I want a little commendation myself.'

'I do not think you do — you seem so uncommonly well satisfield with your exploits,' returned Emma laughing.

'Pray come to breakfast,' interposed Lord Osborne. 'My sister and Miss Carr are in the breakfast-room.'

The young ladies raised their eyes in astonishment and curiosity when the three entered, but Sir William forestalled their questions.

'Where do you think we breakfasted, Miss Osborne? For I beg to inform you, we early risers have had a walk, a breakfast, and a drive this morning, before you have finished your first meal.'

'Really, I cannot pretend to guess where so eccentric a person as Sir William Gordon takes his breakfast, or what his amusements are.'

Emma now hastily declined all breakfast, and proposed to go to her own room to remove her walking dress. It was not until later in the day that she had opportunity to give an accurate account of their adventure, which Miss Osborne received in meditative silence.

CHAPTER 15

THE WHOLE DAY WAS TOO WET to allow any kind of exercise out of doors, and Miss Carr complained bitterly of the stupidity and dullness of a wet morning after a ball. She possessed neither the resources nor the inclination to conceal her feelings at being denied the disdainful gossip about certain guests of the previous evening in which her friend would no doubt have joined her but for Emma's presence. Eventually she was roused from her fretful ill-humour by the entrance of Lord Osborne, but her attempts to be animated and agreeable were evidently thrown away upon him, and he seated himself by Emma, who was engaged in embroidering for his sister, and began to admire her work.

Emma's thoughts were wandering from her admirer's attempts at conversation when she was roused by Miss Osborne's enquiring of her brother if he had seen any of their friends at the Parsonage that day. His answer was in the affirmative; he had been walking with Howard and had a long chat with him about something of importance, and Howard was proposing to go away for a few weeks, if he could find anyone to take his duty; he thought his sister wanted change of air, and it was a long time since he had enjoyed a holiday.

'Going away!' exclaimed Miss Osborne, with a look of utter amazement; 'this does take me entirely by surprise. What in the world can influence him to such a freak as that! Going away, and at such a time!'

'I do not see why he should not go if he likes travelling in the cold,' observed Lord Osborne coolly; 'he has a right to a holiday if he chooses.'

'And he has worked particularly hard of late,' added Miss Carr maliciously; 'he has had double duty to perform.'

'He is always very attentive to the parish,' said Miss Osborne.

'Yes, both to old and young — the charitable visits he pays to *some* old ladies are most exemplary,' continued Miss Carr. 'No doubt he will be rewarded for his exertions, but I fear he will be much missed in his absence.'

Miss Osborne frowned and bit her lip; Emma continued to devote an apparently steady attention to her work, and would not speak. Lord Osborne added:

'I gave him leave to go, as far as I was concerned, but I do not know whether her ladyship will like it. However, I think it rather hard if the poor man cannot have a holiday now and then, whatever my mother may think. He is a very good sort of fellow, and though he was my tutor, I have a great regard for him; don't you think so too, Miss Watson?'

'It is very natural that you should,' replied Emma as steadily as she could, but not very well understanding what he meant.

'I asked him to dine here today,' he continued, 'because he said he should like to see you, Henrietta, before he went, or something of that sort, but he did not seem certain about dining here, or when he should come up. I almost fancy he is not well, he is so different from usual.'

'Something must be amiss with him indeed, if you notice a change, Osborne!' exclaimed his sister. 'For I do not think you in general very quick at observing faces or expressions. I must certainly see him.'

Miss Carr soon departed, and a moment after Miss Osborne rose and walking to the window stood there in deep contemplation for some time. The other two were perfectly silent and — at length — she took her brother's arm, and saying she wanted some conversation with him, she led him out of the room. Emma was trying, but not very successfully, to bring her own thoughts into order, when a gentle knock was heard at the door, and on her inviting the visitor to enter, Mr Howard presented himself.

Both lady and gentleman were excessively embarrassed at this unexpected encounter.

'I expected to find Miss Osborne here,' he faltered.

'She has just left the room,' replied Emma, sitting down again, and then not another word was spoken by either for

129

some minutes. He was trying to be cold, she to be easy and natural; apparently she had the greater success in her efforts, for she found that she could speak with the appearance of calm.

'I hear you are thinking of leaving home, Mr Howard, I hope I shall see Mrs Blake again before you do.'

'I suppose Lord Osborne told you?'

'I certainly heard it from him,' she answered, rather annoyed at his abruptness.

Another pause followed, and then he broke it, by an enquiry if she had enjoyed the ball last night. She was quick to answer that her enjoyment had been less than at the first one she had attended.

'I am surprised,' he said coldly. 'I fancied the friendly kindness of Miss Osborne and the attentions of her brother would have secured you a pleasant evening.'

'I hope I am not ungrateful for Miss Osborne's goodness; and as to the attentions of her brother, to tell you the truth such as they are they are not particularly conducive to my pleasure. There was far more exaltation than excitement in being honoured as his partner.'

'We are perhaps all inclined to undervalue what is in our power,' replied he very gravely.

'I beg your pardon, but I do not see what that has to do with the present case; it is not in my power to think Lord Osborne an entertaining partner, or a good dancer, and though I mean no reflection on him, I should not be sorry to think it was the last time we shall ever stand up together.'

'Possibly it may be,' said he with a peculiar smile.

She could not make him out at all, and resolved not to speak again, since he seemed determined to quarrel with her. Again he broke the silence by an observation.

'I suppose now you have seen more of Osborne Castle, Miss Emma Watson, you have become better reconciled to it.'

'I like it very much,' said Emma, finding she was expected to say something, and not quite certain what would be best.

'I remember not long ago that you expressed very different sentiments. But the circumstances change; you will be much here in the future.'

'I do not think that,' said Emma firmly. 'I have no claim on Miss Osborne which can lead me to expect such an honour.'

'Those who have rank and wealth in their hands have a heavy responsibility,' he murmured.

She made no reply, but continued her embroidery with exemplary perseverance, secretly entertaining a hope that some one would come in, to relieve her from a very uncomfortable *tête-à-tête*. Presently looking up, when about to change the silk in her needle, she met his eyes fixed on her with a look which seemed at once to contradict the coldness of his tones and the gravity of his expressions. She wished to speak, but could think of nothing that could safely be said in the present state of her feelings.

'You do not agree with me, Miss Watson, I perceive; are you convinced that happiness can be secured more easily in an exalted circle, like that of the Castle?'

She reflected for a few moments, and then looking up said, with some warmth:

'Am I to infer from what you say that you think my acquaintance with Miss Osborne or even her brother likely to make me dissatisfied or unhappy; to induce me to disregard former friends, or despise those who have been kind to me? Tell me plainly, Mr Howard; it would be much easier and safer to be at once explicit, if you really wish to act the part of a friend.'

She fixed her eyes on him as she spoke, her bashfulness overcome or forgotten in her eager anxiety for an explanation. His countenance, in his turn, betrayed extreme embarrassment, and he evidently hesitated over what to say. She continued after a short pause, finding he gave no reply:

'I cannot help being afraid from your words, that you have some such charge to lay against me. Tell me, did Mrs Blake think I neglected her last night; that I was too much engrossed with Miss Osborne! I should be extremely grieved were this the case, for nothing could be further from my wishes; if she felt hurt at anything, I fear I must have been wrong, and would willingly do anything in my power to explain the circumstances.'

Mr Howard's countenance betrayed that he was feeling much; but of what nature Emma could not exactly decide. He answered evidently with an effort:

131

'I assure you, you quite misunderstood me; I never intended to give you the impression that Anne was jealous of Miss Osborne. Your mutual friendship need not exclude you from intimacy with others — friendship is not like love — it should not — it certainly need not be encumbered by jealousy. But, Miss Watson, there is a feeling, a sentiment — a species of friendship, which will not bear a rival; an affection which is covetous of the smiles bestowed on others; which can only be satisfied by an entire return —' he paused a moment and then added, 'I beg your pardon, I have said too much, and I cannot expect you to understand me. We are going in a few days to some distance, and, perhaps, I may not see you again — I wish you every happiness — may you never have reason to do otherwise than rejoice in the friendships you contract.' He stopped very abruptly, and after a momentary hesitation hastily quitted the room.

Emma was left alone to try to comprehend, as well as she could, the meaning and object of his very desultory conversation. There began to dawn upon her mind a new idea; he was jealous of Lord Osborne. Her own feelings were in such a state of confusion that she hardly comprehended whether it gave her more pain than pleasure to think this. It was a very great pleasure to feel that he really cared for her; but how unkind of him to go away and leave her merely because Lord Osborne had such a fancy for looking at her.

At that moment Lord Osborne hurried into the room and at once entreated her to come with him into the library as Sir William Gordon very earnestly required her presence. She begged to know what was wanted of her and at last prevailed on the young man to reveal that Sir William had begun to make a sketch of her in the gamekeeper's cottage and was now most anxious for the opportunity of correctly finishing it.

In the library Miss Osborne was looking troubled and unhappy while Sir William was bending over his sketch and Miss Carr had clearly been amusing herself by finding fault with his drawing. Sir William was now claiming with some animation that the defects she saw arose only from the unfinished state of the work. Miss Osborne thereupon begged Emma to oblige Sir William, employing such a grave and earnest tone that Emma was induced to sit for him.

Miss Carr and Lord Osborne stationed themselves behind Sir William, one chattering about every stroke he drew, and commenting on Emma's figure as if she had been an inanimate object, the other staring in his unmerciful way at her face, delighted to be furnished with so excellent an opportunity and so good an excuse.

'Be sure to make her complexion dark enough, Sir William,' said Miss Carr, 'Miss Watson is so very dark — quite a brunette; I think you have made the hand a little too small, it strikes me she has not quite such slender hands — and the hair — surely, you have indulged in a little imagination there — that luxuriant braid — our eyes must see differently if you think that natural and like her own.'

'I have no doubt in the world that our eyes do see very differently, Miss Carr,' replied Sir William. 'I have always observed that to be the case where feminine beauty is concerned.'

'There is not a bit too much hair,' interposed Lord Osborne, 'but she does not wear it in that tumble-down fashion — she is always particularly neat and tidy about the head. I like to see a small head and pretty ear — why don't you show her ear — all ladies should have small ears.'

'So should they all have pretty hands,' replied Fanny Carr, 'but they cannot always get them.'

'My friends,' said Sir William, 'my very dear friends, I really must trouble you to move a little farther off. I think I shall send you out of the room, Miss Carr; be so good as to take Lord Osborne into the conservatory and select a bouquet for my refreshment. I cannot endure all your critical remarks at my back.'

'Come, my lord,' cried the young lady, 'come, do as you are bid.'

'Not I.'

'I shall not make you a copy if you do not,' interposed Sir William, 'nor ever let you see the original again.'

'Well,' said his lordship, moving reluctantly away, 'I'll go on those conditions.'

The couple left the room; Miss Osborne remained in silence.

'I have no objection to Miss Osborne remaining, if she is determined to patronize a poor artist with her presence.'

133

'I am waiting for Miss Watson's sake, Sir William; I cannot for a moment imagine that my presence can make any difference to you.'

Emma thought her friend looked remarkably unamiable as she spoke, and wondered what was the matter.

'Have you seen Mr Howard?' enquired Henrietta in a low voice.

Sir William looked up quickly, in time to catch Emma's deep blush, as she answered in the affirmative.

'How did you find him — my brother said he seemed unwell — what did he appear to you? Something must be amiss.'

Emma could only answer that she did not know, and wished to drop the subject. She turned to Sir William.

'I hope you are not going to try my patience much longer. I only promised for half an hour, you know.'

'Very true, but half an hour of that kind is of an elastic sort, extending from one hour to three at least, as I am sure you must have experienced when obliged to wait for a friend. And, Miss Watson, you are too near perfection to show me such unkindness.'

'Your flattery shall not bribe me to remain. Miss Osborne, may I not go? It was at your request that I stayed — pray release me from the spell.'

'Sabrina fair,
  Listen where thou are sitting —'

murmured Sir William in an undertone, without looking up.

'We will go together,' said Miss Osborne.

'Fair ladies, will you not first condescend to cast an eye on the production of my humble pencil. Have you no curiosity, Miss Watson — no sympathy, Miss Osborne? Do give me your opinion.'

'My opinion, you know, would be of little use,' said Emma, turning round from the door which she had just reached; she stopped in her speech, catching a glance of Sir William's directed towards Miss Osborne, which seemed to say hers was not exactly the opinion he most desired. She left the room without another word, and her exit was followed by a silence.

Sir William broke it first.

134

'Are you absolutely determined against exhibiting any interest in my proceedings — against giving me any encouragement in my efforts?'

Miss Osborne turned away her head, walked up to the easel and affected to be examining the drawing.

'Sir William, you have no doubt an accurate eye for likenesses, but I doubt from the expression you give, whether you possess equal penetration with regard to character.'

'Give me an instance of my failure,' cried he, delighted to have induced her to speak at all. 'Explain your critique, Miss Osborne.'

'No,' she answered, 'you must look for yourself. You are trying to produce a great effect by contrasts, and it has no success but to jar on the senses.'

He fixed his eyes on her with a look of deep penetration, as if trying to read her thoughts. She continued calmly to contemplate the drawing, as if quite engrossed by that object.

'Are you referring entirely to this picture,' enquired he, 'or to some other design of mine?'

She was silent, and he could see that the detachment she affected was no longer easy for her.

'I think you wrong me,' he continued. 'Do you suppose I should dare flatter myself that you would take any interest in my proceedings, that you would condescend to feel any concern about where I went, with whom I associated — what I was doing? Should you not condemn it as unpardonable impertinence if I presumed thus far?'

'Very likely I might, Sir William, but I have an idea that it would not be the first time you had been guilty of impertinence, or expected forgiveness when you were unpardonable.'

He smiled.

'I will be very candid, Miss Osborne,' said he, 'and if I sin in doing so, remember your own accusations are alone to blame for it. I own your caprice and the variations in your conduct towards me have for a moment made me seek the comfort of contrast in Emma Watson — but it was your own fault — you knew I loved you, and you wished to torment me.'

'Sir William, this appears to me a most extraordinary style of address — you have never, to my knowledge, uttered a word indicative of the love you now allude to as a well-known feeling. However, let that pass — the love you say has done the same — why then mention it now?'

'The love has not, and cannot pass, Henrietta — it is of too old and stubborn a nature, has been nursed with too much care in its infancy to be easily extinguished now. You have been unkind — you have refused to speak to me — sometimes to look at me — you have said the most bitter things you could devise — you have been unjust in every possible way — now be candid and kind for once. Tell me how you really regard me!'

'As the most extraordinary of mortals, Sir William. Your manner of address may possibly have the charm of novelty — I have little experience in that way, and cannot therefore tell; but I should suppose there were few men who preface a declaration of affection with violent abuse.'

Now as she really trembled, and had some trouble in commanding her countenance, he seized the moment for his final word.

'What else remains to me? The devotion, the silent adoration of a twelvemonth have been of no avail — you have persisted in slighting me — now I will speak out. I love you, Henrietta — you know it — give me an answer at once — reject or accept — but don't trifle with me any more.'

She tried to speak, but quite overcome, she burst into tears, and seemed on the point of quitting the room, but he resolutely detained her. His arm was round her waist, his hand clasping hers, and as he whispered in her ear 'Henrietta, you *do* love me', she did not deny it.

CHAPTER 16

MR HOWARD WAS A MAN WHO FELT little confidence in his own worth. He also found it hard to believe that he could exert any great influence on the feelings of his friends. Had he been endowed with a bolder temper he would certainly have been aware that there was nothing in Emma's character likely to inspire her with a preference for the young peer over himself. Lord Osborne had made his feelings for Emma perfectly clear to his former tutor, and although Mr Howard had for a moment entertained the idea of asserting his own equal right to compete for her hand, he had not done so. He could not bring himself to confess his own attachment to a young man like his pupil; he could not depend on the secret being preserved, and he shrank from profaning his love by making it the possible joke of Tom Musgrave and his associates. No, he would not be the means of depriving Emma of wealth and rank if she valued them — and if not — if, as was possible, his lordship should be refused, then, with some reason for hope, he would return to try his fate in the same adventure.

For this end it was, in part, that he determined to obtain a holiday; he had long begun to feel that he ought to go for another reason, but Emma Watson's attractions had kept him stationary. The other reason arose from the sentiments which the dowager Lady Osborne had already made very apparent to him.

Even his modest estimation of himself was forced to yield before the conviction which her looks, her manners and her language conveyed to his mind. Most unwelcome this conviction certainly was, as it could end, he thought, in nothing but a positive rupture between his family and the Osbornes; and unless he had the power of obtaining another living, it would certainly render them exceedingly uncomfortable. All hopes of further advancement from the family patronage would be at an end, and he was not sure that even upon the small income his present living afforded him, it would be prudent to marry, as his sister and her little boy were quite dependent on himself.

Yet it was hard, very hard, to give up the charming hopes with which he had flattered his fancy; he did not feel equal to such a sacrifice; he did not feel positively called to it. When he had unexpectedly found himself in Emma's presence, and alone with her, his contending feelings had almost deprived him of self-control, and he had been scarcely conscious of what he said or did, though on quitting her, he carried away a decided conviction that he had behaved extremely ill, and that no doubt she was disgusted with him.

While Mr Howard was thus despondently forming his plans, Emma received a note from Stanton sent over by special messenger. Her father had been taken very ill with a seizure during the night; he had still not recovered his senses and the apothecary had said nothing to give them hope. In less than an hour, Emma was on the way home. Wrapped in fearful anticipations of what would meet her there, she had been almost unconscious of what was passing before her eyes; she had an impression that Miss Osborne had been very kind, that just at last her brother had been there also, that he had squeezed her hand at parting, with much warmth; she thought of it for a moment only, and then her mind again reverted to her father's situation, and her sisters' distress.

The rapidity with which the journey was now performed in the Osborne carriage was a most important comfort, very different from the creeping jog-trot of their old horse, and she felt quite thankful that Elizabeth had spared her such torture as would have been caused by the delay their own chaise would have occasioned.

Before Elizabeth was expecting her, she was at home. Softly she looked into the parlour; the shutters were open, but the room otherwise bore no symptoms of having been disturbed since last night; the candles were still on the table, the supper tray unremoved and the chairs all in disorder. She then proceeded upstairs, and was just on the point of opening the bedroom door, when Elizabeth came out of it. One glance at her face told her that there was no better news in store for her.

Mr Watson was fast sinking — he lay apparently in a deep slumber, and there seemed no probability of his ever recovering sufficiently to recognize those around him, or to speak again.

Elizabeth had been watching beside him, alternately with Penelope, through the night; the apothecary had said there was now no more to do; all the remedies his skill could suggest had proved unavailing, and they must patiently await the result.

Margaret had gone to bed in hysterics, and required Nanny to sit up with her, so that it was a great blessing Penelope had been at home, as she had a head and nerves which were always in good order, and knew as much of medical treatment as the village apothecary.

At this moment Penelope joined them; she had left the patient unchanged; the apothecary and the maid were with him, and hearing Emma's voice, she had come out for a moment to meet her.

'A sad ending to our Osborne Castle festivities, Emma,' said she, as she shook her hand; 'who would have thought it, when we set out? Elizabeth, don't you think we ought to have better advice? I am certain that man there does not know in the least what he is about; there must be a good physician at one of the towns round here — could we not send for him?'

Elizabeth could not tell; they had never had occasion to send for a physician; and she did not know where one could be found. Emma inquired if notice of their father's danger had been despatched to their brothers; it appeared neither of them had thought of this; but it must be done immediately.

They were about twenty miles from Croydon; and by sending a letter by the mail-coach, they knew Robert would hear the same evening, and might be at Stanton easily within twenty-four hours. This much they settled on, and a note was written, and despatched by a trusty messenger, who was to catch the coach at the inn and then try and bring back a physician with him.

The apothecary seemed much relieved when he learnt the project of calling in further advice, and thus shifting the weight of responsibility from his own shoulders. He thought it probable that the patient might linger many hours, possibly two or three days; and with a promise to return in a few hours, he now took his leave for the present.

It is needless to attempt to describe all the feelings which oppressed the sisters as they sat watching the sick-bed — perhaps the death-bed — of their only parent. Hours stole away, bringing no change, and no alleviation of their fears. Margaret did not join the watch; her sensibility, as she designated it, bringing on violent hysterics, which made attention and nursing necessary for her. Emma tried to soothe her, in vain; Penelope was sarcastic; Elizabeth declared she would be soon as well as any of them, if she was not meddled with.

About two o'clock they were roused by the sound of carriage wheels at the door, and Elizabeth stealing into the passage, where a window looked on the entrance, came back with the information that it was a post-chariot, from which a gentleman had alighted, and that there was somebody else in the carriage, but she could not tell who it was.

In another moment, a card was handed into the room, with the name of Dr Denham on it, a name which they knew belonged to a celebrated physician, residing many miles distant. Much surprised, the girls hesitated a moment as to the meaning of this, but, of course, decided that the two eldest should descend to the parlour to receive him.

After a consultation of about ten minutes, Emma, hearing their voices and steps on the stairs, quitted the room of the invalid that she might not be in the way, and when they were safely shut in there, she ran downstairs to refresh herself by a moment's breathing the fresh air.

Great was her surprise on reaching the entrance passage, to see Lord Osborne standing there, and evidently looking about for somebody. Her light footsteps instantly caught his ear, and he turned to meet her with eagerness.

'Ha! Miss Watson,' cried he, 'I hoped to see you here; how is your father, hey — not very bad, I hope.'

'Indeed he is,' replied Emma, with tears in her eyes.

'Indeed, I am sorry — upon my honour — I'm grieved to hear that,' looking quite compassionately at her, 'poor old gentleman — what a pity — but don't fret — I shall be quite unhappy if I think you are fretting.'

140

Emma scarcely attended to what he was saying.

'How came you here, Lord Osborne?' she exclaimed. 'Had you anything to do with Dr Denham?'

'I'll tell you how it was,' replied he, taking hold of her hand, and drawing her towards the parlour door, 'only don't stand here in the cold, that's so uncomfortable. There now, sit down there, and let me sit down beside you — and I'll tell you. We know Dr Denham very well — so when Henrietta heard your father was ill, she wrote him a note, and sent me with it, to ask him as a great favour to visit Mr Watson; she is a favourite of his — and I fetched him in the carriage, and he is to take no fee —'

'I am sure we are exceedingly obliged to you all,' said Emma, colouring from a variety of feelings; 'it was very kind of Miss Osborne to think of it, and of you to take so much trouble.'

'Do you know it gave me a great deal of pleasure — a very great deal; I don't know when ever I was happier than just while I was thinking of obliging you — I did not mind the trouble in the least.'

He was interrupted before he had committed himself to any further declaration by the sound of the physician's return, which startled Emma into a sudden recollection that to be found sitting side by side on the sofa with the young nobleman would produce an awkward impression. She therefore quietly withdrew, to return to her father's bedside, and there it entered her mind that perhaps after all Mr Howard's jealousy was not ill-founded, and that Lord Osborne did entertain a more than ordinary partiality towards herself.

As soon as Dr Denham had taken his leave, her sisters returned to the sick room to tell her what he had said. He had given them no encouragement; had said there was nothing further to be done, that it was true that while there was breath there was hope, but that Mr Watson's advanced age and broken health made a recovery most unlikely, and even a temporary return of his intellect extremely improbable.

The next morning brought no alteration in the situation of the patient, but it brought Robert Watson to the house. He came, cool and self-possessed as ever, and looking decidedly as if his mind at least never quitted his office, but was still engrossed

141

with the business there transacting. There was scarcely any emotion betrayed on seeing his father, and what little was discernible whilst in his sick room, had all vanished before he reached the parlour door.

'Well, I must say this is most unfortunate,' he said, sitting down in his father's chair and stretching out his feet to the fender. 'Heaven knows what is to become of you girls — there will not be more than a thousand pounds to divide between you: and it's so unlucky to happen just now, for of course you must come home to Croydon.'

'That would be very unlucky indeed, at any time,' cried Penelope; 'but I hope not quite inevitable. *I* shall not live at Croydon, I promise you.'

'So much the better, if you have any other plan; three on one's hands are quite enough. There must have been some great mismanagement, or some of you would certainly have married.' In a fit of vexation at his sisters' celibacy, Robert Watson stirred the fire into a vehement blaze.

'Well, to relieve your mind,' replied Penelope, 'I will inform you I am engaged to be married, and expect to be a wife in about a month.'

'Are you indeed? My dear sister, I congratulate you. What settlements are you to have? If the papers pass through our office I promise you I will pay every attention to see it advantageously arranged for you.'

'Your liberality, my dear Robert, is far beyond what I had ventured to expect of you. But I shall not encroach on you as the settlements are preparing at Chichester.'

'It is a very delicate matter to talk of,' whispered Margaret, who had now made her appearance, 'one from which a young woman of sensibility naturally shrinks; but I will so far overcome my feelings as to inform you, Robert, that I too am engaged to be married, and that, therefore, delighted as I should be to reside with my dear Jane, I still hope before long to be able to receive her in my own house, and, as Mrs Tom Musgrave, to return the kindness showed to Margaret Watson.'

'*What!*' said Robert, staring at her with undisguised amazement, 'are you mad, Margaret?'

'Indeed, I hope not,' replied she, simpering; 'I am engaged to my dear Tom Musgrave, that's all I mean; and no doubt we shall be married in time.'

Her brother still looked doubtfully at her, but after a moment's consideration replied:

'Well, Margaret, if that's the case, you deserve more credit than I had ever thought possible, for I would not have given much for your chance with Tom — but, since you say he is engaged to you, I am heartily glad to hear it. Have you any witnesses? Or was the contract in writing?'

'No, it was in the conservatory at Osborne Castle, and as to witnesses oh, dear Robert, you don't suppose ladies and gentlemen choose to have such tender scenes pass before witnesses?'

'I am sure it would be a deuced deal better if they did,' said he sharply; 'there would be much less trouble to their friends.'

The next time she was alone with Elizabeth, Emma heard more of Penelope's engagement. As far as money went, it was decidedly a good match for her; Dr Harding was a physician very well known in the county of Sussex to families of consequence. Elizabeth herself might not fancy an elderly widower, yet she could not expect everyone to have her tastes, and if Penelope herself was satisfied, that was all that could be required.

Emma did not think and feel the same; she wished that her sister should have required more; that she should have been incapable of considering a sufficient jointure to be the principal aim and end of engaging in matrimony. Something must be wanting — something either of delicacy or principle, which could lead her to such results; and she wondered that her eldest sister did not feel as she did.

Elizabeth then proceeded to discuss Margaret's engagement, which she declared seemed to her incredible; she told Emma that while returning from the ball Margaret, after a great deal of nonsense, had spoken of an engagement with Tom, and declared that he was to come the next day and ask her father's consent.

After a little internal hesitation, Emma told Elizabeth that so far as the fact of Tom's having proposed and been accepted was concerned, she could herself answer for the truth of Margaret's statement. She related to her, under a promise of secrecy for the

143

present, the circumstances of her own and Miss Osborne's being accidental listeners. This, of course, settled the point, but did not diminish the wonder of the girls, both that Mr Musgrave should have proposed to Margaret, and that he should since have taken no further steps in the business.

CHAPTER 17

ANOTHER DAY CONFIRMED their worst anticipation. Mr
Watson was no more; and his four daughters were left with
feelings as different as their characters. Emma, who knew the
least of him, certainly experienced the greatest grief. Elizabeth
mourned too — but she had no time to cultivate sorrow as a
duty, or indulge in its appearance as a recreation. Emma, active
and useful likewise, busied herself in spite of her grief. Elizabeth
grieved only in the intervals of her business.

When first Robert came to Stanton, Elizabeth had consulted
him on the subject of sending for Sam, but her brother opposed
it. Emma had listened in silent anxiety to the debate, and in
keen disappointment to its termination. From her sister's conversation, she had an ardent desire to meet her unknown
brother; she had expected to be able to like him — Elizabeth
had, in speaking of him, told many little traits of character,
which convinced her that he must possess a generous disposition
and an affectionate heart; she longed to see him — to know him
— to be loved by him.

But Robert had decided that though he was, of course, to be
informed of his father's illness, there was no need to say anything which should induce him to come himself — no doubt it
would be excessively inconvenient to his master — a needless
expense to himself — perfectly undesirable in every way, and
quite unnecessary; for, what use could Sam be when Robert himself was there? He was nobody — a younger son — the most
unimportant being in the world. As to his wishing to see his
father again, what did that signify? People could not always
have what they wished for — young men in their apprentice-
ship must not look for holidays; he was sure *he* should never

have thought of anything of the sort whilst he was serving his articles; and now, how often did he ever take a holiday from the office?

But Emma's wish to see her brother was not fated to be entirely disappointed, for no sooner did he receive the news of his father's death, than he obtained leave of absence from his master without difficulty, and arrived unexpectedly at Stanton. She was sitting alone in the darkened parlour, when an unknown step arrested her attention; it was not the slow, measured consequential tread of Robert; it was quicker, lighter, more like one which had sometimes made her heart beat before; at least so she fancied for a moment, perhaps only because she had just been thinking of him. The footsteps passed the door, then paused, returned and entered slowly.

His first words and the cordial embrace with which they were accompanied, overcame her firmness, and she burst into tears in his arms. He was much affected likewise, but brought her a glass of water from the sideboard, and then sitting down with his arm round her waist, drew from her all the circumstances of his father's death, and learnt that it was Robert's doing that he had not been summoned sooner. That hour repaid Emma for much that she had suffered at the hands of some members of the family. She had found a friend in her brother. The dearest, the least selfish, the most equal bond which nature ties, laid the foundation of an affection which added greatly to her happiness.

When her sisters entered the room, Emma could not but wonder at the indifference with which he was received both by Penelope and Margaret. Robert's reception, however, was the worst of all.

'So you are come, are you — as your elder brother you might have consulted me, before incurring so much expense.'

The whole of the week which Sam spent at home, was one of consolation and comfort to Emma; he listened to all she could tell him, made her describe her past life, talked of her uncle and aunt, questioned her as to the effects of her change, entered into her feelings, anticipated what they must have been, sympathized warmly in them all, and was in fact a true, warm-hearted brother to the forlorn girl. Together they talked of their father, praised his amiable disposition, sorrowed for his loss; then Sam told

146

her of his prospects and wishes, confided to her his attachment
to Mary Edwards, and his wavering hopes of success; his plans
for his future subsistence, and his anticipation of the brilliant
success which was to await him in his profession.

Emma's future prospects were likewise canvassed. He could
not bear the idea of her having to reside with Robert and his
wife. Sam protested that Emma was in every respect much too
good for such a situation, and that the moment he had a house
and an income, however small, she should share it with him.

When their father's will came to be examined, it appeared
that it was dated three years previously, and that of the sum of
two thousand pounds, which Mr Watson had to bequeath,
neither Emma nor Robert were to receive any share. The latter
had already been put in possession of all that he could reasonably
expect, his father having made considerable advances to estab-
lish him in life, and at the same time when the will was made,
everyone supposed Emma would be provided for by her uncle,
and though that expectation had been entirely frustrated, it
seemed that Mr Watson had never summoned sufficient energy
to alter his will, and give her any share in the little he possessed.

Robert took leave of the family immediately, and returned to
Croydon, having arranged that when everything was settled at
Stanton, three of his sisters should follow him there; Penelope
professing it to be her intention to return to Chichester as soon
as she conveniently could. Sam's week was not yet expired, and
he remained with his sisters.

The morning after Robert's departure, as Emma and her
brother were sitting together, Margaret joined them, and sitting
down beside Sam, described her situation and demanded his
advice.

On hearing the circumstances of the proposal, Sam felt bound
to ask if Tom Musgrave was sober at the time.

'What questions you ask, Sam — sober! You quite shock me
— remember you are talking to a young lady.'

'Well, I will not forget that, but I don't see anything so bad
in the question, and I know no delicate way of putting it. Are
you sure he was not drunk at the time? — will that do?'

'Upon my word — worse and worse, as if I should talk to a
man who was drunk! What do you take me for?'

147

'I am sorry to offend you, my dear sister, but I have known Tom Musgrave a long time, and on occasion seen him very drunk. Indeed, in my opinion, he is just the sort of man to make a fool of himself first, and then of any girl who would listen to him.'

'How excessively unkind you are, Sam,' said Margaret, apparently on the point of crying. 'I am quite sure you are wrong. Tom never could or would make a fool of me. He is not that sort of man at all; but, as I have heard nothing of him since that evening, I wish you to go and call on him — tell him how much pleased you are to hear of the engagement, and beg him to come and see me — there is no occasion to shut him out of the house, though we do not admit other visitors.'

'That's your plan, is it? But suppose he declines altogether — suppose he should say it was a dream on your part — a delusion — a mistake; suppose that is the reason of his silence, what am I to do then?'

'Oh, if he were to do that, you must challenge him! You could not do less for such an insult to your sister; you must send a challenge, and I could bring an action for breach of promise!'

'Well, if you mean to do that, I think I had better let the challenge alone; because the one might interfere with the other. If I were to shoot him, you know your action could not be brought.'

'Do you mean that you will not do as I ask you?'

'Indeed I do.'

'Then I think you most unkind and ungenerous; I always understood it was a brother's duty to fight with every man who insulted his sister or broke an engagement to her.'

'But, allowing us such high privileges, my dear Margaret, I think I am justified in requiring proof; first, that the engagement was made; secondly, that it has been broken. I am not clear yet on either of these points.'

'I see what it is, you are determined not to help me; and I think it excessively ill-natured and cowardly of you to stand by and see your sister insulted and robbed of her best affections, and not interfere for her sake.'

'Indeed, my dear Margaret, I cannot see that my interference has the least chance of doing any good; if Tom was serious and

148

sober, he will need no intervention of mine to remind him of his promises; if he was drunk and did not know what he was saying, the less that is publicly known of such a transaction, the better in every respect for your dignity.'

'I see you will not take my part — I shall have to take my own way. I have never met such barbarous treatment.'

While the silence of Margaret's lover gave so much concern, not a day had passed without Lord Osborne either calling himself at the door, or sending a groom with a joint message of inquiry from his sister and himself; several kind little notes had been received from the young lady, expressing concern and sympathy, and it was quite evident that they did not wish to drop the acquaintance. Nothing had been seen of Mr Howard; but a note from Mrs Blake assured Emma that they had heard every day through Lord Osborne or they would have sent more frequently to enquire for her welfare. This was consolatory, as serving to convince her that she was not forgotten at the Parsonage; but she could not help murmuring a little to herself that Mr Howard should have so entirely withdrawn from personal intercourse.

Meantime all the necessary arrangements for the girls quitting Stanton were made, with all possible despatch. Margaret indeed took no interest in the proceedings, contenting herself with wandering about, and fretting for Mr Musgrave; but the others were busy from the time Sam left them. Penelope still held to her resolution of not visiting her brother; she determined to return to her friend at Chichester, and marry from her house.

Emma was sorry at parting with her — she had got over the shock which her brusque manners had at first inflicted; and they had always agreed very well since the day at Osborne Castle. Consequently, Emma could not help wishing it was Margaret who was going to Chichester, and Penelope who was to share their new home at Croydon.

Things, however, were really better arranged than she could have ordered them, for it would have been impossible for Penelope and Jane Watson to have continued in the same house without the certain destruction of the peace of all around. There was no one in the neighbourhood to regret, excepting Mrs Blake, for Emma would not allow even to herself that the separation from Mr Howard gave her any concern; the Osborne family were all gone to town without her having seen anything more of them, and without the suit of the young nobleman having made any progress. She did not expect ever to see them again. Her own plan for the future was to try to procure a situation as teacher in a boarding school, or private governess; anything by which she could feel she was earning the food she ate, in preference to becoming as her brother expressed it, a burden on his family. She began now to comprehend, more fully than she had done before, what an evil poverty might be, and felt a vivid sensation of regret that her uncle had left her so entirely dependent on others after giving her an education which quite unfitted her for filling the situation of humble companion to her sister-in-law.

Just before quitting Stanton, she had a farewell visit from Mrs Blake and her brother. The lady was the same as ever, and warm in her manners; but Mr Howard looked pale and ill, and was evidently out of spirits. The visit was short; and when they parted, Emma found the interview had only added one more pang to all the distress she had previously endured.

CHAPTER 18

THE JOURNEY TO CROYDON was safely performed and as expeditiously as could be expected by three young ladies and a quantity of luggage travelling with post-horses. Margaret, who was quite at home in the streets of Croydon, pointed out to whom the various houses belonged. Robert's door, with its brass-handled bell, was easily recognized by a large plate bearing the owner's name.

The door was opened by a footman who informed them that master was at work within, missus was out in the town, but they could step into the drawing-room while they waited for her return. With evident nonchalance he assisted the post-boy unload the carriage, and summoning the house-maid, enquired if she knew what was to be done with all *them* things. The waiting-woman decided that nothing could be ventured upon till the missus came home; she had changed her mind so often about the rooms, that it was quite uncertain what would be settled on at last; and if she should happen to alter her arrangements whilst she was out, it was evident they would have had all their trouble for nothing. The three girls were therefore sentenced to sit in the parlour during the interval.

Presently the door opened and Augusta appeared. Margaret instantly rushed up to embrace her, but the child, who seemed peculiarly self-possessed for her age, repulsed her.

'I did not come here to see you, aunt Margaret,' said she. 'Which is Emma?'

'I am,' said Emma advancing, and pleased to be called for.

Her niece considered her attentively with an air of surprise, then said:

'But you are quite tidy and clean — not ragged and dirty!'

'No, my dear,' replied Emma, smiling at her puzzled look; 'why did you expect to see me otherwise?'

'Because the beggars I see in the streets go without shoes, and wear old clothes.'

Emma coloured slightly and made no reply, but Margaret, pressing forwards, again asked what that had to do with aunt Emma.

'Papa and mama said she was a beggar, and I thought she would look like that — but she is nice and looks good-natured, and I will not mind you teaching me at all: will you make me pretty frocks? Mama said you should.'

'I shall be very glad, my love, to do anything I can for you and your mama too; will you sit on my knee and tell me what I shall make your frocks of?'

While Emma was making friends with her little niece, Mrs Robert Watson herself arrived. She received her sisters-in-law with more cordiality than Emma expected. In fact she was rather pleased than otherwise with this accession to her family; she felt that she had secured a careful assistant to the cook in Elizabeth, and in Emma she hoped to find a competent nursery-governess.

After chatting some time with them, she rang for the housemaid to show them to their rooms, and the child declared she would accompany them as aunt Emma's room was close to the nursery. And so Emma found it was, for she was shown into a small closet containing a bed with room to walk round it, an old chest of drawers and a high stool. This was her apartment. There was no chimney, and the window looked out upon a small space of flat leads, surmounted by high, black, tiled roofs. It had commenced raining since they entered the house, and the gurgle of the water in the gutter, and the drip from the window on to the leads had a peculiarly monotonous sound. Emma looked at the forlorn and cheerless closet, and felt she was a beggar indeed. She hoped, however, that when her boxes and books were brought up she should be able to make it a little more comfortable; at least she had it to herself, and should be able to pass her time there in peace.

Her niece dragged her off to see the nurseries — the two

rooms devoted to her occupied the rest of that floor. They were spacious and in every respect comfortable, except that they were littered with playthings which their owner apparently had not learnt to value.

As it drew near to the dinner-hour, Emma ventured downstairs, and found her brother and his wife in the parlour. Robert received her in his usual manner: in another moment her two sisters entered, and they sat round the fire while waiting for dinner.

'I hope you like your rooms, girls,' said Mrs Watson; 'I thought it would not matter putting Elizabeth and you together, Margaret, because I know it's only for a time. I have heard — a little bird whispered to me a certain story which you need not blush about — of a certain young man — I know who — and I am sure I congratulate you: when did you hear from him last, my dear?'

'Oh, my dear Jane, I have not heard from him at all.'

'Indeed! That's very odd. Are you sure that he really proposed to you?'

'I am positive of the fact,' said Margaret, 'as I ever was of anything in my life.'

'Well that is a good deal,' observed Robert, 'for you can be pretty positive when you please. But I only wish, if it's true, you had had some witnesses — then I could have helped you.'

'Would you have called him out?' enquired his wife in a tone of indifference which quite startled Emma.

'No, I should have called him *in*,' said Robert laughing. 'If the fellow refused to marry her, I would have had him up for a breach of promise, without ceremony.'

'And what should I get for that?' said Margaret eagerly.

'You might perhaps have got a couple of thousands — I think I would lay the damages at three.'

'Only three, Robert! I am sure that is not enough for deceiving me, robbing me of my best affections, betraying my trust — oh, three thousand pounds would be no compensation for such conduct, no adequate compensation. I am sure my heart is worth more than that.'

'I dare say you think so, Margaret,' replied Robert coolly; 'but you might not persuade a jury to think it likewise.'

'It would be much better to make him pay damages than compel him to marry you,' said Elizabeth.

'Two or three thousand pounds would secure you a respectable husband, Margaret,' continued Robert. 'My friend, George Miller, would perhaps take you then.'

'I think I would rather marry Tom Musgrave than anybody,' replied Margaret. 'George Miller is only a brewer, after all, and Tom is a gentleman and has nothing to do.'

'But Miller has a capital business, I can tell you,' cried Mrs Watson; 'I should not mind my own sister marrying him. Why I know he used to allow his late wife more than a hundred a month to keep the table and find herself gowns — a very pretty allowance — and very pretty gowns she used to wear.'

'Aye, George Miller could count thousands for Musgrave's hundreds,' said Robert, 'and a capital fellow he is. I only wish you might have such luck as to marry him, either of you girls.'

The conversation was interrupted by the dinner, which was a welcome sight to the hungry travellers, who had tasted nothing since their early breakfast at Stanton. Their brother looked at the table with evident pride.

'Well, Elizabeth, I promised you rather a better dinner than you gave me at Stanton,' observed he. He had the habit of reverting to past grievances.

'You have kept your word, too,' replied she good-humouredly.

'Oh, my dear creature,' cried Jane, 'Robert told me of the shocking dinner he had — poor fellow, you certainly always managed very badly about such things; perhaps it might do you no harm if I gave you some lessons; I have rather a genius for housekeeping — at least so my friends tell me — my uncle Sir Thomas used to like me to order his dinner.'

'My dear Jane, I am afraid your instructions would be quite wasted on me, unless you would give me your income to supply my wishes — when anyone allows me a hundred a month for the table expenses, I will give capital dinners,' said Elizabeth.

'You are not thinking of what you are doing, Jane,' said her husband reproachfully, 'you know I cannot eat the wing of a fowl unless it is torn properly — Emma, I'll trouble you to cut

154

some bacon — good heavens, I cannot eat it so thick as that — you are not helping a Stanton plough boy remember!'

Emma endeavoured to comply but she grew nervous, and her brother was angry, and sent for the dish so that he might help himself. Emma coloured and apologized.

'You should try to oblige, Emma,' said Jane coolly, 'a little pains bestowed on such things, is quite as useful and essential to good breeding as painting or books. Careless ways of carving are very detrimental to the comfort of a family, and though it may seem of no importance to you, it makes all the difference to a delicate palate — one used to the niceties of life — a gentleman in fact.'

After dinner the little girl made her appearance, and immediately required of her mother a share in the walnuts on the table.

'My precious one, you must have them peeled for you.'

'Yes, mama, peel them.'

'No, my darling, they stain my fingers — ask your aunt Emma, I dare say she will do it.'

Emma readily agreed to do so, wishing so far as lay in her power, to show that she really was anxious to oblige.

The conversation about Tom Musgrave still dwelt heavy in her mind; she felt persuaded that the time would come, when she and also Miss Osborne must step forward to prove the truth of her sister Margaret's words, and she shuddered at the idea. She felt that she must make some apology, or at least some announcement of her intentions to Miss Osborne, before she could venture to risk such very unpleasant consequences to them both; and she determined to write to her, and tell her the circumstances as they occurred, and ask her to support and substantiate her word when it came to be questioned.

A day or two passed on, and Emma began to wonder when she should find time for writing; her sister-in-law kept her so fully employed that a spare quarter of an hour was not to be had. Her talents with needle and scissors had attracted Jane's observation when at Stanton, and now they were put into constant requisition in mending the child's wardrobe, or improving the mother's. Her niece's lessons were likewise turned over to her, for she was to learn her alphabet, her parents expecting her to be a little prodigy, and Emma must spare no pains to produce the desired result.

She did her best, but at first little progress could be made with a child so much spoilt by the indulgence and indifference of a mother more concerned to exhibit her own doting attitudes than to foster habits of industry in her daughter. Before Emma had found opportunity to write, she herself received a letter from Miss Osborne. It was of such a nature that her mind was soon made up. No other resort was open to her than that of laying the whole matter before her brother. She ventured therefore to his room of business and handed him the letter. Anything in the shape of business received Robert's strictest attention and he now read with deliberation the following words :

'My dear Miss Watson,

'I am sorry to trouble you with any unpleasant subjects, but I cannot forbear mentioning a circumstance which nearly concerns your family; and when you know the particulars, you can judge for yourself. Mr Musgrave, whom I had, as you know, reason to suppose engaged to one of your sisters, is now in town, and has not only been for some time past paying great attention to a young lady of fortune, a friend of my own, but, as I understand, has denied all engagement to Miss Watson, spoken very disparagingly of her, and even shown letters written by her under the impression that such an engagement existed. Not knowing precisely how affairs stood between your sister and Mr M., I dare not interfere, lest by revealing what she may perhaps wish concealed, I should injure her, and mortify her. I shall not, however, feel justified in preserving silence much longer, unless I am positively assured that all engagement is at an end between them. If she has released him from the promise to which we both are witnesses, it may be important to preserve silence on its previous existence, but if, as I cannot help suspecting, he has only released himself, has deceived or deserted her, I cannot allow my friend to be misled by him, and must insist on having his conduct set in a proper light. I am sorry to be obliged to trouble you, as I feel convinced that whether secretly deceiv-

ing, or openly deserting your sister, he is certainly using her
extremely ill: you know I never had a good opinion of his
character. I am overwhelmed with gaiety, and look back with
a feeling of regret to the tranquil hours at Osborne Castle.

> 'Anxiously expecting your answer,
> 'I remain, dear Miss Watson,
> 'Your sincere friend,
> 'Henrietta Osborne.'

'P.S. Mr Musgrave's address is 75 Bond-Street. — My brother
and Sir William desire all sorts of proper messages to you;
have you seen the Howards lately?'

What did Miss Osborne mean, he demanded, by saying
that she and Emma had been witnesses to the engagement?
Was that really the case? Why had Margaret never alluded
to it?

Emma explained as briefly as possible when and how they two
had overheard the whole conversation. Robert rubbed his hands
with inexpressible glee.

'He's caught then, fairly caught — we shall soon bring him to
terms now; capital, to think of your eavesdropping with so much
effect. But why did you never mention this before, child, when
you heard me lamenting the want of witnesses?'

Emma asserted that she was only waiting to consult Miss
Osborne on the subject, for as they had been mutually pledged
to secrecy, she could not divulge it without her agreeing to it.
Robert saw before him a brilliant perspective of litigation, an
action for breach of promise of marriage to be conducted, with
all the *éclat* that could be given to such a proceeding, and
damages given to his sister which would enable her to marry
decently out of hand. This was delightful. His first step he
determined should be a letter from himself to the culprit, claiming his promise to Margaret, but without alluding to the witnesses to be produced, and he instructed Emma to write to Miss
Osborne, and tell her that her sister had never released Tom
from his engagement, but was still acting on the belief that it
existed, and that therefore she, Miss Osborne, was at liberty to
inform her friend — indeed had better do so at once — that Mr
Musgrave was acting an equivocal part in paying attention to

any other woman, as his hand was positively pledged to Miss Margaret Watson.

Emma enquired what would be the result, if, as was very probable, Mr Musgrave should deny the engagement altogether, and trusting to there being no witnesses, refuse to fulfil it. Robert assured her that in that case he should have the means of compelling him either to fulfil the contract or pay large damages; he should not have a moment's hesitation in commencing an action against him, and with Miss Osborne and Emma to support Margaret's evidence there was no doubt of the result.

She was horrified to hear what was impending over her, and enquired, in a tone of something between fright and incredulity, whether he really contemplated forcing Miss Osborne to appear in a public court of justice.

'Why should she not?' was his cool answer; 'she is as capable of giving evidence, I presume, as any other woman, and her appearance will cause much public notice to be taken of the proceeding.'

'But do you think she will like it?' suggested poor Emma, trembling for her own share of the trial as much as for her friend's.

'I shall not trouble my head about that — I will have her subpoenaed as a witness, and she must come, whether she likes it or not.'

Emma was silent, but looked extremely uneasy. Her brother observed her distressed appearance, and after thinking a few minutes, addressed her.

'As you know so much of the Osbornes, Emma, and it really appears that you can keep a secret, which considering your age and sex is rather remarkable, I will tell you my whole plan, and we will see whether your wit can help me carry it out. Look here — suppose Tom Musgrave refuses all acknowledgement of the engagement, I threaten an action, call on you and Miss Osborne as witnesses; if it really comes before a jury she will be compelled to appear; but say she dislikes it — is too fine or too delicate — well, let her family use their influence with Musgrave to induce a marriage; by threatening to make his perfidy public, by menacing him with the indignation of the family, the Osbornes may work upon his feelings in a way which we could never do. Meantime say nothing; I will explain enough to Margaret, and you have only to answer all enquiries by the assurance that you are not allowed by me to mention the matter. Go now, and bring Margaret to me.'

Margaret was made to wait until Robert had composed his letter to Tom Musgrave. Then he handed it to her and watched her run through its contents.

Margaret's satisfaction was undisguised.

'You never believed that what I said was true; how glad I am that you have come round at last; now, I trust, Tom will relent, and my blighted affections will once more flourish.'

'Don't talk to me of blighted affections,' replied her brother, impatiently; 'don't bother me with such nonsense; do learn, if you can, to think of matters of business *as* business; and in an affair of this kind, try to speak in a rational, sensible way. Do you think Musgrave will yield to this representation?'

'Oh, no doubt of it. At least, I dare say he will; but suppose he should not, what will you do then?'

'It appears that both Emma and Miss Osborne heard what passed between you, and as, in that case, they can both appear as witnesses for you, I have no doubt of getting a verdict in your favour, and very considerable damages from any jury in the country.'

Margaret sat staring at her brother in amazement, and then repeated:

'Miss Osborne and Emma, are you sure?' and turning to Emma, 'Where were you then, I should like to know?'

'We were concealed from your sight,' replied her sister, 'by some orange trees, and thus we heard all you said without intending it.'

'Listening were you — very pretty indeed — honourable conduct — from you too, who make such a fuss about propriety and refined behaviour; but, after all, you are no better than your neighbours, it seems.'

'I am sure I am very sorry,' said Emma, with tears in her eyes, 'if I have done anything to vex you; but indeed, though it may seem strange, I really could not help it.'

'Oh no, of course not!' pursued Margaret, tossing her head back; 'people never can help doing anything which happens to suit their fancy — however, before I venture to talk another time, I will take care and ascertain if you are in the room or not — such meanness — listening!'

'It appears very strange to me,' said Mrs Watson later that evening, 'that we should suddenly hear that Emma knew all about it, when Margaret was so long wishing to have some evidence to prove her words; why did not Emma say so sooner, then?'

'And it seems still more extraordinary to me,' interposed Elizabeth, 'that Margaret should be so angry when she thus, unexpectedly, finds what she wishes for. Emma told me of this long ago, and told me that Miss Osborne had induced her to be silent on the subject for several reasons; but I know, from what she told me then, it was quite accidental, and could not be avoided.'

'And it appears strangest of all to me,' observed Robert contemptuously, 'that women never can keep to the point on any subject, but must start off on twenty different branches, which have nothing to do with the end in view. What does it signify to you, Margaret, when, how, or why your conversation was over-heard — when, on the fact of its being so, depends your chance of getting two or three thousand pounds in your pocket? What does it matter as to Emma's motive for listening, so long as she did listen to such good purpose?'

Margaret replied only by some indistinct murmurs. She was excessively gratified at being talked about, and made the subject of letters to and from Miss Osborne; and the notion of being plaintiff in an action at law seemed to have almost as great a charm for her imagination, as being married; but she was sorely mortified at the information that Tom Musgrave's infidelity was so evident. She was vexed, bitterly vexed, at the idea of a rival, and she could hardly console herself for such an indignity by the expectation of the damages which were to be awarded her.

Emma was very glad when she had finished her letter, and was able to escape from the subject by quitting the house for a walk with Elizabeth. Jane had some errands for them in the town; but, as soon as these were fulfilled, they were able to turn their steps towards the country, and escaping into green fields and pleasant lanes, refresh their eyes and their tempers by watching for the first appearance of the spring flowers. Such walks were a delight to Emma, and gave her strength to endure the numberless petty annoyances which Mrs Watson heaped on her.

CHAPTER 19

THE MATTER OF MARGARET'S supposed engagement was
carried forward on a day following when two letters reached
Croydon. Emma received an answer from Miss Osborne and
Robert a letter from Tom which was short and decisive. This he
read to his assembled household.

> 'Dear Sir,
>   'The receipt of your letter of yesterday surprised me
> considerably. I am extremely sorry that there should have been
> any misunderstanding of the sort; but I am sure your amiable
> sister will at once admit that my attentions to her have always
> been limited within the bounds of friendship, such as our long
> acquaintance justifies, and such as I have paid to twenty other
> young ladies before her eyes. With kind compliments to the
> ladies of your family, I have the honour to remain,
>   'Dear Sir,
>   'Yours faithfully, &c, &c.'

Margaret thought it incumbent on her immediately to go
off in a fit of hysterics, sobbing out between whiles, that he
was cruel and heartless, and she never meant to care more about
him.

'Do have done with that confounded noise,' said Robert
impatiently, 'for there's no getting a word of sense from a
woman when she's in that state, and heaven knows it's little
enough one can reasonably expect at any time.'

Margaret's sobs did not cease at this gentle request, and
Robert grew more angry.

'By jove, Margaret, if you don't stop I'll leave you to make the best of your own matters, and neither meddle nor make any more in it.'

Afraid that he might keep his word, she ceased at last, and then enquired what Emma had heard from Miss Osborne. Emma read the passage in which Miss Osborne replied to her assurance that Margaret still considered Mr Musgrave engaged to her; it merely thanked her for the information, stated that she would warn her friend, and wished Miss Margaret a happy termination to her engagement. The rest of the letter was about subjects quite unconnected with Tom Musgrave, and uninteresting to anyone but Emma. Miss Osborne mentioned one thing which gave peculiar pleasure; her marriage with Sir William was to take place after Easter and they were going to spend the summer months at Osborne Castle, while Sir William Gordon was determining on the plan of a new mansion, which he intended to build on his property. Miss Osborne earnestly hoped that Emma would once more visit there, and declared she quite looked forward with impatience to a future meeting.

She did not wish to read this aloud, as she shrank from the appearance of boasting about her grand acquaintance, but neither Jane nor Margaret would allow her to rest in peace until she had made known the principal contents of her letter; and a sentence containing the information that they had seen Mr Howard, who had spent a few days in town lately, was the only information she eventually kept to herself.

Margaret's curiosity having materially aided in restoring her composure, she was soon able to enquire of her brother what he intended to do. He repeated all he had formerly asserted, and Emma heard it with horror; she escaped from the room to consider what she had better do, and after much thought, decided on writing at once to Miss Osborne, informing her of what was threatened. She sat down and wrote accordingly:

'Dear Miss Osborne,

'I hope you will not consider me in any way to blame, if the information I have to communicate is disagreeable to you. I am sorry to say that Mr Musgrave has been so unprincipled as entirely to deny the engagement, which *we* know subsisted between him and my sister; and what grieves me still more is, that my brother, convinced that there actually was an engagement, declares he will bring an action against Mr Musgrave, unless he immediately fulfils it. The idea that we shall have to appear in a court of justice frightens me very much, and I thought it right to give you early notice of his intention that you might not be taken by surprise. My brother is so fixed in his resolution, that I cannot see the smallest probability of an escape for us unless Mr Musgrave can be persuaded to act up to his promise. I know Lord Osborne has great influence with him, and for the sake of your family, and his own character and respectability, he might perhaps be persuaded by him to do so; but with a man of such character, my sister's chance of happiness would be small, and I cannot wish for their marriage, even to save myself from what I so greatly dread. I feel I am wrong and selfish in shrinking from an exertion which I suppose is my duty, and perhaps after all, when there are so many troubles in life, one difficulty more or less ought not to disturb me so much. I am truly rejoiced at your bright prospects, and shall indeed have great pleasure at any time you name, in witnessing your domestic happiness; I assure you that your kind invitation has given me more pleasure than anything I have lately experienced.

'Believe me, dear Miss Osborne,
'Very truly yours, &c, &c.'

Miss Osborne was sitting in the breakfast-room in Portman Square when the letter was brought to her. Sir William Gordon was beside her on the sofa.

'Here is a letter,' she observed, 'from that charming Emma Watson with whom you were pleased to carry on such a flirtation just before you proposed to me.'

'*I* flirt with Emma Watson! I deny it entirely — I never flirted with any girl in my life.'

'Did you not take a walk with her in the park — a sketch in a cottage — a drive in a cart? Do you mean to deny all that?'

'By no means, I only deny entirely all flirtation — how could I have found time — or spirits, when I was doing hard service to win your most intractable and hard-hearted self.'

As he spoke she opened and glanced over her letter. Then he

saw her cheek glow, and her brow contract with repressed indignation, and she seemed on the point of tearing the letter in two. He extended his hand towards her, and exclaimed:

'My dear Henrietta, what *is* the matter, your looks quite frighten me — do let me see this letter.'

'Take it,' said she, 'and see what intolerable impertinence is threatened me.'

He read it attentively, then said:

'I am quite bewildered — completely mystified — what have you got to do with all this — and what does it mean?'

'Ah, you may well be astonished,' she replied; 'don't you see what is threatened? Imagine *me*, dragged into the Assize Court as a witness in an action between Margaret Watson and Thomas Musgrave for a breach of promise of marriage. Can you realize the scene? It would be novel and startling, I suggest.'

'Extremely so, and I do not see why you should mind it: you will, of course, be treated with all proper respect and consideration, and justice must be done. But tell me how you happened to become the confidante of this charming Margaret; I did not know your friendship extended to the whole family.'

'Neither does it — it is only Emma I care for,' and she proceeded to explain to Sir William all the circumstances attending their involuntary audience of Musgrave's courtship, and her reason for keeping it quiet.

'Caught listening, eh!' laughed Sir William; 'I do not wonder that you shrink from being called on to avow it in public. What a pity you did not start out and cry "bo!" to them both; from all accounts they deserved it.'

'That's all very well, and you may amuse yourself with laughing at me, if you like; but tell me how I can avoid this difficulty — must I appear in court?'

'Certainly, if you are subpoenaed to appear — there is no help for that.'

'How coolly you treat it — why is it not you instead of me it has happened to?'

'Only because I was not one of the eavesdroppers. I am excessively sorry for your distress, my dear Henrietta, but I must think it quite unfounded.'

'Well, there's one thing certain, I warn you; if I have to

appear in this business, we must defer our marriage; I could not appear as a bride and a witness during the same month.'

Sir William started up and looked fixedly at her.

'You are not serious.'

'Perfectly so, William; and I see you are so now,' replied Miss Osborne.

'Then you shall have no occasion to put your threat in execution,' said he, with an air of determination; 'let us talk the matter over seriously, Henrietta.'

'Ah, I am glad I have brought you to your senses, at last; now consider, if we could do as Emma advises, and persuade this Mr Musgrave to marry, as he ought, there would be an end of all trouble in the affair.'

'To you, perhaps, but not to Miss Margaret; I dare say her amiable husband would beat her every day.'

'Now don't relax into your indifference again, and be provoking! Oh, here comes Osborne; see what he says on the subject.'

Lord Osborne entered the room and his sister tried to make him comprehend what had occurred.

'I think,' said he, after hearing her story, 'that Musgrave has behaved very ill — very ill indeed.'

'No doubt of that, my dear brother, but what do you think of this Mr Watson's proposal?'

'Just what we might expect from a lawyer, that he would go to law; it's his business, Henrietta,' replied her brother.

'But it's not my business to be obliged to appear in public as a witness in this ridiculous matter. If he likes to make his sister's *affaires de coeur* the subject for conversation and coarse jokes throughout the county, it is all very well, but I cannot see why I am to be implicated in a transaction which reflects nothing but discredit on all the parties,'

'Especially those who are detected in listening, Henrietta,' suggested Sir William Gordon.

'And poor Emma, too,' continued she, pretending not to hear him, 'she evidently dreads the threatened exposure; I am quite concerned about it for her.'

'Naturally enough,' said her lover, in the same tormenting tone; 'it makes everyone sorry to be found out.'

'Really, Sir William,' said Miss Osborne, drawing up her slight figure with an air of great indignation, 'if you can suggest nothing that is more agreeable than such reflections, we shall be better without you; and I recommend you to leave us to take care of ourselves.'

It was haughtily said — for her quick temper was roused; he knew her well, and did not mean that she should obtain a sovereign rule over him. He loved her for her spirit — but he was determined not to crouch to it — and rising, he made her a grave bow, and left the room. She looked after him anxiously, expecting he would return, or at least, give her one more glance, but he did not, and the door closed before she could make up her mind to speak again.

'What do you want me to do?' said her brother. 'I think it will be easy to prevent all this, if it plagues you and your friend so much; I will speak to Tom myself, and see if I cannot persuade him to keep his promise.'

'Ah! Do, if you can, Osborne; of course the girl wants to marry him; and if he will do that, we shall be left in peace. Poor Emma seems very unhappy — look at her letter.'

Lord Osborne received it eagerly and read it through.

'Poor creature,' said he, quite compassionately, 'how soon, Henrietta, may girls marry after their father's death?'

'Oh! That's a matter of taste! And I don't think it signifies in this matter at all. If we could only get Mr Musgrave to acknowledge his engagement, he may take his own time for marrying.'

Her brother was on the point of saying that he was not thinking of him, but he let it pass — and, after a moment's consideration, added:

'Then you think there would be no harm in *engaging* a girl, even if she could not marry immediately.'

'Oh, I don't know, this engagement was formed before old Mr Watson died, and that makes a difference. Perhaps, if people are very particular, they might not like to commence a courtship under such circumstances.'

'Well, what can I do?'

'Find Mr Musgrave — and tell him that, as the fact of his engagement is known, and, consequently, he is as certain to have a verdict against him, the only thing for him to do is to act like a man of honour. If he refuses, and by that means draws me in to do anything so repugnant to my feelings as appearing in a court, he can never expect to be noticed by us again; and if *we* set the example, everyone will throw him off — he will be scouted in the neighbourhood, and can never dare to show his face again. Tell him this, and if I do not greatly mistake the man he will yield.'

'I will try what I can do, Henrietta, but I wish Gordon had undertaken it — he has so many more words than I have.'

'And if you cannot succeed with him, we must have recourse to Mr Watson, the attorney, and try what we can do to stop his proceedings,' continued Henrietta. 'Perhaps a little bribery, judiciously applied, might induce him to relinquish his intention, and save any further trouble.'

'We shall see about that,' replied he, 'but, in the meantime, I will look for Musgrave, and try my skill on him.'

'Could you find William,' said Henrietta, 'and tell him that I should like to speak to him — or no, perhaps, if you tell him only what you are going to do, it will be better.'

'I heard him leave the house, but, if I see him at the club, I will tell him what you say.'

Miss Osborne bit her lips and made no reply; she did not like to show the empire which Sir William had over her feelings — nor would she readily have acknowledged her anxiety over his quitting her so gravely. She had discovered that he would not be played with and she dared not attempt to trifle with him as she might have done with a less resolute man. She spent the rest of the morning alone, and very uneasy. She told herself it was not because Sir William was absent that she was dissatisfied, it was only because she herself was threatened with a disagreeable incident; then she fell into a train of thought about what Sir William intended to do, where he was gone, and whether he would soon return to Portman Square.

At length, a note was brought to her with an assurance that the bearer was waiting. It was in his handwriting, and she opened it in trepidation. The style surprised her.

'Sir William Gordon's compliments to Miss Osborne, and

he has the happiness of informing her that affairs are placed on a satisfactory footing with regard to Mr Musgrave; but, as Sir W. has undertaken to communicate the result of the interview to Miss Watson and her sister, he wishes to know whether Miss Osborne would recommend him to go in person to Croydon — and if so, whether she has any commands for him.'

Henrietta read the note over three times before she could make up her mind to the answer she should return. She felt it deeply; the tone, the meaning, all conveyed a sort of covert reproach to her. She was sorry and angry at the same moment; and she was quite undecided whether to yield to or resent his conduct. After much deliberation she hastily wrote:

'Miss Osborne's compliments to Sir William Gordon, and as she finds it impossible to give an opinion without understanding more of the circumstances, she begs he will favour her with a call this afternoon, to explain what arrangements he has made.'

No sooner was this note despatched than she bitterly regretted having sent such a one, and felt she would have given anything in the world to recall it. She could think of nothing else, of course, and being quite indisposed for any amusement she refused to accompany her mother in the afternoon drive, but remained sitting alone in the drawing-room. Engrossed with her own thoughts, she did not hear him enter, and was not aware of his presence till he spoke.

'I am here, Miss Osborne, according to your commands; may I request you will let me know your further wishes.'

'You are still offended, Sir William,' replied she, looking up at him; 'I thought you would by now have recovered yourself.'

'I cannot so soon forget the repulse I received; and I presume you intended it to be remembered.'

'Nay, don't look like that, I cannot bear it, I was wrong,' said she extending her hand to him. 'Forgive me and sit down.'

Miss Osborne had not to say she was wrong twice over, nor to repeat the request for forgiveness. He was not tyrannical, though

169

he could not submit to slavery, and a reconciliation was soon effected. When they were able to talk of anything besides themselves, he described to her his interview with Tom Musgrave. He had found him insolent and angry — disposed to resent Mr Watson's threats as insulting, and Sir William's interference as uncalled for. His tone, however, was considerably lowered when he ascertained for the first time that his conversation with Margaret had been overheard by two who were quite able to prove the fact. Sir William told him he was authorized by the family of one young lady — indeed as her affianced husband he considered himself bound to step forward and endeavour to prevent the necessity of her appearing as a witness in a public court; should she, in consequence of Mr Musgrave's persevering in denying the truth, be compelled to perform so unpleasant a task, it would bring down on him the enmity of the noble family of which the lady was a member, and the universal contempt of the county; whereas, whilst affairs stood as they did at present, it was evident the whole business might be hushed up, and when he and Miss Watson were married, they might be certain of the countenance and favour of the family at Osborne Castle, and all their connections.

Tom had hesitated much, and evidently deeply repented the unguarded conduct which had placed him in such an unpleasant predicament; and though he had yielded at last to a conviction of the necessity of the thing, it was with a reluctance which augured ill for the domestic felicity of the future Mrs Musgrave. Indeed he had told Sir William, with an oath, that if she really compelled him to marry her, Margaret Watson should rue the day; so that upon the whole Sir William was of opinion that the young lady had much better not persist in her claim, if she had any value for a quiet home.

'I dare say he will not be worse than other men,' replied Henrietta; 'I have a notion that they are all tyrants to women at heart, only some wear a mask in courtship and some do not take that trouble. But they are all alike in the end, no doubt.'

'Very possibly, Henrietta; suppose you were to carry out your theory and change places with Miss Margaret.'

'Thank you; your liberality is over-powering; but though they may be all alike in temper, they are so neither in person nor in name — and in neither of these particulars does Mr Musgrave please me.'

It was then settled that Henrietta should write to her friend and inform her how matters were going on — it being understood that Tom Musgrave was by the same post to assert his claim to Miss Margaret Watson's hand in a letter to her brother.

Had Margaret Watson possessed one particle of proper spirit, the tone and manner in which Tom Musgrave fulfilled his part of the bargain would have been sufficient to cause a total rupture between them; but far from this was the case with her. The fact of being now believed in her declaration, of being known as an engaged young lady, of having a right to talk about wedding-clothes, and sigh sentimentally at the prospect before her; the distinction which all this would give her in a small country town, where every occurrence, from a proposal of marriage down to the purchase of a new pair of shoes, was immediately known to all the neighbours — this delighted Margaret's weak mind, and set her heart in a flutter of gratified vanity.

The news from Chichester which about this time arrived gave a very flourishing account of Penelope's affairs. Her lover, notwithstanding his advanced age, appeared far more ardent and energetic than the youthful Tom Musgrave. In accordance, it was said, with his earnest solicitations, their union was to take place very speedily, and Penelope hoped that the next time she had occasion to write to her sisters all would have been achieved and it would be to inform them that she no longer bore the same name as themselves.

Mrs Watson found so much for Emma to do, that she had scarcely time to stir from the nursery, except when she took a walk with Augusta, who was now almost entirely confided to her care, and loved her dearly. Had her exertions as nursery governess given the smallest satisfaction to her sister-in-law, had they even been treated by her as an equivalent for board and maintenance, she would have been less uncomfortable. But while she was spending her whole time in unremunerated, and indeed unacknowledged services, she was perpetually reminded of her entire dependence on Robert, and taunted with her uselessness, her idle habits, and her fine lady manners. The numerous visitors, who dawdled away a morning hour in Mrs Watson's parlour, were apt to expatiate on her extraordinary liberality and kindness in receiving her three sisters as her guests, little imagining that the two elder paid for their board out of their scanty incomes, and that the younger compensated for the misery she endured, under the show of patronage, in a way yet more advantageous to her grudging but ostentatious relatives.

CHAPTER 20

THE NEXT LETTER TO REACH Croydon with a coronet on the seal contained the announcement that Miss Osborne's wedding was to be celebrated in about three weeks. She hoped Emma would be able to keep her promise and spend some time with them while they were at Osborne Castle, but she did not assign any particular time to the date of the visit.

Margaret likewise had her share of excitement and pleasure. It appeared that Tom Musgrave had come down to Croydon with serious intentions of persuading her to marry on the same day as Sir William Gordon and Miss Osborne had fixed on. To be distinguished, and to appear connected with the great, was so completely the object of his life, that he was determined to make his wedding as important as the reflected grandeur of the Osbornes could contrive. The credit of this idea, however, was not entirely his own; it was suggested originally by Sir William himself. Miss Osborne, who could not feel quite happy or at her ease with regard to Tom's steadiness of purpose, until the ceremony had actually passed, induced Sir William Gordon to question him as to when he intended to marry, and though he found Tom's ideas rather vague on the subject, he had not much difficulty in persuading him of the advantage of fixing on the same day as their own. The notion delighted Mr Musgrave, and he immediately determined to journey to Croydon and make the proposal at once.

'Well, Margaret,' said he, the morning after his arrival, 'since it seems we must be married sooner or later, do you see any good in delay?'

Margaret simpered and blushed, and did not know very well which way to look or what to say.

'I say,' continued he, 'that there is no use in wasting time, when the thing must be done — unless, indeed, you have changed your mind.'

'Oh dear no, Tom, mine is a mind not lightly to be changed — you know that much of me, I am sure.'

'Miss Osborne is to be married this day three weeks,' observed Tom, 'to my friend Sir William Gordon, and he was proposing to me that we should celebrate ours on the same day. I should rather like it, I own, as they are such particular friends of mine, and we are going to the same county. They come down to Osborne Castle for their honeymoon, and we *might*, indeed of course we *should* be asked up there.'

'Oh, delightful, Tom,' cried Margaret, perfectly enchanted at the prospect, and quite overlooking the coolness of her lover's manner, and the total absence of even any pretence of affection. 'I should like that of all things, only perhaps I might have some difficulty in getting my wedding things ready in time; to be sure, as I must wear mourning I should not want much just at first, but a gown and hat — what should my gown be, dear Tom?'

'Hang your gown! What do I know about your gown? Or what has that got to do with it; I say, will you marry me this day three weeks? — because, if you will not, you may just let it alone, for anything I care.'

'You are always so funny, Tom,' said Margaret, trying to laugh; 'I never know what you will say next. But you do hurry and flurry one so, asking in that sort of off-hand way — upon my word I do not know what to answer — what can I say to him, Jane — is he not odd?'

'For heaven's sake, Mrs Watson, do try and persuade Margaret to act with a little common sense,' cried Tom impatiently.

'Really,' simpered Mrs Watson, 'you are the most unlover-like lover that ever I saw — if I were you, Margaret, I would tease him unceasingly for these speeches. I would say him nay, and nay, and nay again, before I would give him his own way.'

'Oh, I am not so very cruel,' said Margaret. 'He knows my disposition, and how much he may venture on with me.'

'Well, when you have made up your mind, let me know,' said he, settling himself in an easy chair, and pretending to doze.

'Upon my word, Margaret,' said Mrs Watson, 'he gives himself precious airs — would I submit to such a thing from any man in the world — no, indeed — I would see the whole sex annihilated first, that I would.'

'Do not be so dreadfully severe, Mrs Watson,' said Tom, without unclosing his eyes. 'Allow me to enjoy my last few days of liberty; when I have taken to myself a wife, where will my domestic freedom be?'

'Impudent fellow,' said Mrs Watson, going up and pretending to pat his cheek. He caught her hand and told her in return, she was his prisoner now, and must pay the penalty of the box on the ear, which she had so deliberately bestowed on him. She giggled exceedingly, and he was insisting on his right, when Robert entered the room and said, in a cool, indifferent way:

'I suppose, Margaret, Musgrave has told you he wants to marry you this day three weeks, and as I presume, you have no objection, I have resolved to get the settlements in hand immediately. I suppose you have not much to do in the way of preparation, have you?'

'Well, I suppose, as you all come upon me so suddenly, there is nothing for me to do but to submit,' said Margaret, 'and really, I see no harm in it. Of course you will have the marriage put in the newspapers; it must be sent to *The Morning Post*, Tom.'

'I have no objection,' observed the ardent lover.

'Well then, Jane, I suppose I had better be seeing about my gown and wedding clothes — will you come with me and help me choose some muslins, Tom?'

'Not I, by Jove! What do I know about dresses; that's all woman's nonsense, and I will have nothing to do with it.'

'Don't be so dreadfully severe, Tom,' interposed Mrs Watson again; 'you are a naughty, ill-tempered satirist, and we must teach you better manners before we have done with you.'

'Beyond question you will soon do that,' returned he, 'I already feel wonderfully humbled from sitting with you for the last hour.'

Margaret and Jane soon afterwards set off on the important business of purchasing more stuffs than she would know what to do with, whilst obliged to wear her deep mourning.

Tom Musgrave did not stay longer than he had originally proposed, leaving Margaret in such high spirits as plainly showed that she had quite forgotten everything but her immediate preparations.

Three weeks passed and the wedding day brought sunshine as bright as any bride could desire. Emma's thoughts wandered from Margaret and the business of the day at Croydon to the bridal party in London, engaged upon the same ceremony, she imagined, at about the same hour. She had been told that Mr Howard was to officiate and she tried to picture the scene and was then ashamed of herself for doing so. At Croydon she joined fervently in the prayers for her sister's future happiness, but her heart held forebodings. She little knew that a scene of moment to her own future was to take place in Portman Square.

When the ceremony there was performed, the breakfast over, and the new married couple had left the house, Lady Osborne retired to her dressing-room, and thither she sent for Mr Howard. Without the slightest suspicion as to the real object of her wishes, he obeyed the summons, and found her ladyship alone.

She requested him to be seated, and after some attempts at polite conversation suddenly observed:

'The marriage of my daughter makes a great difference to me, Mr Howard.'

'Indeed it must,' replied he, rather wondering what would come next.

'I fear I shall find myself very uncomfortable if I continue in the same style of life as I have done before; without Miss Osborne I shall be quite lost.'

Mr Howard could not help thinking that he should have supposed few mothers would have felt the change so little. They had never been companions or appeared of any consequence to each other. However he felt it his duty to make some observation, and therefore ventured to suggest that her ladyship should not give way to such despondent thoughts: she might, perhaps, find it less painful than she anticipated.

'You are very kind to try to cheer me in my melancholy situation, but, Mr Howard, I have always found you so, and I am deeply indebted to you for the many hours of comfort you have at different times procured for me. You have been my friend.'

176

He did not at all know what to say to this speech, and was therefore silent.

'What do you think of my daughter's marriage?' asked Lady Osborne.

'I think it has every promise of securing them mutual happiness — I hope this as sincerely as I wish it. Sir William is an excellent young man.'

'The marriage is not so high a one as what *my* daughter might have aspired to — she has given up all dreams of ambition — do you not see that?'

'Of course Miss Osborne might have married the equal or the superior to her brother in rank, but she has acted far more wisely, in my opinion, in preferring worth and affection, though not accompanying so splendid an alliance as possibly her friends have expected for her. Sir William has wealth to satisfy a less reasonable woman than Lady Gordon, and if his rank is sufficiently elevated to content her, she can have no more to desire.'

'Do not imagine, Mr Howard, from what I said that I was regretting the difference in rank; on the contrary, I believe most fully that as she was attached to Sir William, Miss Osborne could do nothing better than marry him. Far be it from me to wish anyone to sacrifice affection to ambition. Had there been even more difference in their rank — had he been of really plebeian origin, I should not have objected when her affections were fixed.'

'I cannot imagine that Miss Osborne would ever have fixed her affections on anyone decidedly beneath her.'

'Do you then consider it unsuitable, where love directs, to step out of one's own sphere to follow its dictates?'

'I am decidedly averse to unequal marriages — even when the husband is the superior; but when their positions are reversed, and the man, instead of elevating his wife, drags her down to a level beneath that where she had previously moved, it can hardly fail to produce some degree of domestic discomfort.'

'Yes, but the wife might see it quite otherwise; I can imagine nothing more delightful than for a woman to forego an elevated position, and to lay down her wealth at the feet of some man distinguished only by his wit and worth; to have the proud happiness of securing thus his eternal gratitude.'

'I think a man must be very selfish and self-confident, who could venture to ask such a sacrifice from any woman. I could not.'

'But I am supposing that the sacrifice is voluntary, proposed and arranged entirely by herself — women have been capable of this — what should you say to that?'

'I think your ladyship is imagining circumstances little likely to occur in real life.'

Lady Osborne continued as if she had not heard him.

'And if that man were too modest to be sensible of the preference, if he could not venture, on his own account, to break through the barriers which difference of station had placed between us, should he be shocked if, throwing aside the restraints of pride, I were openly to express those feelings?'

He was silent, and Lady Osborne continued for some moments in profound thought likewise, looking down at the carpet and playing with her rings: at length she raised her head, and said:

'I think you understand my meaning, Mr Howard. Of the nature of my feelings I am sure you must have been long aware. Do you not see to what this conversation tends?'

He appeared excessively embarrassed, and could not, for some minutes, arrange his ideas sufficiently to know what to say. At length he stammered out:

'Your ladyship does me too much honour, if I rightly understand your meaning — but perhaps — I should be sorry to misinterpret it — and really you must excuse me — perhaps I had better withdraw.'

'No Mr Howard, do not go with half explanations which can only lead to mistakes. Tell me what you really suppose I meant; why should you hesitate?'

'I for a moment imagined that your ladyship meant to apply to me what you had just been saying, and I feared you were going to tell me of some friend who would make the sacrifices you so eloquently described. Sacrifices which I felt would be far beyond my deserts.'

'And supposing I did say so — supposing there were a woman of rank and wealth, and influence, who would devote them all to you — what would you say?'

178

'I would say, that though excessively obliged to her, my love was not to be the purchase of either wealth or influence.'

'I know you are entitled to hold worldly advantages as cheap as anyone; but remember, my dear friend, all the worth of such a sacrifice — think of the warmth of an affection which could trample on ceremony and brave opinion. And think of the consequences which might accrue to you from this. Even you may well pause, before preferring mediocrity to eminence.'

'But you forget my profession forbids ambition, and removes the means of advancement.'

'No, *you* forget the gradations which exist in that career — do you treat as nothing the certainty of promotion — of rising to be a dignitary of the church — a dean — a bishop, perhaps — even a member of the Upper House? Has ambition no hold upon your mind?'

'My ambition would never prompt me to wish to rise through my wife — I could not submit to that.'

'You have no heart! How can you not be softened by the deep, though melancholy love which moves me — has that no power over your affections?'

Mr Howard hesitated a moment, then firmly but respectfully replied:

'If I understand your ladyship aright, and I think I cannot now misunderstand, you pay me the highest compliment, but one which is quite undeserved by me. Highly as I feel honoured, however, I cannot change my feelings, or alter the sentiments which I have already expressed. My mind was made known to you, before yours to me, and to vary now from what I then said might well cause you to doubt my sincerity, and could give no satisfactions to your ladyship.'

He stopped abruptly; he wanted to say something indicative of gratitude and respect; but the disgust which he felt at her proceedings, prevented the words coming naturally.

Lady Osborne seemed to be struggling with vehement emotions, which almost choked her; and he hesitated about leaving her alone. By a gesture of her hand, however, she repulsed his offer to approach her; he therefore slowly withdrew, and his mind was relieved of anxiety for her by seeing her maid enter the room before he had descended the stairs. He

179

then hurried away, and tried, by walking very quickly through the most retired paths in Kensington Gardens, to soothe his feelings and tranquilize his mind.

Had there been no Emma Watson in the world, or had she been, as he feared she would soon be, married to Lord Osborne, he must still have refused the proposal which had just been made to him. It never could have presented itself as a temptation to his mind. But under present circumstances, with a heart full of her memory, all the more precious, the more dwelt on, because he feared she would never be more to him, it was more than impossible, it was entirely repulsive.

CHAPTER 21

AS THE DAYS PASSED, Emma made up her mind that the humiliation of life in the house of her brother and sister-in-law was not to be endured. She formed a firm resolution to seek employment as a governess and an opportunity of this kind now presented itself. A frequent visitor at Croydon was a certain Mr Morgan, a man of handsome appearance, but not entirely trusted in the town where he had carried on his profession for about fifteen years. He was generally well regarded as a physician, a man of learning and of independent character with a certain air of mystery about him. Croydon, however, contained some who were jealous of Mr Morgan's social and professional success.

In Emma Mr Morgan recognized unusual intelligence as well as beauty. He sought her company on every possible occasion and did not scruple to take advantage of the fact that the rarity of intelligent conversation in the Watson household inclined Emma towards an interest in him. Having obtained sufficient of her confidence to learn that she was seeking to leave Croydon and take a post as governess, he proposed that she should apply to a certain Lady Fanny Alston — and he offered his services in recommending her qualities to this lady whom he was regularly accustomed to visit. Emma consulted her brother who perfectly approved of the suggestion.

Before anything positive had been arranged, however, the promised invitation to join the Gordons at Osborne Castle reached her. Emma found a score of good reasons to account for her pleasure in looking forward to this visit, but would not allow her mind to dwell on the most important of them.

It was on a June day that she passed between the hay-fields and up the winding slope to the Castle's imposing portal. The

weather was such as to delight every lover of nature. It could
not have been more perfectly fitted for strolling in the shade or
sitting under trees, making believe to read, whilst really watching the birds flitting among the bushes, or the bees humming in
the flowers. It was weather in which scarcely any occupation
could be followed up beyond arranging a *bouquet* or reading a
novel. So thought and so declared the young Lady Gordon as
she awaited her friend. When her husband pressed her to engage
in any serious pursuit, she enjoyed the pleasure of teasing him by
her refusals; she knew now what he would bear, and ventured
not to go beyond it.

'I am glad Emma Watson is coming today,' said she, as she
threw herself on a seat in the flower-garden; 'you will then have
something else to look at besides me, and I shall quite enjoy the
change.'

'Are you sure of that, Henrietta?' said he doubtfully.

'Why, you have not the impertinence to suppose that I value
your incessant attentions. Emma Watson shall listen to the grave
books you so much admire, shall talk of history or painting with
you, shall sit as your model, and leave me in my beloved
indolence.'

'May I enquire if you suppose you are teasing or pleasing me
by this arrangement, Henrietta — is it to satisfy me or yourself?'

'Oh, don't ask troublesome questions; I hate investigations of
motives — all I want is to be left alone, and not be asked to ride
or walk when I had rather lie on a sofa in quiet.'

He returned to the Castle; she remained musing where he
left her, and thus it happened that when Emma was announced,
she found the young baronet alone in their morning sitting-
room. He laid down his pen and advanced to meet her with
great cordiality, desiring a message to be sent to summon his
lady.

After expressing the pleasure it gave him to see her again, he
observed:

'Who would have thought, Miss Watson, when we last met,
that I should be receiving you in this castle; did you guess at
such an event?'

'Not precisely,' replied Emma, 'so far as concerned myself;

but as relating to Miss Osborne — I mean Lady Gordon — anyone must have foreseen it.'

'I assure you, when such things are foreseen, Miss Watson, it most frequently happens that they never come to pass. I have repeatedly seen instances of this kind.' He spoke with an attractive smile, and a faint idea passed through her mind that former encounters with *her* were in his thoughts; an idea annihilated entirely by a more powerful sensation, as the door opened and Lady Gordon entered with Mr Howard.

It was fortunate that the enquiries of the former — her expressions of pleasure, and her caresses — were an excuse for Emma's not immediately turning to the gentleman. Had they been obliged to speak at once, it is probable their dialogue would have been peculiar — interesting but unconnected — as was said of Johnson's dictionary. As it was, they both had time to collect their thoughts — and when they did turn, were able to go through their interview with tolerable calmness; but Emma had the advantage. He still felt that it was contrary to the requisitions of honour to feel any extraordinary pleasure in her company. Had not Lord Osborne made him his confidant, all would have been right, and he might openly have expressed the interest which he now was compelled to smother. His address was cold and formal — the very contrast to his feelings — and extremely ill done in consequence. Emma, chilled by the reception so different from what she had ventured to expect, began to fear her own manners had been too openly indicative of pleasure at the sight of him; and determined to correct this error she almost immediately followed Lady Gordon who had sauntered towards the conservatory.

'Come here,' said the young hostess, linking her arm in Emma's, 'let us leave the gentlemen to discuss the parish politics together. Mr Howard came on business, and Sir William dearly loves meddling with it. Now, you must tell me all the news of Croydon. Have you no scandal to enliven me? — with whom has the lawyer quarrelled? Or to whom have the young men of his acquaintance been making love?'

Emma coloured and laughed a little. Lady Gordon smilingly watched her.

'To you, I suppose, by your blushes, Emma; well, that gives

me a higher idea of country town taste. How many lovers have you to boast of? Tell me all.'

'Indeed, I have no such honours to boast,' replied Emma, 'no one has sought me, and probably no one ever will.' This was followed by a little sigh.

'Nay, do not be so desponding — a little chill is nothing,' cried Lady Gordon, 'but I am not going to pry into your secrets. This conservatory has given us enough of trouble in that way already. By the way, you will, of course, like to go over and call on your sister, Mrs Musgrave — when will it suit you?'

'Tomorrow, if you please,' replied Emma, gratefully; Lady Gordon promised that the means of conveyance should be at her service, and they proceeded to discuss other topics.

She insisted on detaining Mr Howard to spend the afternoon and to dine with them, pleading, as a reason, the absence of his sister, who was away on a visit; and when this point was carried, she led them out into the flower garden again, and loitered away the rest of the intervening time, amidst the perfume of summer flowers, and the flickering lights and shadows of the alcoves, with their gay creeping plants. It was the day and place for love making. Gradually Mr Howard's frozen manner melted away — his purposes of reserve were forgotten, and he became once more the man of Emma's first acquaintance, pleasant and gay — sensible and agreeable. Lady Gordon left them several times together, whilst she occupied herself with her flowers, or her tame pheasants; and each successive time of her absence, there was less check and constraint in his manner; and when, at last, she totally disappeared, and they were left without other witnesses in that delightful spot than the silent trees, or the trickling waters, his reserve had disappeared altogether and she could converse with him as in former times.

'Have you enjoyed your visit at Croydon, Miss Watson?' he enquired.

She looked surprised at the question.

'Enjoyed it,' she repeated — then, after a momentary hesitation, added, 'I wonder you can apply such a term to circumstances connected with so much that is — that must be — most painful.'

He was exceedingly vexed with himself for the question, and attempted to make some excuse for the inadvertence.

184

'It is unnecessary,' she replied, with a something almost of bitterness in her tone, 'I had no right to expect that the memory of our misfortune would remain, when we ourselves were removed from sight. I ought rather to apologize for answering your question so uncivilly.'

'No, no, indeed,' cried he eagerly, 'I cannot admit that — but indeed, Miss Watson, you do me injustice, and the same to all your former friends in that last speech. We cannot cease to regret the dispensation of Providence which in removing your excellent father from among us, robbed us likewise of you and your sisters.'

'My dear father,' said Emma involuntarily, her eyes filling with tears — she turned away her head.

'It was of course a terrible wound to you,' said he softly, and stepping up quite close to her, 'but not one which you need despair of time's healing; your good sense, your principles must assist you to view the occurrence in its true light. It must not sadden your whole life, or rob you of all pleasure.'

'True — but there are other sorrows connected with it —' she stopped abruptly, then went on again. 'However I have no right to complain. I have still *some* friends left — my loss of fortune has not entailed the loss of *all* those whom I reckoned amongst my friends.'

'Can you imagine,' cried he eagerly, 'that such a circumstance can make the shadow of difference to anyone worth knowing. It is, I own, too, too common — but surely *you* have not met with such instances.'

She shook her head and looked half reproachfully at him: in her own heart, she had felt inclined to charge him with this feeling.

He looked very earnestly at her and said gently:

'You fancy friends have deserted you, owing to a change in your prospects — do not — allow me to advise you — do not give way to such feelings — they will not make you happy.'

'They did not make me *un*happy, I assure you,' she said with spirit; 'the value I place on such fluctuating friendships is low indeed.'

He answered her in a low but emphatic tone : 'Even if you have met with one such instance, you should not allow your mind to dwell on it. No good can come of harbouring a secret resentment.'

For a moment she wondered whether he had guessed her true feelings, but she had not the composure to meet his eyes. She had never held him so well as when thus, and with justice, reproving her.

After a pause they walked on through the flower garden and their conversation took another turn. The hour which they thus enjoyed, before summoned to the Castle to prepare for dinner, was one of the pleasantest in Emma's recollection. On Howard's part it would have been the same had his conscience been easy, when he reflected on Lord Osborne's plans and hopes. He tormented himself with the idea that it was unjust to his friend to take advantage of his absence; but *she* had shown no reluctance to the interview; indeed, if his wishes did not mislead him, there was a glance in her averted eyes, and a rich mantling of colour over her cheek once or twice, which spoke anything but aversion.

And if so — if he really had been so fortunate as to inspire her with a partiality so delightful, was he not bound in honour to prove himself deserving of such feelings, and capable of appreciating them. This conviction gave him a degree of confidence quite different from the manners he had exhibited when they had previously met at Osborne Castle, and Emma found him as pleasant as in the earlier stages of their acquaintance.

'Are you still partial to early walks, Miss Watson,' enquired Sir William in the course of the evening, 'or is it only on frosty winter mornings that you indulge in such a recreation?'

'Ah, I had a very pleasant ramble that morning,' said Emma, 'at least till the rain came and spoilt it all.'

'A very mortifying way of concluding,' said Sir William, laughing, 'for I came with the rain. I wish you had not put in that reservation.'

'I am not so ungrateful as to include you and the rain in the same condemnation.'

'But if you wish to indulge in the same amusement now, you will have abundance of time, as Lady Gordon is by no means so precipitate in her habits of rising as to compel her guests to abridge their walks before breakfast. Perhaps as a compliment to you, and by making a very great speed she may contrive to complete her labours by ten or eleven o'clock.'

'Well, I do not pretend to deny it,' said Lady Gordon, 'I dearly love the pleasure of doing nothing. But Sir William is always anxious to make me out worse than I am.'

'But you have not answered my question, Miss Watson, and I have a great wish to know whether you are proposing an excursion tomorrow, because I think it would be much more agreeable if we can contrive to walk together, and if I know at what time you intend to set out, I will take care to be in the way.'

'Is he serious, Lady Gordon?' enquired Emma.

'It is a most uncommon event if he is so, I assure you,' replied the young wife.

'Do not believe what she will say of me,' returned Sir William, 'but just tell me at once that you will walk tomorrow morning, and that you will be particularly happy if I and Mr Howard will join you.'

Emma made believe to consider the proposal entirely as a joke, but somehow, without knowing exactly how, it was settled that the excursion should take place, and that Mr Howard was to meet them at a particular spot, from whence they were to ascend the hill behind the Castle to enjoy the prospect in the morning's sunshine. Lady Gordon privately gave her husband many injunctions not to interfere with the lovers, and while keeping near enough to take away all appearance of impropriety, to be sure to give them plenty of time for quiet intercourse. In return for her consideration he only laughed at her, and accused her of a great inclination to intrigue, assuring her she had much better leave such affairs to take their chance.

The walk, however, took place as was planned, and was exceedingly enjoyed by all three, though Mr Howard did not take that occasion of declaring his passion; indeed he would have had some difficulty in finding an opportunity, as Sir William did not follow Lady Gordon's suggestions of leaving them together.

Mindful of her promise, Lady Gordon sent her guest over the next morning to pay her first visit to Mrs Tom Musgrave. It was with a feeling of some doubt and hesitation that Emma ventured to her sister's house; anxious as she was to see her and judge for herself, and curious to observe the manners which Tom Musgrave adopted as a married man, she could not help some internal misgivings.

She had never seen the house before, and though she had been previously warned of the fact that it had no beauty to recommend it, she was not exactly prepared for the bare, unsheltered situation, and the extreme unsightliness of the building itself. Tom had always spent too much money on his horses to have any to spare for beautifying his house during his bachelor days, and he was far too angry at the constraint put upon him in his marriage to feel any inclination to exert himself for the reception of his bride. She had therefore no additions for her accommodation, no gay flower-garden, not even any new furniture to boast of, and her glory must consist alone in the fact of her new name, and her security from living and dying an old maid.

Most people would have thought that security dearly purchased, but if such were Margaret's thoughts, she had not as yet given utterance to them.

Emma found her lying on a sofa, and in spite of her very gay dress, and an extremely becoming cap, evidently out of spirits and cross, yet wanting to excite her sister's envy of her situation.

'Well, Emma,' said she sharply, 'I am glad you have come over to see me, though I must say I think your friend, Lady Gordon, since she *is* such a great friend of yours, might have paid me the compliment of calling with you.'

'She thought it would be pleasanter if we met first without her,' said Emma cheerfully, 'but she desired me to express the pleasure it would give her to see you and Mr Musgrave at Osborne Castle any day you would name.'

Somewhat mollified by this unexpected attention, Margaret smiled slightly, then again relapsing into her usual pettish air, she observed:

'I think you might say something about the house and drawing-room — what do you think of it?'

Emma was exceedingly puzzled what to answer, as it was difficult for her to combine sincerity with anything agreeable; but after looking round for a minute she was able to observe that the room was of a pretty shape, and had a pleasant aspect.

'It wants new furnishings sadly,' continued Margaret, pleased with her sister's praise, 'but Tom is so stingy of money, I am sure I do not know when I am to do it. Would not pale blue damask satin curtains look lovely here — with a gold fringe or something of the sort?'

'Rather costly, I should suppose,' replied Emma, 'and perhaps something plainer would be more in keeping with the rest of the house and furniture.'

'Do you suppose,' retorted Margaret, 'I do not know how to furnish a house — of course I should have everything to correspond. I have a little common sense, I believe, whatever some people may choose to think of it.'

'It was not your taste that I doubted,' replied Emma, and then stopped, afraid lest she should only make bad worse by anything she might venture to say.

'I should like to know what you *did* doubt then,' said Margaret scornfully. 'Perhaps you thought we could not afford it, but there I assure you you are quite mistaken — Tom's is a very ample income, and he can as well afford me luxuries as Sir William Gordon himself,'

'I am very glad to hear it,' replied Emma composedly.

When Tom joined them Emma quickly repeated Lady Gordon's message, and requested them to name a day for accepting it. A debate ensued as to the most convenient day on which to fix, which presently branched off into a violent dispute as to whether the invitation in question was intended as a compliment to Tom or to his wife; each maintaining the opinion that the honour of the invitation was all due to themselves.

At length, however, Emma contrived to persuade them to settle the point in question; and two days from that time was fixed on for the dinner visit. Emma then took her leave, grieved by what she had witnessed but not surprised at it. Tom was reckless and unkind; Margaret peevish and fretful, without energy of character to make the best of her situation, or strength of mind to bear with patience the evils in which she had involved herself. No doubt if Tom had loved her, she would have been fond of him, and any sensation beyond her own selfish feelings would have done her good; but forced into the marriage against his will, love, or anything resembling it, was not to be expected from him; in consequence, her own partiality could not survive his indifference; and there was a mutual spirit of ill-will cultivated between them which boded ill for their future peace.

Emma reflected on all this as she drove home from her very unsatisfactory visit, and was only aroused from these unpleasant considerations by finding the carriage stopped suddenly soon after entering the park. On looking up, she perceived Sir William and Lady Gordon, who enquired if she would like a stroll before dinner, instead of returning at once to the Castle. She assented with pleasure, and quitting the carriage, they took a pleasant path through a plantation, the thick shade of which made walking agreeable even in the afternoon of a June day.

'Suppose we go and invade Mr Howard,' said Lady Gordon, 'this path leads down to the Vicarage — let us see what sort of a housekeeper he makes, without his sister to manage for him!'

'Always running after Mr Howard, Henrietta,' said Sir William. 'Upon my word, I shall be jealous soon: yesterday flirting in the flower-garden — today visiting at the Vicarage; if things go on in this way, I will take you away from Osborne Castle very soon.'

'Yes, *you* have reason to be jealous, have you not? When men leave off pleasing their wives themselves, they always dislike that anyone else should do it for them,' replied Lady Gordon smiling.

'But the comparisons are not fairly drawn under such circumstances,' suggested Emma, 'for Mr Howard's way of treating Lady Gordon can be no rule for his probable way of tyrannizing over some future Mrs Howard.'

'In fact no,' replied Sir William. 'But I observe, Miss Watson, you take it for granted that he *will* tyrannize over a wife when he has one; is that your opinion of men in general, or only of Mr Howard in particular?'

'Of men in general, no doubt,' interposed Lady Gordon: 'Miss Watson has lived too long in the world not already to have discovered the obvious truth, that all men are tyrants when they have the opportunity, the only difference being, that some are hypocrites likewise, and conceal their disposition until their victim is in their power, while others, like yourself, William, make no secret of it at all.'

'I am glad you acquit me of hypocrisy at least, Henrietta; it has always been my wish to be distinguished for sincerity and openness, I never indulged in intrigue or meddled in manoeuvres or sought for stratagems to carry out my wishes.'

He accompanied this speech with a peculiar smile which made his lady colour slightly, as she well knew to what he alluded.

At length Emma observed that it was a remarkably pretty walk which they were pursuing. Lady Gordon told her that they were indebted for the idea and plan of it to Mr Howard; he had superintended the execution of some other improvements which Lady Osborne had effected, but this one had originated entirely with him. It was the pleasantest road from the Vicarage to the village, and was so well made and drained as to be almost always dry although much sheltered. The idea that he had planned it did not at all diminish the interest with which Emma regarded the road they were discussing; and her eyes sought the glimpses of distant landscape seen between the trees with pleasure materially heightened by the recollection that it was to his taste she was indebted for the gratification.

This sort of secret satisfaction was brought suddenly to a close, by finding herself quite unexpectedly at a little wicket gate opening upon his garden. She had not been aware the house was so near; but the nature, not the source of her pleasure, was changed; it still was connected with him, and the beauty of his garden quite enchanted her. When she had previously seen it in the winter, she had felt certain it must be charming, but now it proved to surpass every expectation she had formed.

They found him hard at work constructing some new trellis work for the luxuriant creepers which adorned his entrance; his coat was off, and his arms partly bare.

'We have taken you by storm today,' said Lady Gordon, holding out her hand to him. 'I like to see your zeal for your house.'

'Really,' said he, holding up his hand, 'these fingers of mine are not at all fit to touch a lady's glove; when we assume the occupation of carpenters, we ought to expect to be treated accordingly.'

'And when we intrude on you at such irregular hours, we ought to be thankful for any welcome we can get,' replied Lady Gordon.

'Indeed, I take it most kind and friendly of you to come,' answered he, his eyes directed with unequivocal satisfaction towards Emma. 'My garden is better worth seeing *now*, than when you were here last,' added he, approaching her.

'It is lovely,' replied Emma honestly speaking her mind. 'What beautiful roses! I do not think I ever saw such a display of blossoms.'

'I am glad *you* admire it,' said he, in a low voice, 'though after the conservatories and flower gardens of the Castle, it would generally be accounted plain.'

'I would not make unjust comparisons,' replied Emma, 'but I think you need not dread it if I were inclined to do so. It is not grandeur or extent which always carries the greatest charm.'

'And would you apply that sentiment to *more* than a garden?' asked he, very earnestly, fixing on her eyes which unmistakably declared his anxiety to hear her answer.

He was not, however, destined to be so speedily gratified as he had hoped; for, quite unconscious that he was interrupting any peculiarly interesting conversation, Sir William turned round to enquire the name of some new shrub that struck his eye at the moment.

Recollecting himself after replying to the baronet's question, he invited them to enter the house to rest; but this Lady Gordon declined, declaring that she preferred a swelling bank of turf, under a tree, to any sofa that ever was constructed. The ladies therefore sat down here, and begging to be excused for one minute, Mr Howard disappeared, going, as Sir William guessed, to wash his hands and put on a coat, that he might look fit for company. Lady Gordon laughed at the idea of a clergyman making himself smart, or of Mr Howard treating her as company; but to dress himself had not been Howard's sole object, for he reappeared with a basket of magnificent strawberries in his hand.

Lady Gordon accepted them eagerly, declaring that she knew his strawberries were always far better than any the Castle gardens ever produced. As to Emma, she was certain she never tasted any so excellent in her life, nor was she ever before pressed to eat with so persuasive a tone of voice.

'I wonder you take so much pains to beautify this place, when you are almost certain of being soon removed from it,' said Lady Gordon.

'The occupation is in itself a pleasure, but I by no means anticipate a change with the certainty which you seem to do.'

'I have no doubt in the least that the moment Carsdeane is vacant, my brother will offer you the living, and as the rector is very old and infirm it seems hardly possible that it can be long.'

Mr Howard was silent for a few minutes, and when he spoke it was on another subject; but not with the gaiety with which he had before conversed; in fact, he was secretly meditating the extreme desirableness of quitting his present vicarage, if ever Lady Osborne came to reside again in the neighbourhood. Nothing could be much more unpleasant than a meeting between them, and he longed to learn from her daughter whether there was any chance of such a catastrophe; but as yet he had not found courage to enquire, fearing her penetration might have led her to guess the past events, or her mother's indiscretion might have made her acquainted with them.

'Mr Howard,' said Lady Gordon soon afterwards, 'you are under an engagement to Miss Watson to give her another lecture on the paintings in the Castle gallery.'

'I remember hoping for that pleasure,' said he.

'Then come whenever you can,' said Lady Gordon; 'the day after tomorrow Mr and Mrs Musgrave dine with us, will you meet them?'

He accepted with pleasure, though perhaps he would have preferred their absence to their company.

After an hour or two had passed pleasantly away, Lady Gordon rose to take her leave, and even then she pressed him to accompany them up the hill. The encouragement which he received from her was so obvious, that had his suit depended only on her alone, he would have felt neither fear nor hesitation as to the result; but as the uncertain wishes of another person were to be consulted, he still debated whether or not he should venture all his hopes on a single effort.

He accompanied them home, but Emma would not accept the assistance of his arm, because she misinterpreted the hesitation with which it was offered, fancying it was done unwillingly, and solely in compliance with her friend's directions. This discouraged him; he did not recover from the disappointment, and in consequence would not enter the Castle, but persisted in

193

returning to spend a solitary evening at the Vicarage. There Emma's smile and Emma's voice perpetually recurred to his fancy, and he occupied himself, while finishing the work which they had interrupted, in recalling every word which she had said, and the exact look which had accompanied each speech.

CHAPTER 22

THE NEXT MORNING AT BREAKFAST, one letter among
many which Lady Gordon received, appeared to excite considerable surprise. She read it over, and then threw it down before her
husband, with an exclamation:

'Pray look at that letter,' she said and then, seeing he did not
take it up, demanded, 'Have you no curiosity?'

'Oh yes, a great deal of curiosity — but no time to spare, and
I know that if I wait a little, you will tell me all without the
trouble of looking at it.'

'I declare I will not tell you a word, as a punishment for such
incorrigible laziness.'

'It is from your brother, my love,' replied her husband, glancing at the letter. 'What does he say to provoke you, and put you
so out of temper?'

'I will not tell you a word, I assure you.'

'Is he going to be married?'

'Look in the letter and you will have no occasion to ask
me.'

'Miss Watson, suppose you were to take it, and oblige me by
reading it out; you have done your breakfast, and I am still busy
with mine.'

'No indeed, I quite agree with Lady Gordon in thinking it
very indolent not to read it for yourself, and shall certainly not
countenance it at all.'

'I see you are in a conspiracy against me, and that is very
unfair when there are two ladies to one man,' replied he
laughing.

'I am going to make you even in numbers at least,' returned
Emma, 'for I am about to leave the room.'

195

She did so, and Sir William immediately taking up the letter read it through quietly and turned to his wife.

'Well,' said she, 'what do you think of that?'

'First, that it is extraordinary that your brother's proposal of a visit should cause you such annoyance; and secondly, that you should think it necessary to make this visit a secret.'

'You are always struck more with my feelings than anything else: I believe if the Castle were to tumble on us, you would be only occupied in observing how I bore it.'

'That is only because you are the most interesting object in the world to me: surely you would not quarrel with me for that, Henrietta?'

She looked gratified, but persisted in demanding:

'But why would you not look at the letter when I asked you?'

'Because if you wish me to read your letters, and do not choose to make Miss Watson acquainted with their contents, pray wait another time till she is out of the room. You see you have driven her away now.'

'I certainly wished to consult you about that; I am so annoyed at Osborne's coming now!'

'And I cannot imagine why!'

'Because I believe it to be only for the sake of Emma Watson, that he has so suddenly resolved to come here. She will be my friend always, I hope, but I would not wish her to be my sister. I do not believe that so unequal a union could be productive of happiness and I think we should all regret the connection. The Watsons are not the sort of people with whom we could possibly desire intimacy.'

'And yet Osborne could hardly do a better thing for himself; she is his superior in everything but worldly position, and were there the least chance of his persuading her to accept him, I should think him a very lucky fellow. But I do not think there is; and therefore you need not be alarmed for him, nor I for her.'

'And why should you be concerned for her at such a prospect — it would be a very good marriage for her.'

'I too do not think unequal connections desirable — and were she your brother's wife, Emma would either grow ashamed of her own family and their station, or she would be pained by being obliged to neglect them. But she will never accept Osborne!'

'I cannot wish the temptation thrown in her way — I should be by no means sure of the result,' said Lady Gordon.

'You cannot prevent it however,' replied Sir William, 'if Osborne has any such thoughts in his head — he is his own master, and cannot be kept away from her. The mischief is of your own doing too — for you invited her here in the winter — and, if I recollect rightly, encouraged the acquaintance.'

'That was entirely for Mr Howard's sake. It never occurred to me that Osborne would notice her.'

'I cannot see why you should have intermeddled between them at all. Mr Howard would have gone on very well alone.'

Lady Gordon did not choose to mention that it was her mother who gave her the principal motive, so she only said:

'Well, it is too late now, so tell me what I had better do, and I will try and obey you.'

'Do nothing at all then, my love; depend upon it, any opposition will only make your brother more decidedly bent on his own way. Let him come, and trust to the evident partiality of your friend, Howard, as our safeguard.'

Lady Gordon had speedily the opportunity of exercising the forbearance which her husband advised. Punctual to his promise, her brother arrived that afternoon. The two young ladies were sitting together when he walked into the room; and Emma bore, with as much composure as she could, the evident warmth and eagerness with which he paid his compliments to her. He seated himself by her side, and after looking intently at her for a minute in the way for which he had been formerly remarkable, exclaimed with great energy:

'Upon my honour, Miss Watson, for all it's so long since we met, you are looking uncommonly well and blooming.'

Emma felt excessively tempted to ask him whether he had expected she would have pined at his absence, or grown old in the last six months. She reflected, however, that he had never appeared at all ready to comprehend a jest.

'Croydon must have agreed famously with you,' he continued, 'I was near there once, and had a great inclination to ride over and pay you a visit; but not knowing the people you were with I

197

felt awkward, and did not like to do it; it is such a horrid thing going entirely amongst strangers.'

'I am honoured by your lordship thinking of me at all; but I should say you were quite right in not coming there; we should have been overpowered by the sudden apparition of a man of your rank.'

'I dare say you created a great sensation in Croydon, did you not?'

'Not that I am aware of, my lord; I never wished to be conspicuous, and I trust I did not do anything while there, to excite observation among my acquaintance.'

'You must have done one thing, which you could not help, at any time,' replied he, in a very low voice, as if ashamed of himself. 'You must have looked pretty; they must all have noticed that.'

Emma met Lady Gordon's eyes fixed on her at this moment with an expression which it was impossible to misunderstand; it spoke so plainly of anxiety and mistrust.

Not knowing precisely what to say next, he began to admire her work, a constant resource with young men who are anxious to talk, and rather barren of subjects; but this did not endure very long, and when he could find nothing more to say on this topic, he suddenly enquired if the ladies did not intend to go out. Emma appealed to Lady Gordon, who declared at first she was too lazy to stir; but her brother pressed his proposition so very warmly, alternately suggesting riding, driving, or walking, that at last she yielded. The vehicle chosen after long discussion was an Irish car which appealed to Lord Osborne because it enabled him to talk to Emma as much as he felt inclined.

The drive at first provided Emma with decided satisfaction. Their road traversed a high ridge and lay through the mysterious enchantment of a forest, until the trees parted and to the south afforded them extensive vistas in the direction of another distant line of hills. It was Lord Osborne's pleasure to halt when they had reached sufficient eminence and to hand down Emma from the car the better to admire the view. On their return from a few minutes' stroll Emma took pains to step forward with the intention of mounting without the proffered aid. In her haste she placed all her weight on one foot without noticing the unevenness of the ground and consequently stumbled forward, twisting her ankle so seriously as to incapacitate her entirely from walking and to occasion very considerable pain.

She spent the evening on a couch near to which Lord Osborne stationed himself, in order to enjoy a good view of her face. He had been almost silent since the accident and he now allowed all the little offices of civility to be performed by Sir William, never offering to hand her a cup of coffee, nor seeing when it was empty, and requiring removal; never noticing when her reel of silk dropped on the ground, or discovering if her embroidery frame was raised at the proper angle. His total neglect of all this, together with the general reserve of his manner, made Emma feel more at ease with him than usual. She did not recognize the shyness of his nature, but made up her mind that had he really been her serious admirer, he would certainly have behaved very differently.

The sprain of her ankle occasioned her great pain all the evening, as Sir William guessed from the paleness of her cheeks, but she did all she could to conceal it, and chatted with him and Lady Gordon as long as they remained together. But she never felt more relieved than when at his suggestion, the proposal for retiring was made early, in order to relieve her, for she had borne as much as she could in silence, and really felt once or twice on the point of fainting.

In the forenoon of the following day, as she was reclining on a couch near the open window, engaged in drawing a group of flowers for Lady Gordon's portfolio, Mr Howard entered the room. He found Emma, to his great astonishment, *tête-à-tête* with Lord Osborne. He had no idea that the young nobleman was then in the country, and not the least expectation of meeting at that moment one whom he could not avoid considering as a dangerous rival. His quick eye did not fail to perceive, too, that some of the flowers in the vase before Emma were of precisely the same kind as the sprig in Lord Osborne's coat, and he came to the not unnatural conclusion that they had been given to him by herself. He now hesitated whether to enter the room or not, but Lord Osborne advanced to meet him with considerable pleasure.

'Very glad indeed to see you, Howard,' he began. 'I dare say you are a little surprised to see *me* here; but I could not help coming. You see we have got *her* back again, aren't you glad?' glancing at the sofa where Emma was lying.

She too held out her hand to him, but as she never suspected his jealousy, not supposing there was any occasion for it, she felt hurt at the coldness of his address, and the hurried way in which he greeted her.

Lord Osborne eyed them both. Although by no means sharp-sighted, he now noticed that Emma was much less pale and the idea suddenly entered his mind that there was danger to his suit in the visits of his former tutor. He sat down in silence, determined to observe them closely.

The consequence of these various feelings was a peculiarly awkward silence, lasting until Mr Howard spoke.

'I called to enquire if you were disposed to fulfil the engagement we talked of the other day, Miss Watson, about the picture-gallery; but I can see that you are not now disposed for the exertion.'

'It is indeed quite out of my power this morning, and I wish I could name a time when it would be possible to have the pleasure.'

'It is only dependent on yourself — but if you have more agreeable engagements, of course it is natural you should defer this one.'

'Do you suppose it to be a more agreeable engagement lying prisoner here?' replied Emma smiling.

'You did not use to be indolent, I know, but no doubt it conforms better with fashionable manners to pass the day on a sofa than in active pursuits.'

'Now do not be satirical, Mr Howard,' said she in a lively tone; 'I never was, and I hope I never shall be converted into a fashionable fine lady, and my lying on the sofa has nothing to do with indolence or inclination.'

'Indeed!' he replied, with a provoking air of incredulity.

'Yes, indeed, it is a downright punishment to me, only alleviated by the kindness of my friends in trying to amuse me.'

Mr Howard glanced at Lord Osborne, as if he attributed the friendship and the amusement alike to him.

'No, you are wrong there — I dare say his lordship is afraid I should be spoilt if I had too much indulgence, so he contents himself with disarranging my flowers and contradicting my opinions: I really must trouble you, my lord, for the bud you stole; I cannot do without it.'

'And I cannot possibly let you have it,' he replied abruptly. 'It's gone, I shall not tell you where.'

'Now is not that too provoking!' cried Emma, 'with all his conservatories and gardens at his command, to envy me my single sprig which Sir William took so much trouble in procuring me. I had a particular value for it on his account, and having sketched it into this group; I must have it, or the whole will be spoilt.'

'Will you promise me the drawing, if I give it back to you?'

'No indeed — it is for your sister. Mr Howard, will you not take my part? I am exposed, without the power of resisting, to his depredations; he knows I cannot move from this sofa.'

'But do tell me what is the matter?' enquired Mr Howard seriously; 'have you really met with an accident?'

'Only a sprain which incapacitates me from moving,' she answered.

'I am exceedingly grieved to hear it,' he said with looks of real concern. 'I had been thinking only of want of inclination, not want of power, when you declined moving.'

'You see in that instance then you misunderstood me, perhaps you do so in others likewise.' This equivocal speech threw Howard into a fit of abstraction from which he roused himself to enquire the particulars of the accident. Emma ended a lively account of it by desiring him to deduce some moral from her story.

'Perhaps you would not like the moral I should draw,' he replied, with a smile; 'it might not be flattering or agreeable.'

'I dare say it would not be flattering, Mr Howard; I should not expect it from you — suppose we all make a moral to the tale, and see if we can think alike. Come, my lord, let us have yours.'

'Give me time to think, then,' said he — for, in spite of his resolution in favour of silence, he could not help yielding to her smiles.

'Five minutes by the watch on the chimney-piece, and in good time — here come Sir William and Lady Gordon to give their opinion of our sentiments.'

'I am quite ready to give mine at once,' returned Sir William, who heard only the last speech.

'I have no doubt that yours, Miss Watson, are very severe — Osborne's romantic — and Howard's common place. Will that do?'

'Not at all — you shall be no judge in the matter, since you make up your mind before you hear the case. Lady Gordon shall be umpire, and if you like to produce a moral, do so.'

'What are you debating?' enquired Lady Gordon, 'I must understand before I decide.'

'Not the least necessary, my dear Henrietta,' said her husband, 'and quite out of character; women always decide first — and understanding, if it comes at all, is quite a secondary consideration with them.'

'A pretty speech to make,' exclaimed Emma, 'when he himself just now answered without understanding at all.'

'I know you would be severe,' replied Sir William to Emma, 'but I was, I assure you, only trying to bring down my conduct to the level of my companions.'

'Shall we not turn him out of the room?' cried his wife. 'He is intolerable today!'

'Oh no! Take no notice of him,' said Emma with spirit, 'I do not mind a word he says.'

'You — all of you talk so much,' complained Lord Osborne, 'that it is impossible for me to settle my thoughts — but I think I have made my moral now — shall I say it?'

'By all means, my lord,' said Emma.

'We are all grave attention,' said Sir William.

'Well, I think ladies should take great care not to make false steps — because, if they do, they will not be able to stand by themselves afterwards.'

'Bravo, Osborne!' cried his sister, 'but rather severe on my friend.'

'And you, Mr Howard,' she continued, 'will you favour us with your opinion?'

'Mine is, that Miss Watson should, in future, avoid any great haste in climbing to eminent situations, lest she be the loser in the attempt.'

Emma coloured slightly at the earnest glance which accompanied the low, emphatic tone of his speech, but laughed it off by observing:

'Yes, my nature is so ambitious, I need that counsel.'

'And now, Miss Watson,' cried Lord Osborne eagerly, 'it's your turn.'

'Well, the moral I draw is, when I am in a comfortable position again, to take care and not lose it in searching for some imaginary advantage — the moral of "The substance and the shadow."'

'And mine,' exclaimed Sir William, 'you must hear mine — it is, that a young lady's strength of limb is less than her will; it is easier for her to twist her ankle than to give up her own way.'

'And mine,' exclaimed Lady Gordon, 'my dear Miss Watson, my moral is, that you should never invite men to comment on your conduct, for they are sure to draw false conclusions and make ill-natured remarks.'

'It is the more hard, as your brother was the origin of my misfortune,' observed Emma, 'but for his persuasion, I should have sat still.'

'Miss Watson, have you air enough here,' said Lord Osborne, coming up to her sofa; 'do let me push you out on the terrace — it would be so pleasant now the sun is off.'

Lady Gordon seconded the proposal, and called on Mr Howard to assist her brother. He did so; and then, distressed to find that the young lord of the Castle took his station closer than ever to her side, he tore himself away from the whole party and went to shut himself up at home till the evening.

'Howard has a prodigious deal to say for himself, which makes him a favourite,' said Lord Osborne thoughtfully.

'I do not think he talked much today,' replied Emma. 'If he did I did not hear it at least.'

'Perhaps you do not care to have men such very great talkers — do you? I never heard your opinion about that.'

'I really believe I have none, my lord, I never made up my mind as to how much a man or woman should talk to make themselves agreeable — some men, I am sure, talk too much.'

'With me in mind, Miss Watson?' interrupted Sir William archly.

'The too much must depend on the quality likewise — if they happen to be very silly or very dull, a few sentences are enough to tire one,' added Emma, 'whereas a lively, clever man may talk for an hour without being wearisome.'

'That is a comforting speech,' exclaimed Sir William. 'Osborne, we will take out our watches next time we begin a conversation with Miss Watson. Lively, clever men — the description just suits us — *we* may talk precisely sixty minutes.'

CHAPTER 23

IT HAD BEEN SETTLED that the Musgraves were to come over early in the afternoon, that they might spend some time with their sister; and in spite of his usual predilection for late hours and unpunctuality, Tom was rendered too proud and happy by the invitation to feel at all disposed to delay the honour. Soon after luncheon they arrived; Margaret adorned in all her wedding finery, delighted at such an opportunity of showing off. Her new bonnet and pelisse were decidedly fashionable; and she was not a little surprised, as well as half-affronted, at the simplicity of dress which her hostess adopted.

On discovering the circumstances that Emma was confined to the sofa, she would not rest till she had heard the whole history of the accident, and then she uttered this sisterly observation:

'Good gracious! How excessively awkward and careless of you, Emma; how could you be so stupid? Well, I am glad it is not me, as of all things I hate a sprain — to go waddling about like an old goose.'

'I don't see anything stupid in it,' said Lord Osborne sturdily, 'it's very unfortunate and very vexatious to us, and I dare say very painful to her, but there's nothing stupid in it.'

'I did not mean stupid precisely,' retracted Margaret, who would never dream of contradicting a peer of the realm, 'I only meant it was very ridiculous.'

Lord Osborne did not condescend to answer any more, but rose and walked whistling away.

Meantime, Tom was trying to be excessively gallant and agreeable to Lady Gordon, who, never particularly prepossessed in his favour, seemed now unusually cold and ungracious. In fact she could not quite forgive the danger she had been in of being called into court, and naturally looking on him as the cause, she felt a considerable degree of repugnance towards him.

His obsequiousness and flatteries did him no service; she would not be accessible to any compliments of his, and to the most elaborate praises, returned him the coldest answers.

'It is very provoking of you to be laid up lame there,' Margaret continued presently to Emma, 'I should like to see the grounds of the Castle; I am always so unfortunate on such occasions: nobody meets with so many disappointments as me.'

'No doubt Emma did it to provoke you,' observed Tom.

'I shall be very happy to show you over the grounds myself,' interrupted Lady Gordon, convinced that anything would be better than the altercation going on between the husband and wife, which must be equally disagreeable to Emma as to herself.

Margaret accepted the proposition very joyfully, and the two ladies left the room together, as Sir William saw no necessity for accompanying them.

'I suppose you enjoy yourself famously here, Emma,' observed Tom, coming close up to her sofa.

'Yes, when I have not a sprained ankle,' replied she.

'And even when you have, your spirits are so good, you seem to enjoy yourself still,' observed Lord Osborne, who had returned from the terrace when Margaret left the room.

'But it makes her of consequence, and all young ladies like that,' answered her brother-in-law. 'I am sure Margaret is always affecting to be ill for no other purpose, and reproaching me because I do not believe it.'

'I do not think your wife at all like her sister,' observed Lord Osborne coolly.

There was silence for a moment.

'How does your stable go on, my lord?' enquired Tom. 'I should like to see it.'

'You are welcome to go and see it if you please, so long as you don't drag me there; I am not inclined for an excursion to the stables at present.'

Tom whistled and walked away, Lord Osborne drew nearer to Emma, and said:

'I hope you do not like him — do you?'

'He is my brother-in-law,' replied Emma, 'you forget that.'

'But one is not obliged to like one's brother-in-law, I suppose.'

'I hope you mean nothing personal or disrespectful by that observation,' exclaimed Sir William.

'No, on my honour, I forgot about you, Gordon,' said he, 'but I should think it quite enough if the husband likes his wife without its being at all necessary that the mother and sisters, and brother-in-law, should all like her, too.'

'Not necessary, certainly, but altogether desirable, and certainly conducive to domestic felicity.'

'If my sister does not like my wife she must keep at a distance from her,' said Lord Osborne, positively, 'and then her feelings will be of no consequence — do not you agree with me, Miss Watson?'

'Not exactly, my lord; I should not in practice, certainly — I do not think I would marry into a family where I was altogether unwelcome.'

'I am sorry for it,' said Lord Osborne, very softly and then, looking remarkably self-conscious and awkward, he walked away.

'His theories sound more unprincipled than his practice would be, I suspect,' observed Sir William, looking after him, and glancing at Emma. 'I doubt whether he would really bear a quarrel with his sister with such indifference.'

'I dare say not,' said Emma, without at all suspecting she had any share in his feelings, or interest in his proceedings. 'Young men often assert far more than they would like to realize, and I do not think worse of him than of many of his neighbours. I dare say he likes his own way —'

'He is very determined in following out his own opinions, but what I meant was, that though from impulse he *might* act in opposition to the wishes of his family, he would certainly repent it, as everybody does sooner or later.'

'Very likely, so for his sake I hope he will not try,' replied Emma, very unconcernedly.

'Shall I go on reading to you, Miss Watson,' enquired Sir William, 'or is there anything you want?'

Emma replied that she should prefer reading to herself, and Sir William, having supplied her with the volumes she desired, left her in solitude.

Thus she remained until she was interrupted by the entrance of Mr Howard, who looked something between pleased and frightened at finding her alone. She told him where the others were gone, so far as she knew herself, but he seemed perfectly satisfied to take her assertions on trust, evincing no desire at all to follow them. He said it was very warm out of doors, that her room was exceedingly comfortable, and that he hoped she would make no objection to his remaining in her company.

She had no wish to oppose him, and a long and amicable conversation followed relative to the books she had been reading. They agreed in admiring the authors in question, and then in praising Sir William Gordon, who had recommended them. He expressed the conviction that the happiness of the Gordons would continue and increase. Both were free from pride of birth; and in Lady Gordon's case, considering what lessons she received from her mother, that showed a very strong character.

'Her friendship for me is one proof of that,' observed Emma, 'she has been invariably kind to me, and I have no claim to equality with her.'

'Not in rank or fortune,' he interrupted, 'but allow me to say, in habits, tastes, and education, you are completely her equal, and she feels it so.'

'Such fulsome compliments, Mr Howard,' said Emma smiling; 'I suppose you think something due to me to make up for your severe reflections on my ambitions.'

'Your ambitions!' he repeated in surprise.

'Yes; no later than this morning you warned me not to climb too high lest I should fall irretrievably; you see I remember your lessons, though you may affect to forget them.'

'I wish I could consider it as a proof that you are not offended at my boldness.' He drew his chair closer to her; 'I almost wished afterwards to apologize for my words; I feared you would think me so impertinent. You were not angry?'

'Not the least in the world — why should I be? Indeed, I did not believe you were serious; you may laugh at my vanity, but I did not feel guilty of ambition.'

'And if you were, *I* had no right, no title, no claim to correct you,' cried he looking very earnestly at her.

'The right of a friend and well-wisher, Mr Howard,' replied

she looking down with a heightened colour — she never could meet his eyes when they had that peculiar expression in them. 'I trust I may consider *you* in that light at least.'

'You have not a sincerer well-wisher in the world,' he replied with emphasis, and then stopped abruptly.

To break the pause which appeared to her to be awkward, she observed:

'You did not tell me where your sister is, Mr Howard — or else I have forgotten: where is it?'

'In North Wales, not far from Denbigh. I am going shortly to fetch her home.'

'I think you are always going somewhere; ever since I knew you, you have been perpetually offering to go away.'

'I must go and fetch Anne, the only question is when?'

'And does that depend on Mrs Blake's wishes, or your caprice?'

'A little of both, if you mean by caprice, the power of absenting myself from the duties of my station,' replied he.

'I wish I had met Mrs Blake,' said Emma. 'Pray make haste and fetch her, for if I leave the country without our meeting now, it is impossible to say when, if ever, I shall see her again.'

'Are you going quite away then?' enquired he with concern. 'I thought your home was at Croydon.'

'It is impossible to say where my home may be — not Croydon certainly — perhaps I may *never* have another. I must in future be content to dwell amongst strangers, and dare not talk of home. I am wishing for a situation as governess.'

A slight shade of melancholy replaced her usually gay expression as she said this, and she added, after a short pause:

'I have one prospect of a home, though an uncertain one at present; my brother — I mean my youngest brother — urges me to go and live with him the moment he can obtain a living for us both in his profession. But it must be quite uncertain when that will be.'

He was still silent, hesitating whether or not he should at that moment offer her one other home more settled and more permanent. He hesitated, and the opportunity was lost. Footsteps were heard in the conservatory. In a low and hurried tone he spoke, clasping her hand in his:

'Dearest Miss Watson, I feel for you! If I had only time I would prove it!'

There *was* no time for more, but with a gentle pressure of his hand he quitted her abruptly, escaping just quickly enough through one window to avoid being seen, as Lady Gordon and Mrs Musgrave entered at another.

Emma remained in a state of feeling which she would have found it exceedingly difficult to describe, such was the confusion in her mind at the moment. Her most prominent idea was, however, disappointment that he had said so little. She really believed he loved her — at least that he intended her to suppose it; but why not speak more plainly, or why speak at all? It would be so very hard to meet him after what had passed, and yet, how could she avoid it?

With these contradictory notions in her mind, and the agitation to which they gave rise evident in her face, it was impossible for her manners to be sufficiently composed, not to attract her friend's notice. Lady Gordon thought she was in pain, and accused her of having been attempting to move; which she attributed to the fact of Sir William having gone out and left her alone. Emma defended Sir William and felt bound to assert with no great respect for truth in relation to her ankle that *her* pain was already somewhat relieved.

CHAPTER 24

MR HOWARD'S FATAL HESITATION had cruel effects on his composure. He spent an almost sleepless night, deeply agitated by turning over and over again in his mind the possible courses of action that now presented themselves. He tried to recall every-thing that Emma had said — the trust that she seemed to place in his friendship, the attention she had paid to his advice, the reproach she had uttered about his being so repeatedly minded to go away. There had been something poignant and unexpected in the frankness with which she had discussed her own future, that she might never visit in the country again, that she had already sought a situation as governess, that she fixed her hopes of an eventual home on the professional advancement of her younger brother, a surgeon's apprentice. How simple, how modest those prospects now appeared to him for one to whom the Lord Osborne was so clearly attracted.

Hoping for respite from his perplexity and hesitation, Howard set off in the morning to visit a sick parishioner. On his way through the village he was overtaken by Lord Osborne on horse-back. This chance meeting had the effect of making up his mind for him; he learned that Lady Osborne herself had already told her son that she intended to come down to the Castle within the near future.

'I think,' added his former pupil lightly, 'she has got it into her head to suspect what I am about and intends to stop me altogether if she can. By Jove, it might do the trick if I got it all settled before she puts in an appearance.'

'Do you believe,' said Howard grimly, 'that Emma Watson will consent to be your wife if she supposes your mother objects?'

'That's the worst of it — I am afraid she may have some scruples, but I mean to try my luck at all events. There's another thing too to be considered, Fanny Carr is coming here — now it would save me an immense deal of trouble with her if I could give myself out as an engaged man. She would not talk half so much.'

'You really think that would make a difference,' said Howard, trying not to smile, but not very successfully.

'I have no doubt of it at all, and the blessing of being freed in some degree from the trouble of answering her is more than I could tell. That girl would talk the hind leg off a horse in no time.'

Howard felt perfectly convinced that Emma never would marry from motives of ambition, but how could he be sure what degree of influence the young peer might have over her heart. Whatever might happen in his absence the idea of meeting Lady Osborne again was so excessively disagreeable that his going to fetch his sister home must now become imperative. But the question arose, what would Emma herself think of it; in what light would she consider his quitting her thus suddenly, after the betrayal of feeling which he had so recently made? Might she not suspect him of trifling with her — might she not think herself extremely ill-used — could he bear to forfeit the esteem which she had sometimes shown for him?

In reality Emma's thoughts were very different. Lying on her couch she had repeated to herself again and again the last words that Mr Howard had addressed to her. Her hand still seemed to feel the pressure of his fingers, and she could hardly believe that after this he could much longer leave her in doubt as to his wishes.

Whether it was the agitation of mind which these reflections occasioned, or solely the pain which for two days she had been suffering, she could hardly tell, but the next morning she found herself so feverish and unwell as to be quite unable to leave her room. She felt this the more because she thus, as she fancied, lost the interview with Mr Howard which she had been promising herself, and until she found all chance of it gone, she had not known how very much she was depending on it.

Howard's intentions were now clear. His departure could not

be postponed, but he believed that out of friendship and sympathy Lady Gordon could be prevailed upon to allow him an interview with Emma, untroubled by witnesses. This idea was doomed to entire disappointment. When he applied at the Castle he learnt with infinite concern that Emma was confined to her room. Lady Gordon pronounced that she was so unwell that if the evening did not find her improved, medical advice must certainly be sent for. Sorrowfully, therefore, and beset by anxieties, as much about his own situation as about Emma's, he was compelled to take his leave.

Emma's indisposition lasted several days, and was probably rather increased than otherwise by the information which her attendant gave her, that Mr Howard was gone to Wales, for no one knew how long. She had no one to whom she could communicate her feelings, and the disappointment was all the more deeply felt from being dwelt on in secret. Lady Gordon possibly guessed her sensations, but was too considerate to show it if she did, except perhaps by an increased kindness of manner. She saw no one else except the apothecary.

Before Lady Osborne could make good her intention of joining them at the Castle, her son had travelled to London. His sudden decision to do so was to be accounted for as much by Miss Carr's behaviour after her arrival as by Emma's confinement to her own room. Fanny Carr's persistent questions about Emma, her reflections on the vulgar pretensions of the Watson family, on the arrogance of a country town lawyer in threatening to contrive that a peer's daughter should appear in the witness-box, all this became more than the young man could bear. When finally she appeared to suggest that Emma's accident was deliberately contrived in order to excite his interest and sympathy, Lord Osborne found the insinuations of his sister's guest quite intolerable. He was a young man in general careless and easygoing as was to be expected in someone of his age, position and upbringing, but his usual composure was now thoroughly disturbed. His anger against Fanny Carr was made the more unendurable by his inability to contend with her in argument. To make a sudden departure on the pretext of duty to his mother was his only possible relief.

Lord Osborne's first evening at Portman Square revealed that his mother's listlessness and indifference were even more marked than usual. In the hope of thereby arousing some interest in her mind he remarked that he had received news that the incumbent at Carsdeane, a living to which he held the right of presentation, was in all probability on his death-bed. He announced his determination that this living, the best at his disposal, should be offered to his former tutor as soon as it became vacant. To his astonishment his mother expressed the most positive opposition to this plan.

Why Lady Osborne should so resolutely set herself against it, he could not imagine; her feelings towards Howard were incomprehensible. She used to be so friendly and favourable to him, and now wished to hinder any improvement in his circumstances, and to prejudice her son against him. He thought his mother hardly in her senses on this subject, so extremely bitter and unreasonable her sentiments appeared. His object, however, in wishing to remove Mr Howard was quite as potent as hers in wishing to obstruct his purpose. His obstinacy in following his own opinion was also at least as great as hers; there was therefore no chance of their coming to any agreement.

Lord Osborne passed most of the next few days at his club. He had supposed that his mother would choose to return with him to the Castle, but when this was suggested she at once indicated that she no longer had any such wish. They parted therefore with cold formality on both sides.

In Lord Osborne's absence Emma's health made rapid improvement. Before her ankle had become strong enough for walking out she had been greeted with the satisfaction of her hosts on her return to the breakfast-room. Her own satisfaction that morning came from the delivery of a letter well calculated to please and excite her. It was from Sam, and contained the agreeable information that a very good situation had presented itself. It was to Penelope that he was indebted for the offer. Since her marriage, she had been anxious to persuade her husband to give up his surgeon's practice, or at least to take a partner in his business, and now she had the satisfaction of making an offer to Sam on such very advantageous terms that he could not hesitate a moment about accepting them. He was to remove to Chichester next month, and though at first he was to live in his brother-in-law's house, if the scheme answered, he was subsequently to have a house of his own, and then he looked forward with delight to the idea that Emma could come and reside with him. The prospect of this gave her courage and strength to support all the disagreeable innuendoes which Miss Carr might throw out, and even to bear with Lord Osborne's presence and Mr Howard's absence. Settled at Chichester, it was not likely that the former of these gentlemen would follow her for the purpose of looking at her, or that the latter, if he wished to see her again, would have any difficulty in tracing her steps. How happy she should be in her brother's little *ménage*, even if she were never to see anything more of those whom she had known whilst at Stanton or Osborne Castle. She could fancy it all to herself, and in her joyous answer, she drew a lively picture of the pleasure she intended they should have together.

Tired of the anxieties attending an attachment which had not progressed very happily, she felt as if it would be delightful to settle for life with her brother and forswear all other and deeper affection. If she could only make sure that he would never marry, it would be all perfect; so she wrote to him, and her letter made Sam smile with pleasure when he read it.

CHAPTER 25

AFFRONTED BY LORD OSBORNE'S sudden departure, Fanny Carr made little effort to conceal her feelings. She was thoroughly mortified by his absence which was not at all what she expected. There was little to occupy her time as she had not learned any species of needlework, and though she could play a little on the harp she never did that with any perseverance. The Castle library was extensive but she had no taste for anything but the lightest literature; a novel was her only quiet resource and in the country it was difficult to procure a sufficient supply of novels.

'William, as I am going to drive with Emma, you must really ride out with Fanny Carr,' said Lady Gordon to her husband on a morning after Emma's restoration to health.

'Why can you not take her with you, my love?' he asked.

'She is very cross today, I do not know what is the matter with her, and really I cannot undertake her, or we shall certainly quarrel.'

'And so she is to be put off upon me, is she, Henrietta? I am truly much obliged.'

'Oh yes, because you are so good tempered, you will be certain to bear with her petulance, so do not refuse me,' said the young wife with a look of entreaty, which her husband could not resist.

'Very well, I am resigned, pray let Miss Carr know the felicity that awaits her; it would be greater, I dare say, if your brother were to be her companion, but I believe any man would dislike a girl who made such a desperate attack on him; I am sure I should for one; I always liked you because you were so capricious and cross; sometimes unkind, and always careless towards me.'

'You loved me purely out of contradiction I have no doubt; but so long as you ride today with Fanny Carr, I shall be satisfied.'

Emma and Lady Gordon fared well that day; the fresh air, after confinement to one room, was delicious to the former; and, as her pleasure kept her nearly silent, her companion was not troubled to make herself agreeable either. As they drove along, each was engrossed by her own thoughts; Emma's were entirely occupied by the charms of the scenes which passed before them — the venerable trees, the groups of deer, the sunshine and shadows. Lady Gordon's feelings were less enchanted; she was reflecting on the visibly growing attachment of her brother, and wondering what would be the result of it.

Miss Carr's reflections on this same theme caused Sir William a very unpleasant morning. In her frustration over Lord Osborne's behaviour and her jealousy of Emma, she was barely capable of the commonest civility. He executed his most ingenious efforts to interest her, as they rode together, in the picturesque qualities of the Osborne property, but to no avail. Fanny had a mind only for the hostility and spite which now ruled her.

'It was a prodigious penance that you inflicted on me, while you and our friend Emma were enjoying yourselves,' were the first words Sir William addressed to his wife when they were together in private.

She had no time in which to express the regret which she sincerely felt, because Fanny Carr directly joined them. It was soon evident that she did so with a precise purpose.

'I feel it to be my duty,' she began, 'to open your eyes to an impudent and dishonourable pretension of which you seem totally unaware. Have neither of you realized that it is the dear aim of Emma Watson to marry your brother?'

'Indeed no, Fanny,' said Henrietta coolly, 'I am aware of no such thing.' Sir William stood aside, and then walked over to the window. While wishing for no part in the conversation that must follow, he felt that his wife was at least entitled to the support of his presence at such an uncomfortable moment.

'I shall not speak of the disparity between them or of the disgrace to which such a connexion must expose your brother in the eyes of everybody; but I am better acquainted with Emma Watson than you think, and I can no longer be silent.'

'My brother is not now a subject I would wish to discuss with

217

you, Fanny, and I am very much astonished you should wish to tell me anything unpleasant about my friend.'

'But perhaps for Miss Carr's peace of mind she should be heard,' said Sir William, leaving the window with a firm step.

'I think you are the two most complaisant people in the world,' said Fanny, now provoked to even more resentment. 'Emma Watson is both artful and unscrupulous — I happen to know that at Croydon she made herself an object of infamous notoriety.'

'How can you talk in that manner? I am positively ashamed of you,' said Henrietta with rising anger.

'You may depend upon it, I am saying nothing that was not well known there, for I learned the whole story when I was staying at my cousin Lady Alston's. Miss Emma was left without a farthing, utterly dependent on her brother, the attorney who had the effrontery to threaten you. She is so discontented and self-willed that nothing would suit her but to go as a governess somewhere else. Lady Alston had recently parted with hers, and who should be recommended to her but a Miss Emma Watson. Of course I remembered the name.'

'Fanny, I know all this already —'

'Let me finish my story — let me tell you this — who was it who recommended her? Why, my cousin's physician, Mr Morgan! He is reckoned a very clever man, and my cousin who is in delicate health depends very much upon his visits. It was he who proposed Emma Watson — and can you guess why? For my cousin judged it wise to make other enquiries and found that Emma Watson had been carrying on a thoroughly discreditable acquaintance with this Mr Morgan, and it was well known in Croydon that her behaviour had given the utmost dissatisfaction to the brother and sister who had taken her into their house. Fanny was quite scandalized and of course returned no answer to the application she had received from such a person.'

There was a pause. Henrietta retained her composure with some effort before making her reply.

'I am perfectly persuaded that you have been deceived in this affair, for your story is nothing but the most slender gossip, but do not let us quarrel. Let us go to luncheon and discuss this no further.'

Sir William looked at his wife with pride, and then conducted the ladies from the room.

News of Lord Osborne's intention to return to the Castle reached his sister on the following day. Henrietta had hoped that her indignant rejection of Fanny's malicious tale might have brought her visit to an end, but this happy prospect was now lost. She foresaw that everything would be extremely uncomfortable and awkward and wondered what was to be done. To arrange a small party for a dance on the evening of her brother's predicted return seemed, after consultation with her husband, to offer the one prospect of some hours in which acrimonious feelings would at least be subdued.

Accordingly the invitations were despatched, although Emma, whose ankle was not strong, felt that dancing would be out of the question for her.

The strange behaviour of his mother had made a considerable impression on Lord Osborne's mind and resolution. His purposes had grown much clearer. In standing firm against his mother in the matter of Mr Howard's presentation to the living in Cadsdeane he had gained a new confidence. He felt that he could trust himself to resist all her outraged opposition to the idea of making Emma Watson his wife. There had been a time, as he had told Emma, when he had almost determined to ride over and see her at Croydon, but in the event he had lacked the resolution to face the Watson family, almost complete strangers and belonging to a class with which he had nothing in common. Now it would be very different. His return to the Castle had one object only — that of asking Emma to be his wife.

It little suited his new frame of mind to discover on his arrival that a dinner and dance for an assembled company of neighbours was immediately to take place. There was some compensation to be had from Emma's resolution not to dance, but nothing could move his sister to rearrange the setting of her table so that Emma could be placed near him.

The Musgraves were of the party, but as the evening advanced Margaret became less than content with her husband's conduct. He attached himself to the wife of his friend Russell, a fine, dashing woman who delighted to make herself conspicuous. Perhaps Margaret would not have minded had Russell himself been in the least inclined to a flirtation, but he was a man's companion, not a woman's. 'What a difference there is in Osborne,' he said to her. 'He used to be quite ready to join in any diversion and now he has just told me that he must attend to his sister's guests. Upon my soul, a precious notion, catch me troubling my head about them if I was a peer of the realm!'

'A monstrous pity he is so altered,' said Tom, whose attention was aroused by this remark. 'I'm sure he's not the same person to me that he was; I really think it is all for the sake of my sister-in-law, that pretty dark girl, who is here now; you noticed her I dare say.'

'Not I; I never look after pretty girls of that class, not my sort at all, Tom,' a remark which caused Mr Musgrave extreme merriment.

The company and the blaze of lights so heated the ballroom that Emma found herself near to fainting. She managed, however, to make her way to the conservatory which was cool and refreshing. There she could walk up and down as her head ceased to spin. There was nobody to disturb her as her friends seemed all to be dancing.

But at length, by the cessation of the music, she learnt that the long country dance had finished, and soon afterwards, couples and groups sought the same refreshment as herself. She sat down in a corner, where amongst the flowers and shrubs the light was soft and subdued. Her white crepe gown showed like the sculptured drapery of a marble statue, and she was suffered to remain in peace, though the conservatory echoed to merry voices. Light laughter and sparkling sallies of wit sounded above the trickling of the silvery fountain.

Presently, the music recalled all the dancers to the ballroom, and she was again in solitude, but not now for long: a step approached, and just as she was rising from her seat, Lord Osborne joined her.

'Now pray sit down again,' said he, 'but how completely you have hidden yourself; I began to despair of finding you and I wanted particularly to talk to you without being overheard: can you listen to me now?'

She acceded with some surprise to the request; he leaned against the wall by her side, and began.

'It makes me happy, my dear Miss Watson, to see you better. I left the Castle with most anxious feelings about your health. It was monstrous awkward of me to allow that accident of yours to happen. I —'

'No,' interrupted Emma, 'that I cannot allow, my lord, the fault was entirely mine. I was impatient and I paid a just penalty.'

'Dear Miss Watson, you are always so good-natured, only please do not interrupt me until I have done. Miss Carr who always says ill-natured things and whom you know I do not like will never let me say what I wish to say.'

'Forgive me,' said Emma simply and a pause ensued.

'I was very unhappy in London,' he eventually continued, 'and here at the Castle my friends, my stables, my kennels no longer engage me as they once did. I have in mind to see more of the world. My life has been indolent and I feel a discontent with it which could perhaps only be put right if I were to travel. Can you understand me? Would you regret my departure? Are you angry with me for asking you that?'

'That could not be,' she answered without hesitation, intending these words as a reply to his last question, but as the change in his expression was so startling she found difficulty in going on.

'Dear Emma,' he said, pressing his advantage, 'you whom I love so very much! Dear Emma — you who are so kind, so good-natured, will you not love me?'

'Lord Osborne,' she said with profound gravity, 'cease, I beg; such words should never have been spoken; they become neither your station nor mine. I must go.'

But he stood before her, and would not let her pass.

'You misunderstand me, Miss Watson, or you would not speak thus. Have I not as much right as anyone to love what is fair and excellent — if I am plain and awkward, can that make my love an insult — and you — are you not deserving to be loved, worshipped, idolized by every man who comes near you. You have everything that I want — everything that would grace a far higher title, or a much larger fortune than mine. What I have is yours if you will accept it; hand, fortune, title, everything — pray give me an answer.'

He paused, and she tried to speak; it was at first with difficulty she could utter a syllable: but then her courage rose and she was able to finish with firmness.

'Lord Osborne, I regret that I should be under the necessity of paining you by my answer; I cannot accept the offer you have made me, but I shall always remember your good opinion, and liberality of sentiment, with gratitude.'

'I did not ask for gratitude,' replied he reproachfully, 'what good will that do me? Besides I do not see that I deserve it.'

'You have judged me kindly, my lord; you have given me credit for rectitude, when others might have thought and acted very differently.'

'I have loved you so dearly, and I never loved any woman before, it is very hard you will not like me in return.'

'I cannot, my lord,' said she, her eyes filling with tears, 'I have no love to bestow on anyone, my heart is —' she stopped abruptly.

He sat looking at her, then said, 'Do not, Miss Watson, pray do not cry — it makes me so very uncomfortable.' He was again silent but with an effort he finished firmly :

'I will not torment you further. Remember you have not a sincerer friend in the world than myself, or one who would do more to prove his good opinion.'

He took her hand this time, and pressed it, looked at it as he held it for a moment, and then as she drew it away, he rose and left the room.

She was quite surprised at the way in which the interview had terminated; he had shown so much good feeling, so much less of selfishness than she had been in the habit of mentally attributing to him; there was no indignation, no wounded pride, no pique or resentment at her refusal; it was almost as if he had thought more of her feelings than of his own. Her opinion of him had never been so high as when she thus declined his proposals. She felt that if he were but as fortunate in his selection of a partner as his sister had been, there was every probability of his equalling her in domestic happiness. She did not regret her own decision, but she regretted that he should have been so unfortunate as to love where no return could be given; if he had but chosen one whose heart was disengaged — but as for herself, *she* was not the woman who could make him happy; she had not the energy and decision of character requisite for his wife; she did not wish to govern, and she felt that she could only be happy, in proportion as she respected as well as loved her husband; unless she could trust his judgement and lean on him, she felt convinced she should despise him and be miserable.

On the following morning a letter was brought to Emma and she perceived that it came from North Wales. An immediate impulse drove her to seek solitude and fresh air. She walked out on to the terrace, down the flight of steps into the flower garden, and there found composure sufficient to examine the letter. From it she learned that Mr Howard's return would not be now long delayed, and then after a short and simple statement of his love there came an offer of his hand; if she should consent to be a poor man's wife, he would do his utmost to make her happy.

CHAPTER 26

MR HOWARD'S ANXIETY to return to Stanton at the earliest
moment possible was very apparent to his sister; but he showed
no readiness to offer her an explanation of his distracted manner.
He would talk only of his parishioners and the pleasure he had
derived from his work in the Vicarage garden. On the subject of
the Castle he spoke little but what he did say left her in no
doubt that the absence of Lady Osborne had provided him with
a freedom much to be valued. He confessed to a dread of being
alone at the Vicarage on her return from London which might
occur at any time. His sister could in some degree offer protection
from the Castle's social demands. Furthermore Charles had
enjoyed a long summer holiday and from the day of their return
he would need to give a great deal of attention to the boy's
tuition.

When at last their long journey home was completed it became
Mr Howard's first concern to discover whether Lady Osborne
was yet at the Castle and whether Miss Emma Watson's visit to
her friends had terminated. On learning that the expressed
intentions of the dowager had not been realized and that the
composition of the party at the Castle remained exactly as it had
been when he left for Wales, his spirits were much raised; he
allowed no further delay in presenting himself before Lady
Gordon whom he knew to be his friend. All his happiness
depended, he frankly confessed, on his seeing Miss Watson in
private.

The meeting with Emma took place in the library of the
Castle, and was procured for him by his friend's good offices.
Emma held out her hand as she crossed the room to meet him; he
took it with a gentle pressure and would not let her go.

'You guess — you must know — why I have hurried home?' was all he could contrive to say.

Emma had given him one glance as she approached, and now found that she could not look up at him again; but he had observed the high colour in her face.

'There was a letter which I wrote, but to which time prevented me from receiving an answer — will you be persuaded to answer that letter by word of mouth?' He took her hand in both of his, but his confidence suddenly gave way to a violent, inward agitation which showed in his face as he added, 'You are too generous to torment me by your silence.'

'Mr Howard,' said Emma, looking up but making no attempt to withdraw her hand, 'you cannot imagine the pain which your departure occasioned me.'

She spoke hurriedly, without considering the full value of her words; but *he* saw the implied meaning — and knew that she was his. Now he could speak from his heart and she could acknowledge that she loved him, and that neither the dread of being poor, nor the desire of being great, could prevent her promising to become his wife.

When his joy had subsided, and he was able to speak in a calm and reasonable manner, he urged her to come out with him into the park, as the first step to securing her company perfectly undisturbed — for, in the library, they were constantly exposed to be interrupted. Here she tried to obtain from him some rational account as to why he had tantalized her so long by deferring an explanation — which, for anything she could see to the contrary, might just as well, or better, have been made long before. Since he professed he had loved her even before she went to Croydon, why did he take no steps to tell her so; or why, since he ended in writing, did he not write to her there? Was it necessary to go as far as North Wales to find courage for such an epistle?

He told her it was doubt and want of courage kept him silent — then he contradicted himself and said it was really jealousy of Lord Osborne. He had believed the young baron loved her.

So he might, perhaps, was Emma's reply — but what had that to do with it; to make the admiration dangerous, it was necessary

225

that she should return his affection, 'and surely, you never suspected me of that?' she added.

'How could I tell? Might you not naturally be dazzled with the idea of a coronet; why, should I have interfered with your advantage or your advancement?'

'As if it would be to my advantage to marry a man like Lord Osborne,' replied Emma. 'Indeed, I think you might have credited me with a somewhat different taste.'

'But, my dearest Emma, did he not love you?'

'What right have you to ask me any such question, Mr Howard? So long as I assure you, I did not love him, that ought to be sufficient for you — let his feelings remain a secret.'

Lady Gordon and her husband learnt with sincere pleasure that a happy understanding had been established between Emma and her lover; they both hinted that the disappointment to Lord Osborne would not be lasting.

As to the young man himself, he felt his disappointment most acutely, but it did not make him more selfish than he had been. On the contrary, it seemed to give rise to a magnanimity of sentiment which could hardly have been expected.

Two days after the engagement he received an announcement of the death of the old rector before mentioned. He now hastened to offer the living to Howard, delighted to have it in his power thus to improve his circumstances.

'This living was always meant for you,' he said, 'you must accept it as my wedding gift.'

'A noble one, like the heart which dictates it, and a welcome one indeed since it removes the only obstacle to my marriage.'

'One day I will come and see you, but it is best at first that we should be apart. Make her happy — you know, I dare say, that she refused me?'

'No, indeed!'

'Did not Emma tell you? She *did* refuse me, and I loved her the better for it, for it was entirely for *your* sake.'

Immediately after this conversation and without any reconciliation with his mother, Lord Osborne quitted the country. Fanny Carr then decided that her visit had been long enough to such dreadfully dull people as Henrietta and her husband were

226

become; so she took leave of her dear friends and returned, unsuccessful, home.

At the end of a week, Mr Howard found it necessary to attend to some business connected with his new living, and a letter from Elizabeth arrived for Emma. Her sister, delighted with the news of her engagement, pressed her to return to Croydon.

She received a far warmer welcome than when she had formerly made the journey. Elizabeth was waiting for her — her face was seen through the flowers in the drawing-room window and she ran down the steps to open the carriage before the footman had time to put on his livery coat. The younger sister was led into the house and in the passage Elizabeth pushed back the bonnet and the dark curls from her cheeks, to see if she was as pretty as ever. Then, before entering the drawing-room, she paused again to make her sister guess who she would find there.

Emma suggested Mr Miller.

'You little goose,' replied Elizabeth, 'as if I should have troubled myself to make you guess that!'

Throwing open the door she ushered her in, and in another moment Emma was clasped in the arms of her dear brother Sam. This was a very unexpected pleasure — she had hoped to see him certainly, but never for a moment anticipated meeting him so soon.

Emma had much to communicate to Sam; besides her own prospects she had other matters which concerned him. A farewell visit which she had paid to the Edwardses had brought another engagement to her knowledge. Mary Edwards was soon to be married to Captain Hunter. She found them *tête-à tête* in the parlour when she entered, and appearances were so very suspicious that even without the direct information which Mrs Edwards subsequently whispered to her, she would have concluded her brother's cause to be lost.

Mrs Edwards appeared on the whole better reconciled to the match than Emma, from her early recollection, would have supposed. Perhaps she had discouraged Mary's partiality for the Captain, from a doubt of his sincerity, which was now removed; or she had given up her previous objections because it was of no use to persist in them. Whatever were her feelings, she had received Emma's congratulations with a good grace, and Emma

227

hoped there was no ill-will implied in the message of compliments which she charged her to deliver to their old acquaintance Mr Sam Watson.

All this she had to communicate to Sam, who listened with philosophy and whistled *sotto voce* instead of answering. Certainly the part which piqued him most was Mrs Edwards' message; for some time indeed he had almost despaired of Mary's affection, but he could not bear that the mother who had never been his friend should suppose he cared at all about it.

Emma had as much to hear as to tell, for Sam had been to Chichester and seen Penelope and her husband, and had arranged the plans for his future establishment. Could he only have commanded a couple of thousand pounds, besides what he possessed, there would have been no difficulty at all in stepping into a comfortable house and flourishing business. As it was, the prospects promised him were sufficient to raise his mind and ease his spirits.

He went on to convey to Emma an invitation from Penelope who expressed her dearest wish to receive her youngest sister in her married home. As she expected very little pleasure from becoming once again an inmate of Robert's house, Emma was delighted to accept. At Chichester she saw at once how well suited was Penelope to her situation in life. Though she did not greatly admire her brother-in-law, he was very superior to Tom Musgrave. It gave her great pleasure to hear him talk of Sam — such a young man must make his way in the world and be a favourite; his skill as a surgeon was most promising; he possessed both intelligence and spirit of a kind decidedly calculated to make for success in the profession. The household was noisy but good-humoured and Emma had to confess to herself that she had been quite mistaken in her earlier feelings about Penelope's marriage.

Another and more unexpected event occurred before a day had been chosen for the marriage between Emma and Mr Howard. To her aunt, whose sudden and ill-advised marriage had originally deprived her of her home, Emma had written to announce her engagement. She now received a letter from Ireland in which Mrs O'Brien first congratulated a niece who she so much loved and then expressed her own immediate intention of returning to England and settling, if a suitable house could be found, in the parish where Emma's home would be situated. Her young husband had proved as unkind as he was unprincipled and, as she still retained the control of her income, she had procured a separation and would never be in Ireland again. Her longing to see Emma was conveyed without reserve and she declared her determination of ultimately dividing her fortune between her youngest nephew and niece.

Thus it came about that it was under the protection of her younger brother and from her sister Penelope's house that Emma set out to church on her wedding day. Before she and Mr Howard had seen the anniversary of their first meeting in the town of Dorking they had become man and wife.

There is but one more circumstance to relate. Lord Osborne's travels occupied him for many months. When he returned to England, Emma was already a mother; he was accompanied by his wife, a charming and beautiful Spanish lady of noble blood. It might have been supposed that her large dark eyes, so reminiscent of Emma's and her habitual silence through lack of power to command our language, had been amongst the strongest causes of his falling in love. But no one who saw Mrs Howard when she visited the young bride at Osborne Castle, or watched his lordship's devotion to the new Lady Osborne, could have imagined that it had such a foundation; nor did anyone at the Castle on that day of reunion recall to mind those earlier events which for nearly a whole year had so much agitated the three persons concerned.

POSTSCRIPT

AT THE AGE OF TWENTY-EIGHT, though not one of her existing stories had been published, Jane Austen began to write another novel — probably her fifth. Her sister Cassandra, always in her confidence, was later to call this fragment 'The Watsons', and so one may assume that Jane had herself referred to it by that title. It first appeared in print as an appendix to the second edition of J. E. Austen Leigh's Memoir of Jane Austen in 1871.

The Watsons has most of the qualities which were to give such delight to Jane Austen's innumerable subsequent readers. All lovers of her writing must experience acute disappointment that she should have abandoned this story with the expression of esteem felt by one sister for another which is to be found at the end of Chapter 5 in this volume. In those first 17,000 words we have what seemed to Dr R. W. Chapman 'so promising a story', what to Virginia Woolf had 'the permanent quality of literature', with 'turn and twists of the dialogue to keep us on the tenterhooks of surprise', and what strikes a contemporary — Margaret Drabble — as 'tantalizing, delightful, highly accomplished'. Why was so much pleasure denied to so many? Why was *The Watsons* left unfinished? Why, for that matter, was it ever begun, for it appears to be the only literary work on which Jane Austen engaged herself during an eight-year period of disenchantment?

Jane Austen wrote her story for her own pleasure and for the entertainment of her family and friends. She began to write as a young girl and she was writing *Sanditon* within a few months of her premature death. For years all attempts to secure publication of any of her manuscripts met with disheartening failure.

Her early novels did not appear until long after they were written.

In the middle years of her life she had to contend with personal and family sadness, but during this period she began *The Watsons*. To judge from the watermarked paper on which she wrote, 1804 was probably the year of its composition. At that time she was living at Bath with her ailing father, her not altogether congenial mother and her only sister with whom her ties were particularly close and affectionate. It was now unlikely that she or her sister Cassandra or her great friend Martha Lloyd would achieve matrimony. It seemed improbable that a real home in the country of which she writes in *The Watsons* with so much longing, drawing on her nostalgic memories of Steventon Rectory, would ever be restored to her. Such attractions as Bath had once possessed had now grown stale. The greatest pleasure in the lives of the Austen sisters seems at this time to have been visits to small watering places in the west. They were at Lyme Regis in 1804 and there, I think, in the month of September Jane began *The Watsons*. The evidence is only circumstantial; it is partly provided by a letter she wrote at Lyme in which their attendance at the local ball is described. It took place on a Thursday, not as in *The Watsons* on a Tuesday; the Austens arrived a little after eight, as did the Edwards party at the Dorking ball. At Lyme Jane found a companion who was 'very conversable in a common way', who had 'sense and some degree of taste', and possessed manners that were 'very engaging', though 'she seems to like people rather too easily'. Emma Watson at Dorking finds in her new friend Mary Edwards 'a show of good sense, a modest unpretending mind and a great wish of obliging.' For the first two dances at Lyme Jane was without a partner. Emma, thanks to her pretty face and the presence of the military, was not so slighted. At Lyme Jane was pleased that her invalid father should have stayed contentedly till half past nine; she and her mother were able to stay an hour later. There then occurred an incident which I believe must have been in her mind when describing the behaviour of Lord Osborne and Tom Musgrave at the Dorking ball. Had they been staying longer, she writes in her letter, she might have danced with 'a new, odd-looking man who had been eyeing me for some time and at last,

231

without any introduction, asked me if I meant to dance again.' He belonged to a party, accounted people of the highest rank at Lyme, the Hon. John Barnwall, son of an Irish viscount, and his wife. 'Bold, queer looking people,' they seemed to Jane, and strange in their manners as was the Osborne set to Emma Watson.

The letter from which I have quoted is dated September 14th. Thereafter Jane, I believe, worked hard on *The Watsons* and had probably completed all that we possess of it by the end of the year. Two tragic events then broke into her creative concentration. On December 16th, Jane's birthday, Mrs Lefroy of Ashe, the older woman whom she most admired and from whom she had received much early encouragement, was killed by a fall from her horse. Less than two months later her own father was dead.

The Watsons breaks off at a point where its heroine has to call on all her resources of cheerfulness to combat the depressing circumstances of her life. We know from Cassandra that almost the next event for the author to describe would have had to be the death of the invalid head of the family and its catastrophic impact on the Watson sisters. Jane felt deep affection for her father and had now to face all that must follow from the disruption of their family life. Would anyone, writing for recreation rather than reward, have chosen to go on with such a story at such a moment?

Eventually all feelings of loss must diminish and in time the Austen sisters and their widowed mother attained a settled, contented mode of life, but Jane's work on *The Watsons* was not resumed. The thirteen years of life left to her were filled by other literary projects crowned with a measure of success. Three of her completed stories were revised and published: three new books, *Mansfield Park*, *Emma*, and *Persuasion*, were written, and *Sandition* was begun. In two of these books a deeper, more committed note has been recognized. Pain, grief, hardship, disappointment enter these later books in a different guise: they assume harder, more positive outlines, cutting their impressions more deeply into the reader's mind. It is not that the darker aspects of life are over-emphasized; the masterly balance of the novels is as marked as ever and they continue to have happy endings, but the flux of human affection is more profoundly felt. Life laid a cold finger on Fanny Price and Anne Elliott, and, though it bestowed on the Bennet and the Watson girls not dissimilar experiences, their impact is quite different in degree of intensity. I find in the events of Jane Austen's life and in the new turn taken by her creative development sufficient to account for her disinclination to pursue the story of *The Watsons*. At first too tragically close to her own circumstances, subsequently the demands which its conclusion would have made must have seemed out of key with the author's more mature approach to story-telling.

The Watsons belonged to Jane's first phase as a novelist which she outgrew. It is a work in the manner of *Pride and Prejudice* with a very similar structure. Essentially it deals with the fortunes of a family, the youngest sister being the central figure. Our interest is unevenly distributed over the other five, three daughters and two sons. This is a replica of the Austen family with the sex distribution reversed and two omissions — George an invalid and Edward who was adopted by the Knights. The central interest of the book was clearly to lie in contrasts between the three or four social settings in which the heroine was to be placed. The fragment leaves us in no doubt what they will be — the respectable poverty of Stanton, the modest comfort of Wickstead Vicarage, the arrogant grandeur of Osborne Castle, the pretentious vulgarity of the lawyer's house at Croydon. It is not only that the story foreshadows its own fulfilment but also that the themes against which the action is to take place are already indicated.

A year after Jane's death, the last volumes of her work containing *Northanger Abbey* and *Persuasion* were published. Coincidentally a fourth daughter was born to the wife of her brother, Captain Francis Austen of the Royal Navy. This baby was given the names of the new books' two heroines, Catherine and Anne. She grew up in a large and lively family of brothers and sisters and she lived an eventful life in England and in America where she died in 1877.

Catherine Anne Austen lost her mother at the early age of five, and her father, eventually to become Admiral Sir Francis Austen, K.C.B., married Martha Lloyd as his second wife.

Cassandra made long visits to his house at Portsdown. Thus his younger children were largely brought up by the two women with whom Jane had been most intimate. They carried on conversations in the style of Jane's characters, they read aloud from her novels, they discussed characters and plots with the bright young people who made up the family. The Watsons must have provided endless entertainment and a great deal of speculation amongst them. The beginning of the story, in particular, was so often read and repeated that years later one of the young people seems almost to have had the opening pages by heart. Those early recollections were to be of advantage to her.

Catherine married a Chancery barrister named John Hubback. He earned himself an early reputation and then suffered a mental collapse which incapacitated him for life. Catherine met this tragedy with a resilience and courage characteristic both of her father and her aunt Jane. She was a spirited young woman with energy and will-power. She had three young sons to bring up. Her talents were both artistic and literary and she used the latter, as her aunt had done, to write novels. The first of these was published in 1850 under the title of *The Younger Sister*. Nine more were to follow and to attain a fair success on both sides of the Atlantic. The construction of a plot for a first novel is normally a major problem, but Catherine faced none of the usual difficulties. She simply used her vivid recollections of *The Watsons* and built on them the subsequent developments which Jane had revealed to Cassandra who in her turn had retold them within the family.

The manuscript was not in Catherine's possession as Cassandra had bequeathed it to one of the other nieces whom Jane herself had known. But the opening chapters of *The Younger Sister* are extraordinarily close to the text of *The Watsons*. Many turns of phrase and indeed whole speeches have been memorized. She did not recall all the names accurately, but little of the detail is missed and when put side by side it is not easy to distinguish the early pages of *The Watsons* from their counterpart in *The Younger Sister*.

The present continuation of *The Watsons* is the second to be based on Catherine's novel. The first, though carried out by Catherine's grand-daughter, so greatly compressed the plot's development that it did less than justice to Jane's own work when all it yielded was so perfunctory a conclusion.

The author of this version, a reader of Jane Austen since childhood, has made a study of Catherine Austen's life and writing. This has led to the conviction that between aunt and niece there were resemblances of character and temperament. On many matters they held the same views. The belief that Cassandra and Martha knew more about *The Watsons* than has been supposed, and that Catherine absorbed from them an accurate picture of the author's intentions, is in my view well founded. Any merit in this present telling of the story derives from that belief.

I must add an important acknowledgement. Without the initial help of one of Jane Austen's great-great-great nieces and the continuous help of another, this book would not have been produced.